"You know, folks say I'm a pretty good listener."

Adam looked at her then and, tucking in one corner of his mouth, shook his head. "Seems you're pretty good at lots of things." Blue eyes blazing, lips trembling, he added, "Wonder how good you are at forgiveness."

Forgiveness? What in the world could a man this good, this decent, have done to make him feel unworthy of forgiveness?

While she stood there, trying to decipher his comment, Adam grasped her upper arms. "How much do you know about me?" he demanded in a raspy voice.

Kasey had never seen a man more tortured, more troubled. She felt helpless, inept, unable to put a stop to his misery. And so she did what she'd always done in times of trouble, and turned to God.

Lord, she prayed, *guide me. Help me know what Adam needs to hear right now....*

Books by Loree Lough

Love Inspired

*Suddenly Daddy #28
*Suddenly Mommy #34
*Suddenly Married #52
*Suddenly Reunited #107
*Suddenly Home #130
His Healing Touch #163

*Suddenly!

LOREE LOUGH

A full-time writer for nearly fifteen years, Loree Lough has produced more than two thousand articles, dozens of short stories and novels for the young (and young at heart), and all have been published here and abroad. The author of thirty-seven award-winning romances, Loree also writes as Cara McCormack and Aleesha Carter.

A comedic teacher and conference speaker, Loree loves sharing in classrooms what she's learned the hard way. The mother of two grown daughters lives in Maryland with her husband and a fourteen-year-old cat named Mouser (who, until this year—when she caught and killed her first mouse—had no idea what a rodent was).

His Healing Touch
Loree Lough

Published by Steeple Hill Books™

STEEPLE HILL BOOKS

Steeple
Hill™

ISBN 0-373-87170-8

HIS HEALING TOUCH

Copyright © 2002 by Loree Lough

Visit us at www.steeplehill.com

Printed in U.S.A.

The Lord is gracious, and full of compassion; slow to anger, and of great mercy. The Lord is good to all: and His tender mercies are over all His works.

—*Psalms* 145:8-9

To my family...the heart of my stories...and my life!

Prologue

Halloween Night

Buddy's instructions had been simple: Dress in black. Smuggle the assigned item out of the house. Meet at the graveyard, near the angel tombstone, eleven-thirty sharp....

It was eleven twenty-five, and Adam Thorne's skin prickled with uneasiness as he walked along the eerie-looking iron fence surrounding Crescent Lawn Memorial Gardens.

He didn't like the way the moonlight, slanting down from above, turned tree branches into gnarled, witch-finger shadows. Didn't like the way it glinted from the wide golden eyes of the owl, perched above his head, either. He couldn't decide which caused the dread coiling around his spine...the winged hunter's hollow hoot, or the dried leaves scuttling across the sidewalk like rodents fleeing the owl's crooked beak.

The nippy October wind moaned. Dogs howled. Cats screamed. Sixteen-year-old Adam couldn't have asked for

a more perfect Halloween. So why did he have this...
feeling?

Crouching, he slid between several missing spike-topped
fence pickets. He hadn't been here in years, but if he remembered right, the appointed meeting place was just on
the other side of the caretaker's toolshed.

Sure enough, like a tiny red beacon, the telltale glow of
Buddy's lit cigarette signaled him.

As Adam got closer to his buddies, a bigger-than-life
marble angel came into view in the graveyard. In the bright
silvery moonglow, it seemed that she stared...directly at
him. Distracted by the creepy-crawly sensation, he tripped
over a tree root, nearly dropping the basketball-size pumpkin Buddy had ordered him to bring.

"You're such a klutz, Thorne," Buddy taunted, grabbing
the jack-o'-lantern and handing it to Luke.

The others watched as Luke jammed it onto the metal
rod—his "assignment"—that served as the dummy's neck.
Travis brought the hay, and Wade, a faded plaid shirt and
torn work pants. Good ole Buddy, never one to overlook a
detail, added boots and a grease-stained fedora to the en-
semble.

"Man," Travis said, snickering, "he could make *The
Guinness Book of Records,* he looks so real!"

Wade said, "Y'mean cuz his head's so big?"

"That," Luke put in, "and there's so much hay stuffed
in him, he can practically stand on his own."

Adam didn't join in their laughter.

Luke gave him a playful punch on the arm. "What's
your problem?"

"Nothin'. I just...I think this whole thing is...it's stupid,
that's what."

Buddy wrinkled his face in disapproval. "Put a lid on it,

mama's boy.'' Sneering, he looked at the others. ''Who thinks Thorne is a mama's boy?''

Luke, Wade and Travis exchanged guilty glances. ''Well,'' Luke started, ''what we're doin' *is* kinda—''

Quick as a bullet, Buddy's hand shot out, knocking off Luke's baseball cap. ''*You* put a lid on it.'' With one icy glare, he silenced any further disagreement.

Of the five gathered round the tombstone, only Buddy hadn't made the Centennial High football team. Adam thought it odd that the outsider did the best Coach Jones imitation of the lot of them: '''Get with the program, boys,''' Buddy aped, as they waited for his next order. '''Time's a-wastin'!'''

As if even the B & O Railroad was afraid to disobey, a tremor pulsed beneath their feet, a sign that the midnight train was fast approaching.

Buddy leaped up, punching the air with a hard right cross. ''Yes-s-s!'' came his hoarse whisper. ''I've been lookin' forward to this all day!''

Shaking his head, Wade wrapped his arms around the dummy's waist and, half dragging, half carrying it, headed for the tracks. Luke and Travis followed, muttering to one another as they huffed up the grassy incline. When the foursome crested the hill, their leader looked back at Adam, who lagged behind.

''C'mon, mama's boy,'' Buddy said, his voice a sarcastic singsong, ''or you're gonna miss all the fun....''

The uneasy feeling that had been dogging Adam all night took another nip at his heels. Was he edgy because Buddy's harebrained ideas had gotten them into trouble, dozens of times? Was it that this time, Buddy had decided to hone the fun-slash-risk factor by tossing a Halloween dummy onto the railroad tracks in front of a moving train?

Or was it simply that despite their obvious reluctance,

the rest of them had agreed to go along with one of his schemes...*again?*

Engineer Al Delaney wished he could belch. Just one good healthy burp, and maybe this discomfort would end.

All day, he'd been feeling, well, odd. He blamed a sleepless night. Overwork. The bologna-and-sauerkraut sandwich he'd stuffed into his mouth an hour ago. Cranking his left shoulder in a clumsy forward-then-backward circle, he peered through the train's front window, wondering what to blame for the pressure that had been tightening across his chest for the past half-hour or so.

Wincing at this latest troubling twinge, Al thumped his chest. *Well,* he thought, taking a deep, difficult breath, *I'll be clockin' out in half an hour, and then—*

Movement up ahead caught his eye. Something—looked to him like a man—on the tracks.

"What the—?"

Heart pounding like a parade drum, Al reached for the whistle with one hand, the brake stick with the other. The high-pitched squeal of locked wheels strained against polished steel tracks.

But it was too late.

Kasey Delaney woke to the repeated dinging of the doorbell. Knuckling her eyes, she padded into the upstairs hall and croaked a sleepy "What's going on?"

"Probably just Buddy and his gang," her mother said.

It would be just like the neighborhood juvenile delinquent to need a Halloween finale, but why he'd think ringing people's doorbells in the middle of the night was fun, Kasey couldn't guess.

"Mrs. Delaney?"

Her mom stood at the top of the stairs, one hand on the

newel post, the other clutching her bathrobe tight to her throat. Kasey reached for her hand, but froze when her mother whispered, "Dear God, don't let it be—"

Her mother had always been calm, practical, easygoing. Hearing the fear in her voice frightened Kasey, too. Heart beating double time, she said, "What, Mom? Don't let it be *what?*"

She watched as her mom took a deep breath, smoothed back her bangs. Despite the outward attempts at bravado, her voice trembled when she exhaled. When she opened her mouth to answer her daughter's question, the grandfather clock chimed, announcing two o'clock, tolling in odd harmony with the doorbell.

A cold chill wrapped around Kasey's shoulders. "Where's Dad?"

"Oh, you know your father," she said, squaring her shoulders. "I'll bet he took Jimmy's shift. His wife was supposed to have her baby tonight, you know."

Kasey nodded. That would be just like her dad, all right, stepping in to help out a pal. Still…wouldn't he have called?

"Mrs. Delaney? Mrs. Al Delaney!" The man on the porch had stopped ringing the bell and started banging on the door.

Lifting the front of her nightgown with her right hand, her mother started down the stairs, the left hand making a soft, hissing sound as it dragged over the polished banister. "Go back to your room," she said from the tiny foyer.

"But Mom—"

"Don't argue with me, Kasey Delaney!"

Kasey took two reluctant steps back, shut her eyes tight and leaned her forehead against the doorjamb. *"Please, God, please, God, please, God,"* she chanted, hands clasped in prayer, *"let Dad be okay."*

Kasey opened her eyes in response to the loud, grating sound of the deadbolt. Its echo, resounding up the uncarpeted stairs, reminded her of the noise her father's hammer had made when it drove in the steel pins that secured the landscape timbers surrounding her mother's flower garden. Seemed he was always doing things for others....

"Mrs. Delaney?"

The door was open now, and the overhead porch light cast the man's shadow on the foyer floor. He was a policeman, as evidenced by his short-billed hat.

"What is it?" her mother asked in a thin, little-girl voice. "What's happened?"

In the instant before the officer answered, a thousand pictures of her father flashed through Kasey's mind: tossing her a softball; sitting beside her at the piano, playing corny duets; helping her with math and science homework. He'd taught her to tie her shoes, to swim, to twirl spaghetti like a Rome-born pro, forced himself to eat every bite of every oven-baked fiasco she'd ever cooked up.

Kasey pressed the heels of her hands against her ears, but she still heard the policeman say, "Ah, may I come in, Mrs. Delaney? I think this might be easier to hear if you were sitting down...."

Easier? Was the man out of his mind? Kasey slammed her door, knowing even before her teary face met her pillow that nothing would ever be easy again.

The radio alarm jarred Adam awake.

"...and the vagrant reportedly hit by the train was never found," the rise-and-shine announcer was saying. "Engineer Al Delaney is survived by his wife and daughter."

Heart pounding, Adam leaped from bed, bare feet slapping on the hardwood as he raced toward the kitchen. "Mom," he gasped, "where's the *Sun?*"

Without looking up from the Today section, she pointed.

Adam paged through the rest of the paper scattered on the tabletop, eyes narrowed as he searched for a corroborating story. And then, on page twelve of the main section he found it: Vagrant Missing; Engineer Dead. The article explained how, just before he'd breathed his last, Al Delaney told paramedics that a vagabond had staggered onto the tracks behind Crescent Lawn Memorial Gardens.

Thirty-five-year-old Al Delaney, the report said, had a long history of heart disease. The tidbit didn't matter one whit to Adam. What mattered was that Mr. Delaney probably wouldn't have died *last night* if it hadn't been for—

Adam's gaze froze on the black-and-white photograph of the Delaney family—Al, his wife Karin, their daughter, Kasey, age twelve.

Twelve. Same age Adam had been when his own dad died, four years earlier.

Overwhelmed with guilt and shame, Adam stood and, taking the paper with him, trudged woodenly back to his room.

"Do you see the time, young man?" his mom said from behind the paper. "School starts in less than half an hour, y'know."

Yeah, he knew. But he wouldn't be going to school today. Too much to think about….

Five minutes later, when he opened the back door, his mom was at the sink, rinsing her coffee mug. "Where's your book bag? And what about your lunch?"

"Don't need 'em."

She started toward him. "Adam Thorne, where—?"

"Got stuff to do," he muttered.

"Stuff? What stuff?"

Truthfully? Adam didn't know *what,* exactly. But he knew this: A man had died last night because he hadn't had the guts to put a stop to a moronic stunt—and now, he had to do *something*.

Shrugging, he stepped off the porch. "Love ya, Mom," he said over his shoulder. "Have a good day at work."

Today, Adam intended to work, too...at finding a way to make right something that had gone so very wrong.

Chapter One

Fifteen years later—Halloween Eve

Kasey Delaney squinted through the windshield.

Should she turn right or left? Exhaling a sigh of frustration, she threw the car into park and grabbed the directions, written by her so-called assistant in purple ink on lavender notepaper.

Yes, she thought, she'd followed each instruction to the letter. Which meant there should be a sign at this crossroads that read Kaplan's Herb Farm. Kasey looked up. There was a sign, all right. A big white one in the shape of an arrow. But it said Thorne's Getaway in bold, black letters.

She glanced around, at thick underbrush spilling onto the gravel, at autumn leaves, at deep murky puddles that had collected beside the road following last night's downpour.

She hated to admit it, but she was lost. And if there was anything she hated more than being lost, she couldn't name it at the moment. But she had no one to blame but herself.

Not two hours ago, she'd barely sidestepped a run-in with Aleesha.

"I wrote the directions down 'zactly as the lady told them to me."

"But Aleesha…"

The girl's lower lip had jutted out and her dark eyes misted with tears. She tucked a black cornrow braid behind one ear. "You ain't *never* gonna trust me."

The last thing Kasey had wanted was to hurt the kid's feelings.

She leaned her forehead on the steering wheel, remembering how they'd met three years ago through an inner-city mentoring program. Fact was, Kasey couldn't love Aleesha more if she were a flesh-and-blood relative, which was why, despite the protests of half a dozen well-meaning friends and relatives, she'd legally adopted the girl. Hoping the action would prove her trust, Kasey had tucked the directions into her pocket.

"Should've known better," she muttered now.

Immediately, she felt guilty for the harsh thought. Aleesha had come a long way in the year they'd been a bona fide family. And she'd go even farther, "with a little more patience and a whole lot more love," Kasey said to herself.

She reached for her purse. She'd call Information, get the herb farm's phone number, and call for directions *herself*…if only her dinosaur of a cell phone would work way out here in the middle of—

The phone wasn't in her purse. Grimacing, Kasey realized that Aleesha had borrowed it earlier that afternoon, and returned it with a dead battery.

"You shouldn't leave here without it," her mother had warned, when Kasey plugged it into the charger. "Marty

Bass said we're in for severe thunderstorms tonight." Then she said, "What's wrong with the charger in your car?"

Kasey's silent nod toward Aleesha had been hint enough: misplaced. "I'll only be gone an hour or so," she said with a reassuring smile. "What could possibly happen in an hour?"

"A million things," her mother said.

One of which, Kasey admitted now, was getting lost.

Well, no point dwelling on it. "When life gives you lemons, you quote tired old clichés."

Grabbing her pruning shears and a wicker basket for cuttings, Kasey decided to take advantage of the acres of wildflowers on either side of the road. She climbed out of the sports car, immediately wrinkling her nose at the sucking sound her hiking boot made when she lifted it from the mud.

What could happen in an hour? "You could get lost *and* mired in mud."

Squaring her shoulders, Kasey plunged into the hip-high grass. The whole area was lush with seed pods and willow branches. Better to concentrate on work than the occasional cricket. "Now I remember what I hate more than being lost," she grumbled, lurching at every insect's hip-hop. "*Bugs.*"

Shouldn't a person who traipsed through fields on a regular basis be used to things that crawled and flew and stung? She'd been the proud owner of Fleur Élégance for more than five years, after all. The floral creations she designed for hotels, restaurants, department stores and art galleries had won numerous awards—and secured Kasey impressive contracts. Her trademark, right from the get-go, had been the gnarled branches, wild mushrooms and dried leaves she'd artistically interspersed among realistic-looking silk flowers.

Fortunately for her, very few insects lurked in late October. But there were enough. Too many for her liking! Dusk was settling over the field as a yellowjacket buzzed near her head. "Isn't it time for you to go to bed, or hibernate," she said, waving her free arm, "or *some*thing?"

Soon, she'd gathered a basketful of cuttings for her next project. Smiling, Kasey could almost picture the arrangement she'd create with them on a marble pedestal in the center of the Columbia Bank's main branch.

A glance at her watch told her that more than an hour had passed while she'd snipped and trimmed. She could almost hear her mom, her neighbors, even Aleesha teasingly referring to her as a scatterbrain for letting time slip so easily away from her. Kasey had never let the jokes get to her. Instead, she told herself that becoming immersed in projects, losing all track of time, was a trait that almost always guaranteed—

That's weird, she thought, approaching her car. *I never realized that it sat so low to the ground—*

And then she understood *why* it looked that way. Kasey hadn't noticed when she'd stopped alongside the narrow, rutted road, but she'd parked in a huge mudhole. In the hour that had passed as she collected flowers, her tiny convertible had sunk to its floorboard. "Oh, fine. That's just great," she complained. "Stuck in the middle of nowhere, no phone, no food…"

She smiled and shrugged. "When life gives you mud," she mused, "pucker up!"

She decided to think of this as an adventure, a compelling tale to tell when she got back to civilization. Worst-case scenario, she'd have to spend the night here in the car, and walk to the main road in the morning to flag down a tow truck.

Right?

As if in answer, thunder rumbled overhead. Couldn't be a good sign, Kasey thought, especially not this late in the year. Seconds later, a sizzling flash of lightning sliced the darkening sky. Suddenly, her predicament didn't seem quite so funny. In fact, it didn't seem funny at all.

Because, for one thing, she hadn't seen another vehicle as she'd driven out here. Not a farmer's truck. Not a horseman's van. Not even a kid on a bicycle. And, though she'd been in that field for over an hour, she didn't remember hearing anything drive past, either.

Kasey had never admitted it, not even to her mother, but thunderstorms scared the willies out of her. Waiting one out in a minuscule convertible didn't seem the least bit appealing. And, though she'd given up her night-light more than a decade ago, she wasn't overly fond of the dark, either. Especially when, thanks to an impending storm, it fell as fast as a stage curtain.

But being alone *in the woods* in the dark…

Shivering, Kasey squinted toward the horizon. Was that a light? Heart pounding, she did a squishy little jig, right there in the mud. Yes, yes it *was* a light! Now, if she could just make it that far before the storm hit….

"Please, God," she prayed, *"let it be a cozy little cabin with a nice, happy family in it."*

Her stomach growled. "And I hope they'll be sitting at the supper table, eating cheesy lasagna and buttery garlic bread." She licked her lips. "And that there'll be cold lemonade in the fridge."

Kasey reached for the sports car's door handle. No point lugging the overflowing basket of wildflowers through the—

Something scurried across the toe of her boot, and Kasey let out a wail. Whatever it was wouldn't get a second chance to tramp on her foot! She took off like a sprinter and headed straight for that light, and didn't stop until she stood on the porch of a tidy log cabin.

She stared at the wide wooden door. Golden light, filtering through the curtained window beside it, glowed with welcoming warmth. Would the people inside be warm and welcoming, too?

She was drenched by now, and shivering in the wind. Kasey frowned. Much as she hated to admit it, her mother had been right. She never should have come all the way out here so late in the day.

No sleep last night. Nonstop supervision of Aleesha. Her mother's up-again, down-again health. If she wanted to, Kasey could make a long list of excuses for her rash decision. But right now, all she wanted was to get inside, out of the wind and rain. Summoning what was left of her courage, she knocked.

Scurrying—much like what she'd heard in the underbrush on the way from the car to the cabin—sounded on the other side of the door. Then, footsteps. Big, heavy footsteps.

She held her breath as her fertile imagination went to work: Maybe the cabin was a hideaway for a gang of jewel thieves. Maybe a murderer had holed up in there. What if a serial killer had slaughtered all the people inside, so they'd never be able to testify against—

"Who's there?"

The suddenness of the deep baritone startled her so badly, she let out something that sounded like "Eek!"

Sighing, Kasey rolled her eyes, because she'd always hated it when women did that in the movies. And yet, when the door jerked open, she said it again. On the heels of a silly giggle, she sputtered, "Uh, um, h-hi!" in a tiny voice.

Backlit by the interior light, he was little more than a shadow on the other side of the screen door. And it was definitely a "he." A tall, very broad-shouldered man who said nothing, nothing at all.

"Um, my, uh, my car got stuck in the mud back there?" She used her thumb to point behind her. "I was gathering flowers?" She held up the basket, in case he needed proof. "My, um, assistant gave me the wrong directions, so I'm lost?"

He continued to stand there, one hand on the frame, the other holding the brass knob of the inside door. He didn't nod, didn't smile, didn't speak.

What's with you? she wanted to ask him. *Cat got your tongue?* "I, uh, well, then it started to rain." She giggled again, and this giggle sounded even sillier to her own ears than the last one. "There was thunder and lightning and the whole nine yards, y'know? And I thought, 'Uh-oh, what're you gonna do now?' And then I saw your light? And—"

Kasey clamped her teeth together, wondering what on earth was making her spew out information in the form of questions. She'd never done anything like it before.

Maybe she was dreaming. Sure. Why not? That made sense, because this whole situation was beginning to feel like a nightmare. The darkness, the weather, this house and its owner—if this huge, silent man hadn't *killed* the owner—all had the makings of a Hitchcock flick. She'd always wondered why heroines seemed to deliberately put themselves in danger in those movies. Now, feeling enormous empathy for the poor, delicate things, Kasey believed they'd probably only been desperate to get in out of the cold rain.

And speaking of rain, how long did this guy intend to let her stand here, dripping and shaking? Didn't he have any manners at all?

"Oh, sorry," he said, opening the screen door. "Where are my manners?"

Had he read her mind? Or had she, in her high-strung state, been thinking out loud? She decided she could just as easily do the rest of her thinking inside.

She slipped past him, taking care not to touch him—no easy feat, big as he was—and made a beeline straight for the heat of the fire. She'd prayed for a cozy cabin and a nice hot fire, something to eat and drink. *Two outta four ain't bad,* she thought, thanking Him. Now what were the chances her host was a normal, decent guy? She'd settle for anything less than a criminal at this point.

He closed the door just then—a little louder than necessary, Kasey thought. When he bolted it, she swallowed, hard.

"I don't get much company way up here." He laughed softly. "Especially not during a thunderstorm."

Well, she told herself, at least he has a nice laugh. Then her smile faded as she remembered that lady reporter's interview with Ted Bundy. *He'd* had a nice laugh, too.

Frowning darkly, the stranger said, "You're soaked to the skin."

Which should have been the least of his worries. Between the mud that had clumped in the treads of her boots and the rain that dripped from her pants cuffs, she'd tracked in quite a mess. And now it was puddling on what appeared to be a polar bear rug. "Oh, wow. I'm so sorry," she said. "When I get back to town, I'll—"

"Easy. I know how to use a scrub brush."

With no explanation whatever, he disappeared through a nearby doorway, leaving her alone near the fire. Had he gone to fetch his hatchet? A handgun? Maybe a rope and a roll of duct tape, so he could tie her up and torture her before—

He clomped back into the room on brown suede boots. *Who is this guy?* she asked herself, staring at the big shoes. *Paul Bunyan?* Then she noticed that he carried something white, and something red, neatly folded and stacked on his hand. On his unbelievably *large* hand. Larry from *Of Mice and Men* popped into her mind.

They stood for a moment, blinking and clearing their throats, as if trying to come to grips with the fact that she was stuck here, at least for the time being.

"You can change," he said, nodding toward the room he'd just vacated, "in there."

She nodded, too, as he handed the clothes to her. "Wow. Neat. A sweatsuit. And a towel, too," she said. "This is great. This is good." What inane thing would pop out of her mouth next? she wondered. *"Let us thank Him for our food"?*

Smiling, both dark brows rose high on his forehead. "Lemme guess," he began, "your name is Red."

"No, it's—" She followed his gaze to the basket of cuttings still clutched in her free hand. Getting his Red Riding Hood joke, she laughed. Way too long and way too loud, but what did he expect after the chilly greeting he'd given her?

"I—I own a... These are for..." She put the basket on the nearest end table. Maybe she'd explain later. *And maybe you won't.* "I'll just go and change now." And backing through the door, she said, "Thanks. Really. I appreciate it."

The instant she closed the door, Kasey checked for a lock. "Rats!" she whispered through clenched teeth. "Whoever heard of a door without a lock?"

You have, was her silent answer. Her own bedroom door didn't have a lock on it. Neither did her mom's, or Aleesha's. And while her bathroom door had one, it had been broken for as long as she could remember. Besides, if the guy on the other side of this door aimed to harm her, a lock wouldn't stop him. And if that was his aim, wouldn't he have done it by now?

Possibly.

And he might just be one of those killers who got his jollies by watching his victims suffer....

Trembling, Kasey leaned her back against the door. *Get hold of yourself, 'cause if he is a murderer, you'll need your wits about you!* Then, trading her wet clothes for his gigantic, fleecy sweatsuit, she vowed to get her overactive imagination under control.

Adam had just placed two mugs of hot chocolate on the coffee table, when she came out of the bedroom. He hadn't known what to expect, considering the shape she'd been in when she arrived, but surely not this....

No way she could've been taller than five foot five. He knew, because when she'd slunk past him to get inside earlier, the top of her head had barely reached his shoulder. Somehow, she looked even tinier in his bulky sweatsuit.

Her hair had looked darker, straighter, when it had been all plastered to her head by the rain. Now, thick waves that fell almost to her waist gleamed like a new penny in the firelight.

"I suppose it's too much to hope that you have a phone way out here...."

"Cell phone," he said, "but the battery is dead."

"Seems to be a lot of that going around lately." Then she noticed the mugs. "Oh, wow," she said, smiling. "Hot chocolate, my favorite."

The smile put a deep dimple in her right cheek at exactly the same moment as a loud, gurgling growl erupted from her stomach. She placed a hand over it. A very tiny, dainty hand, he noticed.

"Hungry?"

Her cheeks turned a rosy red. "Well, I hate to put you out. I can make myself a sandwich, make one for you, too…if you have the fixin's."

"You just sit there by the fire and get warm. I'll whip us both up a bite to eat." He headed for the kitchen. "Do you like grilled cheese?" Standing at the counter that separated the kitchen from the living room, Adam picked up a can of tomato soup, opened his mouth to offer that, too, when she spoke up.

"Do I!" She sat on the hearth, hugged her knees to her chest. "Only way I like it better is with a bowl of tomato soup."

"Well, then. We have two things in common."

Well-arched brows disappeared behind wispy, coppery bangs.

"An aversion to being cold and wet, and grilled cheese with a side of tomato soup."

Either she hadn't heard his response to her unasked question, or chose not to respond, for his surprise houseguest was leafing through a copy of *Architecture Today*. He wondered which house had her wrinkling her nose that way. Hopefully, the ridiculous-looking one the magazine had decided to feature on the cover. Adam didn't know why, especially when his own house was a glass-and-wood contemporary in Ellicott City, Maryland, but he'd never been overly fond of modern-looking houses. Give him an old Victorian, like his grandma used to live in, and—

"I could never live in one of these."

"One of what?"

"These houses that have more windows than walls." She

met his eyes. "Where's a person supposed to hang pictures?"

He'd been trying to butter the bread when she said it, and buttered his hand, instead. After wiping it clean on a kitchen towel, he stirred the soup and shrugged. He didn't have anything on the walls at his place, so the question had never occurred to him.

She stood, returned the magazine to its pile, then bent to make a tidy fan shape of the stack. "So," she said, walking toward him, "mind if I ask you a question?"

"Fire away."

"Actually," she added, sliding onto a stool, "it's more like a couple of questions."

What was it with women? Did they all need name, rank, and serial number before they could carry on an ordinary conversation? "Name's Adam Thorne," he began dryly, adjusting the flame under the frying pan. "I'm thirty-two, unattached, and practice medicine for a living."

"Whoa." She held up a hand, traffic-cop style. "A doctor without a phone? How will your patients get hold of you in case of an emergency?"

"My partner takes over when I'm away, and when he's gone, I do the same for him."

"I didn't see a car out front—"

"Friend dropped me off." *As if it's any of your business,* he added mentally. "He needed to borrow my pickup and—"

She stopped his explanation with a weary sigh.

"Sorry," Adam said, "but it's too late to hike out of here tonight, especially with this weird weather—"

"When will your friend be back?"

He grinned at her interruption. "First thing tomorrow morning."

She straightened her back, tucked her hair behind her

ears and bobbed her head. "Oh, well…" she said, shrugging.

He liked her grit. For all she knew, he was a madman. Yet there she sat, pretending not to mind that the wind had blown her into a stranger's house.

"…lemons and puckers and all that."

He would have asked what that meant…if he hadn't looked into her eyes. Adam couldn't help noticing how big they were, how long-lashed, how *green.* And then she smiled, and he had to add *beautiful* to the list.

There was something about her, though, something vaguely familiar….

He set the thoughts aside when she made a thin line of her mouth, slid the pucker left, then right. "What I really wanted to know was, what are you doing way out here in the middle of nowhere, all by yourself?"

Man, but she was cute! Adam cleared his throat. "I come up here every other weekend or so. You know, the old 'get away from it all' routine."

She nodded. "How in the world did you ever find this place? I mean, it's so…" Fingers drawing little arcs in the air, she hummed the tune to an old Beatles' song. "It's so *nowhere, man!*"

Chuckling, he said, "Inheritance. The property belonged to my grandparents."

"They lived here?"

Adam shook his head, biting back the sadness the thought aroused. "Not exactly. Theirs was a traditional farmhouse, swing on the porch, potbellied stove in the dining room…. Unfortunately, it burned to the ground a decade or so ago." He swallowed as the flash of memory prickled his mind. "I had this one built a couple of years back."

Another nod, another glance around. "I like it. I like it a lot."

So now I can go to my grave a satisfied man, he thought, grinning. Adam sliced each sandwich in half, poured the soup into two deep bowls.

"I feel like a lazy oaf, just sitting here while you do all the work. Let me set the table, at least." She hopped off the stool. "Where do you keep the silverware? And the napkins?"

Adam opened a drawer, saw her eyes widen and her mouth drop open. "What?" he asked.

Blinking innocently, she said, "O-o-oh, nothing."

"Seriously, what?"

"Well, if you hadn't already told me you were single, I'd have figured it out after poking my nose in there, that's for sure!"

What *was* she rambling about?

"How do you ever find anything?"

"I just dig 'til I come up with what I went hunting for."

She bobbed her head from side to side. "Makes sense, I guess." She pointed at the contents of the drawer. "You need a license to hunt in there, 'cause it looks dangerous."

If she hadn't punctuated the comment with a wink, he might have taken offense. But then, it seemed he took offense at just about everything these days. Adam put the food on the counter, topped off her hot chocolate with more. "Now then—"

She held up a hand to forestall the question. "I know, I know. Turnabout is fair play and all that." Laughing softly, she said, "My name is Kasey Delaney. I'm twenty-six years old—well, I'll be twenty-seven in a couple of weeks—and I, too, am single. I'm a floral designer by trade and—"

"Floral designer? What's that?"

"You know those big bouquets you see in department stores and hotel lobbies and what-not?"

He hadn't. But he nodded, anyway.

"Well, that's what I do."

"You make them?"

"I make them."

He came around to her side of the counter, sat on the stool beside hers. "So, you're artistic, then."

"Maybe." She held her thumb and forefinger half an inch apart. "Just a little."

But wait just a minute here…. What had she said her last name was? Something French. No, Irish. De-something. Devaney.

Delaney.

His pulse raced and his mouth went dry. She couldn't be *that* Kasey Delaney, could she? But then, how many Kasey Delaneys could there be in the Baltimore area? "'Scuse me a sec, will you?"

She blew a stream of air across the soup in her spoon. "Sure, but don't be gone too long. Might not be anything left when you get back."

He hadn't prepared the meal to satisfy his own hunger, anyway. The main reason he'd made a sandwich for himself was so she wouldn't feel uncomfortable eating alone. But now Adam was the uncomfortable one. Because what if…what if she was—

Only one way to find out.

He'd carried the photograph in his wallet for fifteen years, to the day, almost. He'd cut it out of *The Baltimore Sun* the morning after Halloween that wretched year. For a few years after that, he'd carried it as is, but as it yellowed and turned up at the edges, Adam began to worry it might disintegrate. And he couldn't have that. He needed the article to remind him who and what he'd been, who and what he could become if he didn't force himself to remember what he'd done that night. It had been encased in plastic since his eighteenth birthday.

In the bright overhead light of the bathroom, he slid his wallet out of his back pocket. It required no hunting to find the article; he'd read it numerous times since…since the night that stupid, *stupid* prank went so wrong.

He looked at it now, reminding himself that the girl in the black-and-white photo had been twelve when the picture was taken. She wore braces, a ponytail, one of those dark-plaid, private-school–type uniforms. One look at those big, smiling eyes cinched it. The Kasey pictured here and the one in his kitchen, who'd made him laugh and smile— and mean it for the first time in years—were one and the same.

Why did life have to be so full of bitter irony? he wondered.

How much should he tell her, if indeed he told her anything at all? Was her visit here truly an accident? Or had she shown up for a reason?

He doubted that. He'd always been very careful to keep his identity a secret from the Delaneys, hand-delivering cash payments in the middle of the night, never at the same time of the month, so he wouldn't risk having Kasey or her mother catch him making "deposits" in their mailbox.

It had started small, just ten dollars that first month, earned from his part-time job changing oil filters at the local lube center. Remorse-ridden that his cowardly silence had been partly responsible for a man's death, for a woman's widowhood, for a child losing her father, Adam had taken a second part-time job, upping the amount to twenty dollars the next month. And although the amount in the last envelope had increased to nearly a thousand dollars, the guilt hadn't decreased.

"Hey," she called, "you okay in there? Should I send up a 9-1-1 smoke signal?"

Adam slid the article back into his wallet and tucked the wallet into his jeans pocket. Heart beating against his rib cage, Adam did the breathing exercise that always calmed him before surgery. Smiling, he headed back to the counter.

"So," he said, forcing a brightness into his voice that he didn't feel, "did you save me any soup?"

She insisted he let her do the dishes, and he insisted right back. "Okay. All right," she conceded. "But I'll wash, you dry, since you know where everything goes...more or less...." And that's how they ended up side by side in his tiny *L*-shaped kitchen.

Sharing this everyday chore with a virtual stranger felt good, felt natural, making Kasey wonder if she'd lost her mind somewhere between that field of flowers and this isolated cabin. In an attempt at rational balance, she tried to rouse some of the fear she'd felt earlier, when thoughts of murderers and robbers had her heart beating double time.

But it was no use. Rational or not, she felt safe with Dr. Adam Thorne. It didn't seem to bother him, either, that as the minutes passed, neither of them had said a word. Kasey added "comfortable" to the things he made her feel.

"So tell me, what kind of medicine do you practice?"

"Cardiology."

"In Baltimore?"

"I'm affiliated with several area hospitals—GBMC, St. Joseph's, Sinai, Ellicott General—but my office is in Ellicott City."

She looked up at him. "You sound like a TV commercial."

He laughed at that.

"I live in Ellicott City, too. Small world, huh?"

Adam looked away suddenly. "Yeah. *Real* small."

Kasey didn't know what to make of the dark expression that accompanied what should have been an innocuous agreement. "So why cardiology instead of—"

The plate he'd been drying shattered on the floor.

"Careful," she said, squatting beside him, "you don't want to cut yourself."

But he didn't seem to have heard her. And his hands shook slightly as he reached for the fragmented ceramic.

She grabbed his wrists. "I'll do that. You probably have surgery scheduled bright and early Monday morning. I'd feel terrible if you had to cancel, get your partner to do the operation, because you cut your finger on my sandwich plate."

One side of his mouth lifted in a wry grin. "How do you know it was your plate? Could have been mine."

"True, but it'd still be in the cupboard now if I hadn't shown up. Now really, let me clean this up," she repeated. "It'll make me feel better about all the trouble I've put you to."

When he hesitated, she put on her best "do as I say" look, hoping it would have more effect on Adam than it did on Aleesha.

Amazingly, it did.

"Do you have a dustpan?" she asked as he stood.

He pointed to a narrow door.

She pulled out a hand broom, too, then proceeded to sweep up the remnants of the plate. "What would you be doing if I wasn't here?" she asked, eye-level with his worn hiking shoes.

"Watching something on TV, I guess."

It was just a broken plate; the miserable way he sounded, a person would think he'd killed someone! "Then go watch something on TV. Pretend I'm not even here."

The shoes—and their owner—hiked into the living room, and seconds later, the theme from the Channel 13 news filled the air.

When she joined him after cleaning up, he was in his recliner, TV listings in one hand, clicker in the other. Kasey sat on the end of the couch nearest his chair and hugged a quilted toss pillow to her chest. "Anything positive happening tonight?"

"Nah. Typical news day." He brightened slightly to add, "The Dow Jones is up a couple of points, though."

Yippee, she thought. Kasey knew as much about the stock market as she knew about cardiology. "Have they said anything about the weather yet?"

"Only that we're in for a doozie of a storm."

Yippee, she echoed silently. It'd be just her luck for the tail end of that hurricane that had been wreaking havoc in the Atlantic to choose tonight to head up Chesapeake Bay. If that happened, they could be stranded here for…for who knew how long! Several years earlier, when the weather had taken a turn like that, downed trees and power lines had Baltimoreans fighting in store aisles over the dwindling supply of ice and batteries. Kasey sighed inwardly.

A huge clap of thunder, followed immediately by crackling lightning, shook the cabin.

Wonderful, Kasey thought. What else could go wrong?

As if in answer to her question, the lights went out. She watched as the TV's picture shrunk to a bright white pinpoint, then disappeared altogether. She'd never seen such total darkness, not even in the basement furnace room at home.

"Stay right where you are," Adam said. "I'll get a flashlight."

"Don't you worry, I'm not gonna move a muscle. I can't even see my hand in front of my face."

She could hear him, rummaging somewhere off to her left. Hopefully, he hadn't stored the flashlight in that kitchen drawer, because he was likely to pull out the proverbial bloody stump instead of a flashlight.

Much to her surprise, he was back in no time, illuminated by the pyramid-shaped beam of a foot-long flashlight.

"Here," he instructed, handing her a battery-powered lantern, "turn that on."

And before she could agree or object, he was gone again, leaving nothing but a bobbing, weaving trail of light in his wake. Kasey fumbled with the lantern until she found a switch on its side. Minutes later, Adam placed a glass-globed lantern beside it, and once lit, the oil-soaked wick brightened the entire room. He placed a matching lamp on the kitchen counter.

"Well," she said, laughing, "what in the world will we do without the TV to entertain us?"

Adam leaned back in his recliner. "Oh, I have a feeling you'll think of something."

For a reason she couldn't explain, the way he sounded just now matched the expression he'd worn earlier. *Suspicious* was the only word she could think of to describe it. And she couldn't for the life of her come up with a reason he'd have to feel that way. "We could play a game, I suppose. Do you have a game cupboard up here?"

"Actually, it's a game *chest*." He nodded at the coffee table. "What's your preference? Scrabble? Monopoly? Life?"

Last thing Kasey wanted to do right now was *think*. She wrinkled her nose. "How 'bout War?"

"That baby game?" he said, grinning.

"Truthfully, if it's all the same to you, I'm not really in much of a game-playing mood right now."

Adam sighed. He'd never liked games. Not even as a

kid. "Good, 'cause I'm *never* in much of a game-playing mood."

"Really?"

He watched her tuck one leg under her, hug the other to her chest. In the lantern light, her hair gleamed like a coppery halo, her eyes glittered like emeralds. "Why's that? Are you a sore loser?"

She had a lovely, lyrical voice, too, he thought, smiling when she laughed. "Sore loser? Hardly. For some reason, I rarely lose."

"I see. So you turn *other* people into sore losers, then."

And that smile! Did she realize it made him want to kiss her?

"Something like that, I guess."

She started to get up. "So, how 'bout I snoop around in your kitchen, whip us up a cup of hot chocolate. Or tea."

Somewhere under that thick, oversize sweatsuit, was a curvy, womanly figure. He knew, because earlier, her soaking-wet blouse and trousers had acted like a second skin, making it impossible not to notice. He was surprised at the caustic tone of his *"Mi casa, su casa."*

She padded into the kitchen on the thick-soled athletic socks he'd loaned her and turned on the gas under the teakettle. And as she opened and closed cabinet doors in search of tea bags and sugar, he said, "So tell me how you got into this flower business of yours."

"It's a long boring story." She shook an empty box. "And by the way, you're out of hot chocolate."

"Well, one thing we're not out of is time." He linked his fingers behind his head.

And you'd better spend it wisely, he cautioned, because he couldn't afford to give in to his feelings.

He had a pretty good life, all things considered. His mom was still healthy, thank God, and he had good friends, a good job, a nice house, a place to hide from the everyday stresses and strains of the world. Only thing missing, really, from his American Dream lifestyle was a wife, two-point-five kids and a golden retriever. The scene flashed in his mind—he and Kasey and a couple of rosy-cheeked, red-haired tots....

Ridiculous! He could see it now: *"Hey, how would you like to marry me? And by the way, I killed your father...."* He wouldn't live his dream life with Kasey.

Yes, he'd lived a pretty good life, but aspects of it had been less than fair. Tonight, for example. He'd been sitting here, alone, browbeating himself yet again, knowing full well that he had no one but himself to blame for his solitary status.

Still, if he'd shown a little courage fifteen years ago, Al Delaney wouldn't have died—at least, not on *that* night. Adam knew, even back then, that he'd pay for his moment of cowardice for the rest of his days. And if he needed proof of it, he only needed to look into his kitchen, where a gorgeous creature was humming as she prepared him a cup of tea.

He couldn't afford to fall for her, no matter how cute and sweet she was, no matter how funny. If he did, well, eventually she'd find out he was responsible for her father's death. And he'd rather die himself than have her hate him because of it.

Keep it casual, keep it friendly. She'd be gone in the morning and he'd probably never see her again. Not outside the confines of his own private thoughts, anyway....

"So," he said in a calculatedly easygoing tone, "tell me the so-called long and boring story about how you got into the flower business."

Chapter Two

A filled-to-the-brim steaming mug in each hand, Kasey trod slowly toward him. The tip of her tongue poked out from one corner of her mouth as she concentrated on every cautious step. Adam could think of just one word to describe her at that moment: *Cute*.

Knees locked, she bent at the waist and carefully centered his mug on a coaster on the end table beside his chair. After depositing her own cup on the tile-topped coffee table, she flopped onto the couch.

"Whew," she said on a sigh. "I've developed a whole new appreciation for waitresses." One dainty forefinger indicated the hot brew. "That's dangerous work!"

Chuckling, Adam lowered the recliner's footrest, rested ankle on knee and steepled his fingers beneath his chin. "You were about to tell me how you got into the flower business."

Her laughter reminded Adam of the wind chimes that once hung outside his grandma's kitchen window.

"I guess you'd have to say I just fell into it."

Adam continued to watch, transfixed as she gestured with

small but clearly hardworking hands, her incredible green eyes flickering with wit as she smiled, pursed her lips, tucked in one corner of her mouth.

"'Falling into it'...now *that*," Adam interjected, "sounds dangerous."

Her brows knitted in confusion. "How so?"

"Well, look at those things—" He indicated the basket of cuttings. "Briars big enough to saddle, spears that could harpoon a Great White." He met her eyes. "*I* sure wouldn't want to 'fall into' any of that!"

She laughed again, and again Adam noticed the way the sound of it rang inside him, like the silvery note of a bell. *Get back on track,* he thought. "So how, exactly, does one 'fall into' floral design?"

Resting both elbows on her knees, Kasey leaned forward, puckered her lips and blew across the surface of her tea. "This stuff is hot enough to fog your glasses...if you were wearing any."

He wondered when—*if*—she intended to tell him about her work; how she'd try to keep him distracted if she decided not to. Wondered *why* she'd want to keep something so everyday-ordinary from him. The only reason he wanted to know, really, was to prove to himself that what he'd done fifteen years ago hadn't destroyed her.

She sat back suddenly and crossed her legs. "My shop is called Fleur Élégance, and—"

"*Your* shop?"

Wearing a proud little smile, Kasey nodded. "Couple of years ago, I paid off my mother's mortgage. We'd always had this big shed out back, but I was never allowed in it. Dad always said, 'You could poke an eye out in there.'" She imitated a deep, growly voice. "Which was probably true. The thing was filled to overflowing with...*stuff.*"

Kasey laughed softly. "He used to call Mom a clutterɔug. *That* was true, too.'' Resting her head against the sofa's back cushion, she continued. ''Mom saved everyhing. Rusted tools, extension cords with bared wires, broken-down lawn mowers, bald tires, bent lawn chairs...a lifetime of junk.''

Adam thought he could listen to her talk, hours on end. She loved life, and it showed in every movement of her curvy little body, in every syllable that passed those wellshaped pink lips.

''Dad had been gone nearly ten years when I struck a bargain with Mom—I'd clean out the shed and set up a yard sale, and Mom could spend the proceeds in the bookstore.'' Smiling, Kasey rolled her eyes. ''The woman has more books than a public library! Anyway, she agreed to the deal, so I cleared everything out, installed new windows—''

He knew the answer to his next question even before he asked it. ''Installed windows. Yourself?''

Her expression said, *Well, sure. Doesn't everybody?*

If he hadn't made that promise to himself to keep a safe distance from her, Adam would have given her a hug— maybe more than just a hug—while trying to convince her that not everybody installs their own windows. Especially not pretty, petite girls.

''Once I'd put down a new floor and painted the walls, I had myself a right nice little place to do business.'' She gave a nod. ''Now *getting* the business, *that* was the hard part. At least, at first.''

She sat forward to take another sip of tea, a length of cinnamon hair falling over one shoulder when she did. She flipped it back, exposing the delicate creamy-white skin of her inner wrist, and dangly silver earrings.

He had a new word to describe her now: *Stunning.*

Adam shook his head. *Snap out of it, man.* He couldn't

deny how much he liked Kasey. Couldn't deny how much he disliked what he was beginning to feel for her, either.

Which is *what?* he wondered.

He was attracted to her, to be sure. And what man wouldn't be captivated by a gorgeous, green-eyed redhead with a knockout figure and the voice of an angel?

But there was more to it than that. So much more.

Somehow, being with Kasey these few hours had forced him to admit he didn't like his solitary lifestyle. She hadn't done it with smoke and mirrors. Hadn't done it with feminine wiles. Rather, she'd made him see how much he yearned for love and companionship, simply by being, well, by being *Kasey.*

During the past fifteen years, he'd probably looked at her picture a thousand times. Each time he'd seen that sweet, innocent face looking back at him, Adam had prayed she'd stay that way, forever. He'd likely said a thousand prayers for her, too; he may never know if all the heavenly requests made on her behalf had been met, but he could see, looking at her now, that *that* prayer, thankfully, had been answered.

Better get a grip, Thorne, he reminded himself. He'd had no way of knowing it at the time, but when he made the choice to go along with Buddy's prank all those years ago, he chose his destiny. His cowardice had been one of the reasons she'd lost her dad, and his throwing a little money at her family once a month hadn't changed that.

He chalked up what he'd begun to feel for Kasey to guilt. Had to be some kind of cockeyed contrition, right, because what else could it be? They'd only known each other for a few hours.

Several times over the years, he'd considered digging deeper, finding out more about Kasey and her mom. But nothing he might have learned could replace Al Delaney, so why try? Protectiveness had spawned that idea—was it also responsible for what he'd been feeling since he opened the door, saw her standing there, drenched and dripping and shaking like the last autumn leaf? Had he confused protectiveness for something deeper?

"How's your tea?" she asked, interrupting his thoughts.

Mechanically, he picked up the cup, took a sip. By now, it was cooler than he liked it. Fact was, he preferred coffee to tea, but he didn't say so. "It's good."

"Sweet enough?"

On the rare occasions when he did drink tea, he used no sugar at all. But he'd have eaten the stuff raw, right off the spoon, if she'd asked him to. "It's perfect. Thanks."

Then, more to get his mind off his roller-coaster emotions than for any other reason, he asked, "So how'd you get your first job?"

"Well..." She tucked stockinged feet under her. "A friend was getting married, and she had no money for a bouquet—for floral arrangements of any kind, for that matter. My dad always said I had a green thumb, that I was pretty good at arranging flowers from Mom's garden...."

Her smile went from friendly to whimsical, telling Adam that one memory had conjured another. *I miss him still,* said the mellow look in her eyes.

She sat up straighter, cleared her throat. "Anyway, Claire ended up getting ten wedding gifts from me—" One finger at a time popped from her closed fists as she counted: "The bride's bouquet, one for her maid of honor, the groom and best man's boutonnieres, mother of the bride and groom corsages, and vases for the front of the church."

Adam nodded. "Let me guess...and all the nice ladies who attended the wedding saw your pretty flowers, and when *their* daughters got married..."

Kasey clapped her hands together. "Exactly! Word of

mouth was all it took. Before I knew it, I had more orders than I could handle.''

''Good news travels fast.''

''Then I got smart.''

He blinked. ''Smart, how?''

''My dad used to say 'why work hard when you can work smart?' I didn't figure out what he meant until I'd been in business a year or so.'' Staring straight ahead, she lowered her voice, as if what she was about to say was a state secret: ''He died when I was just twelve, and he had a *lot* of 'sayings,' so there was a lot to figure out.'' Facing him again, she continued in her normal tone of voice. ''Anyway, I finally realized I could make more money, a *lot* more money, if my arrangements were b-i-g.''

Scratching his head, Adam said, ''I'm following you...I think.''

''Well, at first, all my clients were individuals. They wanted flowers for weddings, to decorate their homes and vacation properties. Small arrangements, you know? I was barely covering my overhead costs.''

Eyes wide, she clasped her hands under her chin and whispered, ''And then I saw a huge urn of flowers at one of those offbeat art galleries downtown. It hit me like *that!*'' She snapped her fingers. ''What I needed was a whole new kind of customer. *Businesspeople* instead of...regular people.''

''So that's where the shopping malls and department stores came in,'' Adam said.

''And financial institutions, and legal firms...any company that wants to set a certain atmosphere for their customers and clients.''

Adam added *smart* and *savvy* to his quickly growing list of reasons to like Kasey Delaney. ''You've accomplished quite a lot in your twenty-six, er, almost twenty-seven years.'' *Imagine what she could have become...if she'd had a father to nurture and guide her,* he tacked on.

''It hasn't been all that much, really.''

Even in the dim lamplight, he could see that she was blushing. He didn't understand why she'd feel self-conscious about all she'd accomplished, and said so.

Her voice was soft and sad when she repeated, ''It just...hasn't been much.''

Adam wanted to know more, so much more, about this lovely, talented young woman. Wanted to know what put the sadness in her voice, dimmed the light in her eyes. He'd always made his monetary deliveries in the dead of night, so had no way of knowing if she'd taken a husband, if she had children. Might she be available...?

He'd stayed on the fringes of her life, quite by choice. Every month, like clockwork, he dropped a cash-filled envelope into the mailbox of the house where she'd grown up. He hadn't felt right about poking his nose into other areas of the Delaneys' lives. But now, hearing that a home of her own and a successful business didn't seem like much of an achievement to Kasey, he couldn't help but wonder what her dreams and goals had been.

His goal hadn't changed in fifteen years: Fill in for Al Delaney in the only way he knew how...with money.

''I'm going to warm up my tea,'' she said. ''Care for a refill?''

He shook his head. ''You said you lost your dad when you were twelve?''

She nodded over her shoulder, and he winced inwardly as a wary expression darkened her pretty features. What did she know? he wondered. Had the look been prompted by something she suspected...about *him?*

He thought of that old saying— Just because you're

paranoid doesn't mean they're not out to get you—and wondered again if her visit here had been happenstance...

...or part of a plan.

And speaking of plans...

"Your father must have planned well for you and your mom."

Brow furrowed, she gave him a sidelong glance. "Planned well?"

"Well, you seem to have done pretty well for yourself. House that's free and clear of bank attachments, a successful business... Did you go to college, Kasey?"

"Sure did. Graduated the University of Maryland with a BS in business administration."

"Well, it's not as expensive as Harvard, but the tuition sure ain't free."

Her frown deepened. "True." Kasey perched on the arm of the sofa, wrapped both hands around her mug. "My tuition wasn't paid with funds from my dad's estate, if that's what you're implying. He was a good, hardworking man, but he wasn't rich. Not by a long shot."

She focused on some unknown spot behind him. "We had bills, lots of them. In fact, we found bills we didn't even know we had until after he died."

Clearing her throat, she stood, walked around to the front of the couch and sat down. "Which is why, first chance I got, I wrote a check to that mortgage company."

"Sorry," Adam said. "Didn't mean to pry."

She met his eyes and sent him a smile so warm, so sweet, it made his heart ache. Oh, to have a woman like this...so kind and nurturing, so resourceful and dedicated...for his very own!

"You're not prying, exactly," she said offhandedly.

"So you made it through college on scholarships, then?"

That made her laugh. "No. I did okay in the grades department, but not okay enough to earn scholarships."

That surprised him, a fact that must have shown on his face.

"Oh, I think if I'd had the luxury of time to study, time to turn in detailed reports, if I'd had a dad at my elbow, making sure I'd dotted all the *I*'s and crossed all the *T*'s, I probably could have done better in school."

Shame and remorse thudded in Adam's chest.

"I had to work two, sometimes three, part-time jobs to help out. Mom did what she could, but she's never been particularly healthy...."

There had never been any indication that Mrs. Delaney was anything but hale and hearty. "What's wrong with her?"

Kasey shrugged. "Little of this, little of that. My grandmother always blamed it on self-pity. Me? I call it loneliness."

Mortified, Adam scrubbed both hands over his face. If the woman was lonely, there could be but one reason.

"Lonely for *what*, I never quite figured out," she tacked on.

He raked his fingers through his hair, waiting, hoping she'd explain.

"My folks didn't have the most loving, romantic relationship in the world." A harsh, nervous laugh punctuated the statement. "And if you had known them, you'd realize what an understatement *that* is!

"They rarely spoke, and when they did, it was only to insult one another. So it took me by surprise how hard my mom was hit by my father's death."

Kasey hugged her legs to her chest, rested her chin on her knees. "I'll never forget the look on my mother's face when the grim-faced cop arrived on our front porch to deliver the news," she whispered.

She met Adam's eyes. "She looked so lost and alone—like a little girl. It frightened me so much." She sighed. "Turned out she loved him in her own way, despite all their problems."

Adam didn't know what to say, and so he said nothing.

"I was a mess, crying and blubbering like a two-year-old. Mom was too distraught to provide much comfort. Things only got worse the next day, when the cop came back to tell us about the evidence the department had found all around the railroad tracks."

"Evidence?" His heart thundered. What did she know...and could she connect *him* to that night? He recalled the article in *The Baltimore Sun* and the other papers. "Evidence of what?"

"Cigarette butts, footprints and pieces of a *pumpkin*, of all things, in the cemetery near the tracks."

Holding his breath, Adam waited for her to hit him, square between the eyes, with the accusation.

"The police found what was left of a scarecrow-type dummy, just down the tracks from the graveyard. They figured it was just a silly Halloween prank—kids probably, who were curious to see how far the train would carry their ingenious little creation. At the time, the cops decided the shock of thinking it had been a real person in front of his engine scared my dad so badly, he had a heart attack."

What did she mean "at the time"? Adam stiffened, waiting for further explanation.

But she shook her shoulders, instead, as if casting off the dour turn the conversation had taken. "Enough about me," she said in a deliberately brighter voice. "Tell me how you got interested in medicine. Were you a fan of *Marcus Welby, M.D.* reruns?"

He'd seen the television show a time or two and had enjoyed it, but he hadn't made a career choice because of it. He hadn't gone the route of most students interested in medicine, who, after interning in pediatrics or obstetrics or geriatrics, changed their specialty until they found one that "fit." Adam had known almost from the morning after that life-changing night which field he'd choose.

But how could he explain that to Kasey?

Just then, the oven timer began chiming.

"Oh, my," Kasey said, dashing into the kitchen to turn it off. "I must have pushed the wrong button when I was looking for the overhead light."

Saved by the bell, Adam thought. With any luck, when Kasey came back to her perch on the couch, she wouldn't pick up where she'd left off.

"I wish there was some way to call home. They'll be so worried."

"They?"

Nodding, she snuggled back into her corner of the sofa. "My mom and Aleesha. Who knows what they're thinking, what with this storm and all. And it's the night before Halloween."

The night before Halloween. Fifteen years ago tonight, Adam, Luke, Wade and Travis were huddled in Buddy's basement, making plans for "the great prank," each agreeing to bring one element vital to its success....

"Well, you know how it is in Maryland," he said. "Chances are fair to middlin' it isn't even raining in Ellicott City."

His words seemed to reassure her, for she sent him a small smile.

"True. Still, I've never been gone this long without telling them where I was. They're probably thinking something terrible happened to me."

"And maybe because they know you so well, they're thinking you're a feet-on-the-ground kind of gal who's riding out the storm in a safe place."

"You're very sweet to say that."

The warmth of her gaze lit a fire in his soul, and as much as he wanted to warm himself by it, it was a blaze Adam knew he had to tamp, immediately.

"So who's this Aleesha person you mentioned?"

"She's seventeen now, but I met her three years ago, when I volunteered for the Big Sister program in Baltimore. Her parents died in a house fire at just about the same time my dad was killed. She'd been bounced from foster family to foster family ever since. Poor little thing doesn't even remember her folks, she was so small when she lost them."

Kasey hadn't said her father *died,* he noticed; she'd said he'd been *killed.* All the more reason not to stoke what he was beginning to feel for her, because sooner or later, she'd find out *he* was one of the killers.

"Aleesha and I hit it off, right from the get-go," Kasey continued. "She's the most wonderful, loving girl. She has some problems but we're working around them."

"Problems? What kind of problems?"

"Learning disabilities, for starters. Plus, she's very myopic, and wears braces on her legs. I adopted her just over a year ago."

"Legally?"

She gave one nod. "Legally."

So the girl who'd grown up without a dad had learned enough about loving, about giving, to share her life—her *self*—with a needy child. "You're something else, Kasey Delaney. Something else."

She blushed, waved his compliment away. "Seemed the least I could do. I mean, God has been pretty good to me."

God? Adam failed to see what God had to do with who

and what Kasey had become. Seemed to him she was self-made, that she'd fought adversities of all kinds, and won—and Adam said so.

"No." She said it emphatically, in a no-nonsense voice. "I am what I am, if you'll pardon the Popeye quote, because God saw fit to give me my own little miracle."

What kind of nonsense was she spouting? She'd seemed perfectly rational and reasonable, until that "miracle" business came out of her mouth. It was ridiculous enough to be laughable. "A miracle, huh?" he asked, hoping the sarcasm he felt didn't show in his voice.

"Yup. In the form of a generous, anonymous benefactor."

Adam's heart beat harder. A generous, anonymous benefactor. So she *did* know about him! But how? He'd been so careful about his deliveries.

"For fifteen years now, once a month, someone has been leaving money in our mailbox." She held up her hands. "I know, I know, it sounds like something out of a Dickens novel, but it's true! He started small, just a few dollars at first, and worked his way up. Last envelope contained over a thousand dollars. Cash."

Adam swallowed, hard.

"I have a pretty good idea who he is, too."

He held his breath, grateful for the semidarkness that hid his blush. "But how…how do you know it's a 'he'?"

She grinned and tapped a fingertip to her temple. "Two and two, Dr. Thorne, usually equals four."

"I—I'm afraid I don't follow."

"Well, we have this neighbor, see, and after Dad died, he began looking in on us. A lot. Never had two words to say to us before that night—unless you count boyhood pranks—and then suddenly, the day after Dad was killed, he came over to ask if Mom and I needed anything. Day after that, we found an envelope with ten dollars in it stuffed into the mailbox.

"A month or so later, he cut our grass—using his lawn mower and gas!—and we got fifteen bucks in the next envelope. Another time, he trimmed the hedges, and, yep, a couple days later, there was a twenty-dollar bill in the mailbox."

"That was...nice of him."

"Not *was*," she corrected. "He's still doing it!" Kasey laughed softly. "Not the chores, of course. He's a big important businessman now, far too busy for that kind of stuff. But he's still leaving envelopes full of money every month."

Adam cleared his throat. "Very...uh, very generous man."

"I'll say. If it hadn't been for him, I would never have been able to afford to go to college. When Mom was able, she'd take in ironing, decorate cakes, things that didn't tax her delicate system too terribly...."

There was no mistaking the sarcasm in her voice. Kasey didn't believe for a minute that her mother had a physical condition that prevented her from working. And yet, she'd taken care of the woman *all these years*. He had to wonder why a girl who'd suspect her own mother's intentions had such complete faith in the do-gooder from across the street.

"I always managed to find steady work, and pretty much kept the wolf from the door, as they say. But college?" She shook her head. "No way that would have been possible without him."

It gave Adam a good feeling, knowing his monthly contributions to the Delaney household had served the intended purpose: to make life easier for Kasey and her mom. Suddenly, it didn't matter who got the credit.

"I say a little prayer for him, every morning. Say another one every night, before I turn in."

Did she have any idea what she was doing to him, sitting there, pretty as a picture, telling him things like she'd been praying for his miserable soul? Looking into her innocent, trusting eyes, it made him ashamed. So ashamed that he would've stood up and walked right out of the room...if there had been anywhere else to go.

"I just wish I knew for sure that it *was* the man across the street."

He leaned forward, drawn closer by the sincerity of her tone. "Why?"

Her eyes misted with tears and yet she smiled. "Because I'd like to tell him that, much as we appreciated everything he did for us, we don't need his help anymore, that we're doing fine on our own, thanks to him."

"And this man across the street...what makes you think it might *not* be him?"

She shrugged one shoulder, wiped the tears from her eyes. "Well, he must know that I've guessed what he's been up to all this time, and yet he seems to think it'll buy him certain—" she frowned "—favors." Kasey shrugged. "That just doesn't quite jibe with the kind of man who'd leave regular payments."

"What kind of favors?"

"Oh, nothing, really. Drops in last-minute for meals. Stops by unannounced with laundry, mending. Things like that." She frowned and a huge sigh whispered from her. "He has enough money to buy and sell Mom and me ten times over. And his lifestyle, well, that's another story altogether!"

"His lifestyle?"

"It's...well, let's just say it doesn't fit the profile of—"

"—a generous benefactor," they said together.

After a moment of friendly laughter, Kasey said, "I'll bet you've heard of him. Buddy Mauvais?"

A punch to the gut couldn't have knocked the wind out of him more effectively. Yeah, he'd heard of Buddy Mauvais, all right. Anybody who hadn't been living in a cave these past ten years knew Buddy...as a two-bit con man. But Adam had a whole different reason to know the name that had appeared in countless newspapers, and been mentioned on local TV news stations every time a crooked stock deal or a get-rich-quick scheme scammed some poor fool. Somehow, Buddy always managed to slither through one legal loophole after another. Not that it surprised Adam; Buddy had been lying and conniving his way out of trouble since he was a boy.

Why hadn't Adam made the connection earlier? He'd known all along that Buddy lived across the street from the Delaneys. That's one reason he'd been so careful when dropping envelopes in their mailbox; he wouldn't have put it past good old Buddy to steal the money, if he'd seen Adam delivering it!

A slow rage began to burn inside him at the thought that Buddy had been taking the credit for *his* generosity. And to make matters worse, trying to take liberties with Kasey in repayment of it!

"So why don't you tell me about it?"

He blinked, turned his attention back to her. "Tell you about what?" It came out gruffer, angrier than he'd intended, especially considering *she* wasn't the one Adam was furious with. If he could get his hands on Buddy Mauvais right now—

"Obviously, you and Buddy have a history of some kind...."

He put a concerted effort into staying calm. "What makes you say that?"

"Well, just look at you," she said. "Ever since I mentioned his name, you're tight as a drum." Grinning, Kasey added, "And if you don't stop gritting your teeth, you're sure to crack your molars."

He hated to admit it, but she was right. He opened his fists, unclenched his jaw, relaxed his shoulders. Adam shook his head. He needed to get off someplace, be by himself, think this thing through in a rational, logical way. Until then, he knew, he'd better zip his lip. *And do a whole lot better job of keeping a lid on your temper while you're at it.*

"Nah," he said, forcing a grin. "I'm just frustrated with the power company, is all. I mean, you pay through the nose for service, and half the time you're sitting in the dark, waiting—"

"Adam, do you mind my being completely blunt?"

Well, he thought, that all depended on what she intended to be blunt *about.* "No. I guess not," he said carefully.

Adam clamped his lips together and waited, searching for the inner strength that would be required to react appropriately to whatever idea was percolating in that pretty head of hers.

"What I read on your face just now wasn't frustration at the power company. It was anger, plain and simple." She scooted to the edge of the seat, leaned toward him and said, "Now, I don't know why you feel the way you do about Buddy, but don't you think it'd be a good idea to tell me about it?"

He looked into her eyes, so big and bright, so filled with sincerity. "Buddy and I go way back," he began. "We were…" He couldn't bring himself to say "friends." "We hung around together some when we were in high school."

"Then, you probably know him better than I do."

She clasped her hands together in what he read as a gesture of quiet supplication.

"I need to know everything I can about him, and if you can shed some light..." She extended her hands, palms up, beseechingly.

Her voice was trembling, and that made no sense at all. Especially when Adam reminded himself that Kasey thought Buddy was her own personal God-sent "miracle."

"I'd really appreciate it, Adam."

"But why?"

She lifted her chin a notch, squared her shoulders and straightened her back. "Because," she said in that matter-of-fact way of hers, "Buddy has asked me to marry him."

Chapter Three

Kasey pretended to be so engrossed in pulling up her too-big socks that she hadn't seen Adam, bobbing his head right to left, working out the tension in his neck. She'd struck a nerve of some sort, mentioning Buddy's name, struck another by admitting he'd proposed to her. She began searching her mind for an appropriate question, one that would explain *why*.

"I'm whipped," he said, getting to his feet. He stretched, gave an exaggerated yawn, then headed for his room. "Back in a flash," he added over his shoulder.

Adam was carrying a pillow and a blanket when he reappeared a moment later. "I'll bet you're even more anxious to start countin' sheep than I am. Good thing I put fresh sheets on the bed this morning, eh?"

Her head was still swimming from the abrupt change of subject. "Adam, I'm not taking your bed."

"You're not taking it, I'm giving it to you."

"But you've done so much already. I can't let you—"

"Trust me, schweetheart," he said in a barely recognizable Bogie imitation, "nobody *lets* me do anything." He dropped the bedding on the coffee table, as if to underscore his statement.

Kasey put her hands on her hips, to underscore her determination.

Eyes locked to hers, he said, "Okay, but I think it' gonna be pretty uncomfortable out here, both of us tryin to share this lumpy ole couch."

She glanced at the huge, overstuffed sectional. If need be, two adults and maybe a couple of toddlers could spen a comfortable night here...provided, Kasey thought, look ing at Adam, one of them wasn't built like a Baltimor Ravens linebacker.

"I've sawed logs out here plenty of times," he said "Believe me, I'll be fine."

But why would he put himself through a long, torturou night, when he had every right to the big brass bed, visibl from the living room?

She already knew *why*.

Smiling, Kasey recalled that several times since her ar rival—as he rushed around to find her something to wear as he grilled her a cheese sandwich—she'd thought what a nice man Adam was. It had taken only a few minutes o his hospitality to blot out her fears that he might be a mur dering maniac. She'd prayed for a warm, dry place fille with warmhearted inhabitants. True to form, God had pro vided...not "people," but certainly someone big enough— and big-hearted enough—to be two people! Silently, sh thanked Him.

Adam's quiet baritone broke into her thoughts.

"Would you be more comfortable if I tried to scare u something more, uh, more jammie-like for you to slee in?"

His fumbling, awkward suggestion added yet anothe item to her quickly growing Reasons to Like Adam list

Kasey patted her thigh. "You're sweet to offer, but the sweatsuit is terrific."

She stood and faced him. "I'd like to sleep right here." Being able to read people's faces could sometimes make or break a sale. It appeared she hadn't yet managed to convince Adam she was serious. "Look at it this way—how many chances does a city girl get to fall asleep in front of a roaring fire?"

He lifted his chin, telling her he still planned to spend the night on the couch. Well, she had "stubborn" down pat herself. "I hate to be a pushy guest, but I insist."

Adam regarded her for a moment before saying, "Okay, but I think it's only fair to warn you, I set a trap a couple of hours before you showed up."

A trap? Kasey rolled her eyes and sighed. "Do I seem like the kind of girl who'd leap onto a chair at the sight of a teensie-weensie mouse?"

Her stomach did a little flip in reaction to the quick once-over from his brown, brown eyes, flipped again when she saw a flirty grin lift one corner of his mouth. Then one dark brow rose on his forehead.

"I'll admit, you don't look like the 'eek' type."

Kasey recalled the way she'd behaved when Adam first opened the cabin door. "Do I detect a 'but' in that statement?"

His grin grew. "Never said the trap was for a mouse."

Why was her mouth suddenly dry? "Chipmunk, then?" He stood, feet shoulder-width apart and arms crossed over his chest. If he shaved his head and got a big gold earring, he'd look even more like that cartoon sailor in the cleaning commercial.

"Nope."

She licked her lips. "Squirrel."

He shook his head.

Her heart began beating a tad faster. "What, then?" She prayed he'd say "fox" or "bobcat," *anything* but "snake."

He looked at her out of the corner of one eye. "Maybe I need to revise my statement."

"Excuse me?"

"Maybe you *are* the type who's scared of things that go *bump* in the night."

To her knowledge, snakes didn't "bump." But then, her encounters with reptiles had been few and far between…deliberately. Still, it was far too early in their relationship to show him what a scaredy-cat she could be. Kasey grabbed the poker from the hearth and struck a fencer's pose. "Anything that goes *bump* in *my* night will leave here *wearin'* a bump!"

Wait—had she thought the *R* word? She'd only met the man a few hours ago! Just because he'd been *nice*—and she'd appreciated it—didn't mean they'd started a…a *relationship*.

Did it?

Adam laughed, and she realized he was just teasing her.

"All right," he said, "you win. But if you're going to sleep out here, at least let me get you some clean sheets, another pillow, a comforter, maybe."

Kasey was still reacting to the delicious sound of his laughter when she said, "You must be kidding. There's so much wood on that grate, I'll probably roast during the night."

"Then, maybe I oughta come back in a couple of hours," he mumbled around a yawn, "to turn you over and baste you."

She headed back to the fireplace, to put the poker back into its stand. Looking over her shoulder, she began, "And maybe you oughta—"

Kasey's right foot came down on the toe of the too-big left sock Adam had loaned her, throwing her off balance. The poker clattered onto the brick hearth as she held out both hands to soften the landing.

Adam, lightning-quick, grabbed her wrist. One well-timed tug kept her from falling face-first into the blazing fire—and put her directly into the protective circle of his arms.

Pressed tightly against his barrel chest was just about the last place Kasey should be, she knew. And yet, it was precisely where she wanted to be, where she'd pictured herself—a time or two, anyway—during the past few hours.

She looked up slowly, past the wide shoulders and the broad chin. She hadn't noticed before—perhaps because they'd stayed a careful distance apart, perhaps because of the semidarkness—but a shadowy stubble peppered his face. It made him look even more rugged, even more handsome, if that was possible. When had he last shaved, Kasey wondered. Yesterday? The day before? And what might it feel like if that slightly fuzzy upper lip should graze her mouth with a soft, searching kiss...?

She saw a similar question simmering in his dark brown orbs. Her heart thudded, because she sensed that Adam was going to kiss her, and soon. Sensed, too, that she'd like it, that she'd want another, and maybe another after that.

Dear Lord, she prayed, *if You're trying to tell me Adam is 'the one,' I'm getting the message loud and clear!*

Adam held her close, torn between pushing her away and pulling her nearer still. Relief—that he'd managed to keep her from falling into the fire—mingled with the exhilaration of having her so near.

Looking deep into her eyes, Adam understood for the first time what the poets meant, for he felt as though he were drowning in a sea of bright green.

Long ago, he'd taught himself to mask his emotions, had made it a regular part of every doctor–patient relationship. Obviously, something in his carefully practiced routine had short-circuited. How else could Kasey have known how very much he wanted to kiss her? And he could see that she *did* know; she had closed her eyes, tilted her head, lifted her chin.

The logical side of his brain ranted, *Stop it! You're getting in over your head!* But the emotional side prodded, *She'd be good for you! Why not make hay while the sun shines for a change?*

He all but laughed at the irony: sunshine, when it was nearly midnight, and during a raging thunderstorm, yet!

Kasey opened her eyes—her magnificent, glittering green eyes—at the exact moment that a rib-racking clap of thunder shook the cabin. Startled, she instinctively squeezed closer; involuntarily, he tightened his protective embrace.

And that's all it took to melt the last of his resolve.

Adam leaned down as Kasey stood on tiptoe. *You're gonna be sorry,* pealed a warning in his head. But it came too late....

The instant their lips touched, a soft sigh bubbled up from somewhere deep inside her and swept over him like a tepid ocean wave. One moment, he'd been an empty, castaway bottle, bobbing in the sudsy surf. The next, her warmth spilled into him, soaking into his soul and filling his hollow heart. How long before he'd sink completely?

The question caused reality to rear its ugly head, reminding him of the promise he'd made to himself, not an hour ago. *You have no business doing this,* he ranted inwardly, *no business at all!*

He was about to disconnect himself from the exquisite sensations of peace and contentment the simple human contact had awakened, when her hands slid up his chest, came to rest on his shoulders. If her reaction to their kiss was any indicator, Kasey, too, had waited a lifetime for...for whatever this wonderful feeling was called.

He'd known her for a long, long time, in a distant, detached way. He realized now that by staying in the shadows of her life, he'd deprived himself of the pleasure of watching Kasey make that graceful change from bony, freckle-faced girl to curvaceous, charming woman. It was probably better that way, because if he *had* witnessed the transformation, even from the sidelines, living his life on the fringes of hers would have been impossible.

The documentary he'd been watching on TV when Kasey showed up popped into his head; suddenly, Adam felt great empathy for the scraggly gray wolf who, driven from the pack, died of grief and loneliness. Difficult as it would be, now that he'd crossed the invisible line he'd drawn between them, he intended to step back into the shadows, for his sake as well as hers.

Gently, Adam curled his fingers around Kasey's upper arms, took a careful step back.

One hand still resting on his shoulder, she blinked, and the disappointment in her eyes made his heart ache. As she touched the fingertips of the free hand to her lips, she sighed. "Thanks, Adam."

His lips were still tingling from their kisses, his mind a muddle from having had to force himself to come up for air long enough to do the right thing. He had no idea why she was thanking him.

Kasey tidied the collar of his shirt. "Earlier, you said you might come out here during the night, to turn me over and baste me." She looked him full in the face. "Well, if it hadn't been for your quick thinking just now, I would've been *toast*, not a roast!"

The smile not only curved her mouth up at the corners,

but lit her eyes...and every dark place inside him, too. He'd seen TV movies where people fell head-over-heels in a heartbeat. Adam had always scoffed at the silly, romantic plots, because only buffoons and simpletons believed in love at first sight. Evidently, he was a buffoon. Or a simpleton. Or both. Because he believed in it now, with every beat of his Kasey-filled heart!

"So, thanks for saving my life," she said again. And fluttering her long, thick lashes, she added in Scarlett O'Hara fashion, "You're mah hee-roe!"

Hero?

The word echoed, thudded like a hammer in his head, because he was anything *but* a hero, and he knew it. Luke knew it, and so did Wade and Travis. And Buddy—the man who'd asked Kasey to marry him—*he* knew it best of all!

"Well," Adam said, taking another step back, "guess I'll let you get a little shut-eye. Quite a day you've had, what with getting mired in the mud, lost in the woods..." His voice trailed off...*meeting up with your father's killer,* he finished silently. "If you need anything, anything at all, just make yourself at home, okay?"

She nodded. "Okay, and—"

Unable to listen to another word of gratitude, he held up a hand; what he'd done for her to date wasn't *half* what he owed her. He turned quickly and headed for the bedroom, amazed at how difficult it was to walk away, to put even these few yards of hardwood floor between them.

"G'night. And thanks again, for everything."

"You're welcome," he muttered, closing the door.

Adam rubbed his jaw. He should've stoked the fire. Should've double-checked the door and window locks. Should've made sure she had everything she needed. *Should've kept your hands to yourself!*

The memory of Kasey—so tiny in his arms, so strong

and yet strangely vulnerable—sparked in his mind. Adam rubbed his eyes, but the vision seemed tattooed on the insides of his eyelids. "What you don't know can't hurt you," he whispered. The old adage made perfect sense, suddenly, because he'd given in to a weak moment, and more than likely, he'd be sorry in the morning.

In truth, he was sorry *now*.

Moments ago, he'd held perfection in his arms.

And he'd never again be able to settle for less.

The quiet *pop* and *crackle* of logs burning in the grate and the steady thrum of rain on the roof lulled Kasey into a near-sleep state. Drowsily, she glanced around the cabin's living room, where everything, from the deep green plaid valances above the dark wood-trimmed windows to Adam's well-worn brown recliner, reflected the flames' buttery glow. It was a tastefully designed space that made her feel safe and secure. Had he hired a professional to create the cozy atmosphere, or had he chosen the furnishings himself?

No, more than likely, the woman in his life had helped Adam make the decisions. And surely there *was* a woman, right? Not a wife—he came and went too freely to be a married man, as evidenced by his 'get away from it all' weekends—but maybe a fiancée, or at the very least, a girlfriend....

The picture of him holding another woman the way he'd just held her started an ache inside her, and considering the suddenness of their relationship—

There it was again...the *R* word. *You're behaving like a silly schoolgirl in the throes of your first crush!*

Well, that made sense, sort of. After all, she'd been stranded in the middle of nowhere, during a wild thunderstorm. She'd been afraid, cold and wet, and hungry, and he'd come to her rescue, even before he saved her from falling into the fire. Maybe what she was feeling wasn't the beginnings of love, but gratitude.

Their embrace, their kisses, sizzled in her memory. Hugging the pillow to her, Kasey sighed dreamily. If that was gratitude, she could live a lifetime feeling grateful!

She rolled onto her side, one arm crooked beneath her head. Eyes closed, she inhaled the manly mix of pine needles and bath soap clinging to Adam's sweatshirt sleeve. It was a scent she'd recognize anywhere, especially after he'd held her so very close, and—

Buddy's dark-eyed, smiling face flashed in her mind, blotting out the beautiful memory. She couldn't say how it had happened, exactly, but somehow Buddy had gotten the mistaken impression that he and Kasey were a couple. "Meet my soon-to-be fiancée," he'd say when introducing her to visiting dignitaries. "One day soon, you'll dance at our wedding!" he'd tell politicians and lobbyists. "What do you think of my beautiful wife-to-be?" he'd ask businessmen who came from all over the world to seal one of Buddy's many "deals."

Kasey would have to guess that in the two years since he'd started announcing to the world that she was his "intended," Buddy had kissed her dozens, maybe even hundreds, of times. Kisses had concluded quiet dinners, had been stolen in dimly lit movie theaters and while dancing at one of the many galas he was so frequently invited to.

But not once had Buddy's kisses stirred anything in Kasey's heart. The fact that Adam's *had* made her feel like a cheating wife. And how ridiculous was that!

On her back now, she pressed the fingertips of her right hand to her mouth, remembering the way her pulse had accelerated in response to Adam's kiss. In all honesty, the knee-wobbling, heart-hammering reaction started long before his lips connected with hers; a mere glance from those chocolate-brown eyes was all it had taken to make her realize *this* was what the songwriters meant when they referred to ''love.''

She had no business feeling this way about Adam, not after all Buddy had done for her family. And Adam had no business *waking* these feelings in her, because a man as handsome and wonderful as that simply *had* to be involved with a woman, and—

Kasey rolled over again and faced the sofa's back cushions. Tomorrow, she'd figure out a way to get out of this place, away from the man who owned it. Like it or not, she'd get back to living the life that had been laid out for her.

Like it or not?

Too many people depended on her. Her mother, Aleesha, her customers—even Buddy, in his strangely distant way. She buried her face in her hands and shook her head, wishing she hadn't worked quite so hard to earn her Do-the-Right-Thing-Kasey nickname.

''Didn't realize scrambled eggs could be so…so…''

''Fluffy?'' Kasey finished for him the next morning, as they sat down to breakfast.

''Yeah. Fluffy.'' The sissy word would never have occurred to him, yet for some reason it described her egg dish perfectly. Adam couldn't help but be impressed. He'd scrambled eggs, possibly hundreds of times. His mother had made them when he was a boy, as had several lady-friends, hoping to impress him enough to give up his bachelor status. So why did these taste so special?

''Glad the power is on again,'' she was saying as she filled two small glasses with orange juice. ''What time will your friend be back?''

Adam looked at the clock above the stove. Fifteen

minutes to eight. "Shouldn't be long. He said eight, and Wade's a fairly punctual guy."

Kasey held the milk carton above his coffee mug. "Say when...."

"Thanks, but I drink mine straight."

She tilted her head. "No kidding? So do I."

As she put the milk back into the refrigerator, Adam wondered how many other things they had in common. So far, he counted grilled cheese sandwiches, tomato soup, hot chocolate. Neither of them enjoyed board or card games. And she sure liked kissing as much as he did! Seemed a sorry shame to let a woman like this get away—

Wade burst through the door, then stopped dead in his tracks when he spotted Kasey at the stove. Adam could almost read his partner's mind: The woman looked familiar, but he didn't know *why*. He'd seen the photo Adam carried with him, plenty of times, but so far Wade hadn't put two and two together.

"There's plenty to eat, pal," Adam invited, gesturing to an empty chair.

A wary half smile on his face, Wade took a seat as Kasey rose and walked directly to the cabinet where Adam kept the plates. She slid one in front of Wade and laid a butter knife and fork on a neatly folded paper napkin beside it.

"Juice?" she asked, fingers wrapped around the refrigerator handle.

Wade nodded dumbly, and as Kasey filled his glass, he met Adam's eyes. *She's pretty comfortable in your kitchen,* said the look on Wade's face. *Shut up* was the message Adam sent back.

"So, who's your pretty friend?" Wade asked, grabbing a slice of toast. He narrowed his eyes and, using his butter knife as a pointer, added, "Hey...she's wearing the sweatsuit you won in that marathon last month."

Kasey's cheeks glowed and she ran a hand through her curls. "I, um, I was picking flowers," she told Wade, "j-just down the road, when the storm hit last evening. My car got stuck in the mud, and—"

"You don't owe this palooka any explanations," Adam interrupted, shooting Wade another heated "zip it" look. Then he said, "Kasey Delaney, meet Wade Parks, my partner."

"And pal," Wade stuck in, grinning around a mouthful of breakfast. "Y'know, these are some of the best scramblers I've ever had the pleasure of—"

"Stow it, *pal*. I'm not buying it, and neither is—"

Suddenly, Wade's smile faded. Eyes wide, he swallowed, hard. "Wait…" He took a sip of his juice. "Kasey, what did you say your last name was?"

"She didn't. I did," Adam pointed out, aiming a look at Wade that said, *Careful*….

"Delaney," Kasey said, wiping her right hand on a dish towel before extending it toward Wade. "Pleased to meet you."

The stunned expression on Wade's face prevented him from shaking her hand. Suddenly, he was overcome by a coughing fit. After a few moments of sputtering and gasping, though red-faced and watery-eyed, he managed to catch his breath.

"Whoa," he croaked. "Sorry, guys. Hope I didn't spoil your appetites."

Nice save, Adam thought, relieved. But "Fat chance!" is what he actually said.

"So," Kasey said, "how long have the two of you been partners?"

Wade, still clearing his throat, signaled that Adam should answer the question.

Anything to keep you quiet, Adam thought. "Eight years," he said.

"But I've known this old dog since we were pups," Wade added, stuffing another forkful of eggs into his mouth.

Kasey sighed. "Would've been nice if there had been a couple of good cardiologists in Ellicott City a few years back. Maybe my dad could have survived his heart—"

A whole new coughing fit rendered Wade speechless.

Kasey's large eyes narrowed as she gave Wade a look that, from Adam's point of view, seemed a blend of suspicion and mistrust. Could she know that fifteen years ago, the men now sharing breakfast with her had been partially responsible for her father's death?

Adam took a deep breath and said to Wade, "So, did you get your woman all moved into her new place?"

"Yeah," he rasped. "Marcy's all set. Told me to invite you to supper. But let's not get too hung up on that 'woman' thing, shall we? We're friends."

Adam harumphed. Wade had more "friends" than he had fingers and toes. "Supper? I thought you said she can't operate a can opener."

"She can't." Wade grinned. "She's a real whiz at orderin' pizza, though." He cleared his throat. "Supper is a bribe. She was kinda hopin' you'd help me get her stereo, TV and VCR hooked up." He looked at Kasey. "I'm terrible at that stuff. My own VCR still blinks twelve o'clock, and it's three years old!"

Kasey laughed. "So does mine."

"Well, then," Wade said, "maybe after we get Marcy's equipment up and running, me and Einstein here can stop by your place and fix *your* clock."

Adam wished there had been a flyswatter nearby, because he would have used it to smack Wade alongside the head. The coughing spasms were evidence enough that his friend knew who Kasey was. What could he be thinking, suggesting a thing like that!

Wade must have read the heated expression on Adam's face, because he quickly threw in, "Well, I guess that's a pretty stupid idea, considering it'll take a while to finish at Marcy's." He punctuated his statement with a burst of nervous laughter, then changed the subject. "The road's all but washed out just around the bend to your place, Adam. All I can say is, I'm thankful for four-wheel drive."

Kasey groaned.

Which made Wade say, "What?"

"I don't have four-wheel drive. In fact, I don't have *two*-wheel drive."

He looked from her worried face to Adam's. "Huh?"

"She drives a car so small you could carry it in your pocket," Adam explained, "and it's stuck in the mud."

Wade waved the problem away. "We'll get you unstuck and have you on your way in no time. Right, partner?"

Getting Kasey on her way didn't seem nearly as important as getting *Wade* on his way, before he spilled the beans. "Sure. Why not?"

Grinning, Kasey got to her feet. "'Here's your hat, there's the door, so what's your hurry?'" She began stacking plates. "Never let it be said Kasey Delaney doesn't recognize when she's worn out her welcome!"

Despite Kasey's wide smile, Adam couldn't tell if she was kidding. Maybe she'd gotten good at pretending to feel what others expected her to feel, same as he had. True, he wanted to be rid of her, fast as possible, but only because he couldn't bear to have her know about his past. If his and Wade's conversation had hurt her feelings....

He grabbed her hand without a thought as to how it

might look to Wade, or to Kasey, for that matter. "You could never wear out your welcome," he blurted.

From the corner of his eye, he saw Wade's eyebrows rise. But it didn't matter, because Kasey had tilted her head, smiling so warmly that she could have melted the ice in the freezer without opening the door.

"What a nice thing to say, Adam."

She tilted her head the other way, and gave his hand a squeeze before turning to load the dishwasher. "Were you guys serious—about helping me get unstuck, I mean?"

"'Course we were," the men said in unison.

Without facing them, Kasey said, "Then, when you're finished at Marcy's, the three of you can come to my place. I'll fix you all a nice dinner, to thank Adam for taking me in last night, to thank both of you for getting my car out of the mud."

Adam opened his mouth, intending to say, *Thanks, but no thanks,* when Wade spouted, "Hey, that sounds great! What time should we be there?"

Hanging his head, Adam heaved a sigh. Well, just this once. But after tonight—and after he had a moment alone with Wade—that'd be *it*.

No more Kasey Delaney in his life—at least not up close and personal....

Kasey's mother had left an hour earlier to help her Ladies' Auxiliary friends prepare for the upcoming silent auction. And moments ago, Aleesha had climbed into the Resurrection van, headed for a Halloween costume party in the basement of the church.

Kasey had spent the better half of the morning cleaning the house, part of the afternoon shopping for groceries, and the past few hours preparing the meal she'd serve Wade, Marcy and Adam. The table had been set since three, and she'd been dressed and ready since four. Hopefully, the threesome would arrive at five, the scheduled time, because the lasagna would be ready to come out of the oven by then. She wanted to have everything cleaned up before the trick-or-treaters began to—

As if on cue, the doorbell chimed. Drying her hands on a blue-and-yellow plaid dish towel, she hurried to the door. One last peek in the mirror. Yes, her lipstick was fine, and no, her hair hadn't slipped out of the loose braid. Taking a deep breath, she felt reasonably ready to let them in. Smiling, she threw open the door—

—and froze when the first face she saw belonged to a tall, willowy blonde.

"Hiya," the woman said, pushing past Kasey. "So nice of you to include me, last minute and all." She gave her wad of pink gum a final *pop*, then giggled.

"Kasey," Wade said, sliding an arm around the petite brunette beside him, "this is Marcy. Marcy, Kasey Delaney."

"Nice to meet you." Kasey stepped aside. "Please, won't you all come in?"

"It's gettin' dark early these days," said the blonde. "You get many trick-or-treaters in this neighborhood? I imagine you do…all these little tiny houses so close together. I'll just bet there are five kids in every one of 'em." The gum went *snap*, and she giggled again.

"This is Carole," Marcy said, once Kasey closed the front door. "We've been friends since junior high and—"

"What's that…that *smell?*" Carole wrinkled her nose.

Kasey held her breath. She usually didn't wear perfume, but had decided that for tonight she'd spritz on a bit of her mother's Ambrosia.

"What smell?" Wade asked. "All my schnoz detects is something good to eat."

Carole shook her head and grimaced. Holding her stomach, she said, "Eww…I hope it's not something *Italian*." One hand over her stomach, she added, "I can't do spicy food, y'know."

Kasey was doing her best not to meet Adam's eyes, because it was fairly obvious that Carole had come as his date. The notion hurt more than she cared to admit, considering she'd only met him yesterday. Still, it seemed an insensitive, inconsiderate thing to do—bringing an uninvited guest. But then, to be fair, she hadn't told him he couldn't bring his…*woman*.

Well, that'll learn ya, she thought, straightening her back. "Let's go into the family room," she suggested, forcing a bright smile, "and I'll get us all some iced tea to sip while we're waiting for the—"

Carole waved a red-taloned hand in the air. "Oh, no. No can do," she sputtered around the wad of gum. "Caffeine makes my li'l heart go pitter-pat, pitter-pat." Winking at Adam, she sidled closer to him. "I'm savin' that for—" she batted her eyelashes suggestively "—later."

Kasey searched Adam's face, hoping for a sign there had been some mistake, that this loud, aggressive woman was not his date. Because she would never have guessed Carole to be his…type. Unfortunately, his lopsided grin told her nothing.

"Carole's in public relations. She just relocated here from Washington, D.C.," Marcy explained, as they filed into the family room.

Kasey managed a stiff smile. "Congratulations." And to Adam, she said, "You must be very proud."

He blinked. Looked from Kasey to Carole, from Marcy to Wade, then back at Kasey. "Proud? Well…sure," he said, as Carole snuggled closer still.

"I'll get the iced tea," she announced. "Carole, would you prefer a soda? Or maybe some herbal tea?"

"Got any wine? Wine I can do." She winked at Adam. "It makes me…*mellow*."

"No." Kasey thought of Aleesha, and the example she'd tried to set for the girl even before becoming her adopted mother. "We don't have alcohol in the house. Ever." She wondered if Carole chewed gum to cover up the odor of tobacco on her breath. "No tobacco products, either."

Carole sighed deeply. "Okay. I guess I can settle for some herb tea. You got honey? Or do I hafta use sugar? 'Cause processed sugar is really bad for a woman's complexion…."

She fought the urge to say, *I've got honey,* honey. Instead, Kasey simply said, "Make yourselves comfortable."

Alone in the kitchen, she pressed her forehead to the cool, smooth surface of the white refrigerator. As she had lain on the sofa in his cozy living room last night, she'd considered the likelihood of a woman in his life. But *that* woman? Surely Carole hadn't helped decorate the cabin….

She held her breath and said a quick prayer for forgiveness. "You're acting like a jealous girlfriend," she whispered, turning on the flame under the teakettle. And she had no right to feel that way. Had no right to judge Carole, either. There must be *something* redeeming about her personality, because Adam was kindhearted and good and decent. If he'd chosen her—

"Need any help?" Marcy asked, peeking around the doorway.

"No, but thanks."

"This is really nice of you, having a bunch of strangers over for dinner. I feel like Mother Hubbard, because my cupboards are totally bare!"

Kasey laughed. "I'm happy to do it. Adam was such a wonderful host last night, and he and Wade were such good sports, even after they got all muddy getting my car unstuck."

It seemed Marcy hadn't heard a word she'd said. "So tell me...what do you think of him?"

"Wade? Oh, he seems very nice. I think—"

"Not Wade, silly," she said, grinning. *"Adam."*

She poked around in the freezer, grabbing ice cubes for the tumblers she'd lined up on the countertop. Considering what a fool she'd already made of herself, fussing over her hair and makeup, taking forever to choose *just* the right outfit to impress Adam, Kasey had no intention of admitting her real feelings to this perfect stranger. Even if Marcy did have a wide, friendly smile and big, honest brown eyes.

"He seems very nice. Polite, gentlemanly, intelligent—"

"You make him sound like a Boy Scout leader! C'mon, you can tell me. You like him, don't you?"

Kasey poured iced tea into each glass. "Well, of course I like him. As I said, he's very nice and—"

"Sure you like him. Everybody likes him. But do you *like* him?" She wiggled her eyebrows.

Kasey simply couldn't bear to admit that she'd allowed herself to develop a crush on a man she barely knew.

A horrible thought suddenly occurred to her.

Maybe Adam, suspecting she'd grown too fond of him, too quickly, had brought Carole along tonight as a polite yet firm way of telling her he wasn't interested in a relationship. If that was the case, what difference did it make whether or not she liked him *that* way?

"Seems he's already spoken for," she blurted.

"You mean Carole?" Marcy's laughter echoed from the yellow-tiled kitchen walls. "Adam isn't interested in her!"

"Could've fooled me," Kasey muttered.

"Hmm?"

"Nothing." The teapot began to whistle, and Kasey busied herself spooning honey into Carole's cup.

"What *is* that delicious aroma?"

Kasey sighed. "Lasagna. I have no idea what I'm going to feed Carole...."

Marcy looked in the freezer. "Fish sticks, frozen macaroni and cheese, hot dogs, and two diet TV dinners." Smiling, she met Kasey's eyes. "You eat like a teenager, you know that?"

"Those are for my daughter."

"How old is she?"

"Almost seventeen."

"Seventeen! You don't look old enough to *have* a kid, let alone one that old."

"Well, she's adopted. But I couldn't love her more if she were my own flesh and blood."

Marcy closed the freezer door and stood, one hand on her hip, nodding. "You're one cool chick, Kasey Delaney. I think I like you."

Now, how could anyone help but smile at a comment like that! Kasey flushed.

"Want my opinion?"

"Depends."

"Feed Carole the macaroni and cheese. Seems right up her alley." With that, she grabbed two iced tea glasses and headed for the family room. "How long 'til supper," she said in a loud voice, "'cause that lasagna smells *wonderful* and I'm starving!"

Balancing the remaining tumblers in one hand and the teacup in the other, Kasey followed Marcy into the family room. It might not be the evening she'd planned, but it sure wasn't going to be boring!

Chapter Four

"**I** keep thinking I *know* you from somewhere," Carole said around a mouthful of sticky macaroni and cheese. Using her fork as a pencil, she drew a circle in the air. "Your name is just...*soooo* familiar."

Kasey shrugged. "Guess I have one of those names."

"No, no. It's more than just your name. You *look* familiar, too. I've seen your face someplace, I'm sure of it." This time, she jabbed at the air with her fork. "But don't worry, it will come to me."

The woman's smirk and intimidating tone of voice gave Kasey the opinion that Carole secretly hoped "it" would be something humiliating.

Marcy gasped. "Wait! *I* know why Kasey looks so familiar!"

Kasey held her breath and said a quick prayer for protection. Marcy seemed nice enough, but she'd been Carole's friend for years. If there was any truth in the "birds of a feather" rule....

"Remember when we were in junior high, there was all

that news coverage about an engineer who died near Crescent Lawn...the night of Halloween?''

Carole narrowed her eyes, as Wade and Adam exchanged puzzled glances.

"Weird," Marcy continued, leaning forward and lowering her voice, "that fifteen years later, to the exact day, we're sitting in that same guy's house!"

Carole's brow furrowed. "What *are* you talking about?"

"Oh, c'mon. You were glued to the TV, 'cause like just about every other kid around here, you planned to go to Crescent Lawn on Halloween, too!"

Carole put down her fork. "You mean the guy who died of a heart attack that night was your father?" She lay a hand atop Kasey's. "So *that's* why you look so familiar. Your picture was all over the news." She gave the hand a little squeeze. "Oh, wow. Oh, no. Kasey, I'm *sooooo* sorry."

Kasey snatched back her hand, hid it in her lap. "It was a long time ago, and I don't—"

"No, really," Carole droned on, "it was heartless of me to bring that up. I'm sure it's tough enough for you and your mom the rest of the year. But tonight..." She expelled a heavy sigh. "I'll bet you were making last-minute adjustments on your costume when you got the terrible news that night, weren't you!" Groaning, she sat back in her chair and buried her face in her hands. "I feel *soooo* awful!"

If she felt so awful, Kasey wondered, why didn't she just shut up? "There's fresh coffee," Kasey said, rising. "And I've made spumoni for dessert." She forced a bright smile. "Who's interested?"

"I'm in," Wade said. "If the spumoni is even half as good as that lasagna..." He smacked his lips.

Marcy nodded. "Me, too."

Kasey met Adam's eyes, and couldn't help but wonder why he suddenly looked like a boy caught with his hand in the cookie jar. She thought she heard a slight tremor in his voice when he said, "Sounds great."

"None for me, thanks. I'm watching my weight." Carole patted her flat abdomen. "But you guys go ahead and enjoy. I don't mind watching you eat."

"Good," Adam said, none too gently, "because to tell you the truth, I don't think any of us mind if you mind." He stood, too, and grabbed the lasagna pan. Ignoring Carole's indignant gasp, he faced Kasey. "Dinner was delicious."

She couldn't put a name to it, but something akin to guilt glittered in those dark brown eyes. "Glad you enjoyed it."

Alone in the kitchen, he deposited the glass pan on the stovetop. "I apologize for Carole's behavior."

"Why?"

"Seems *somebody* ought to apologize for it."

"Didn't you say earlier that you'd only just met her?"

He nodded.

"Even if you'd known her for years, why would I hold you responsible for anything she's said or done?"

He stared at the floor. "I don't know," he muttered. "I just feel bad, is all."

She fixed the big smile on her face once more. "Hey, no biggie." Sliding the plates into the pan of sudsy water she'd fixed earlier, she shrugged. "People like that keep us on our toes. They're really good for character building, if—"

"You're something else, you know that?"

Kasey blinked. "Because I refuse to let a few rude comments spoil my whole evening?"

He only stared.

"What?" she asked, after a few seconds of intense scrutiny. "Do I have mozzarella between my teeth or something?"

Adam smiled. "Or something," he said softly.

She swallowed, cleared her throat and prayed like crazy that he couldn't hear the wild beating of her heart, because for the life of her, Kasey didn't know why his mere presence was having such an effect on her.

"So," she said at last, "what say we get dessert on the table?"

He took a step forward, placed both hands on her shoulders.

The clock ticked, ice clunked into the freezer bin, her pulse pounded as he looked into her eyes. She could see an image of herself mirrored in the dark gleam of his pupils. Could he tell, as those dark-lashed brown orbs bored into her, that she felt almost as small and helpless as her minuscule reflection?

Adam slid his arms around her, pulled her close and rested his chin amid her curls. "Ahhh, Kasey," he said huskily, "if only..."

He sounded so sad, so lonely. And she couldn't help but wonder why a handsome, healthy doctor, with lots of friends, a home of his own and a successful medical practice, would be either one. "If only what?" she whispered.

The heat of his sigh warmed her scalp while the muscles of his chest hardened under her palms.

"If only we could get the dessert and the coffee into the dining room in just one trip." And holding her at arm's length, he said, "You gonna dish up the spumoni, or shall I?"

After dinner, Adam insisted on staying to help Kasey with the dishes. And though Carole protested, whimpering that she didn't like riding in the back seat—which was where she'd have to sit if Wade and Marcy took her home—he refused to back down.

"So," Kasey said, rinsing a plate and sliding it into the dishwasher, "what do *you* remember about that night?"

Immediately, Adam's mouth went dry and his palms began to sweat. "What night?" he asked, though he had a sinking feeling he knew.

"The night my dad died." She feigned a tough woman-cop voice. "Where were you on the night of October thirty-first, nineteen and—"

"Carole is an idiot," he interrupted. "An insensitive, coldhearted, brainless idiot."

Kasey's eyes widened. "Wow. Don't be so wishy-washy, Adam." She grinned. "If you have an opinion, you're free to voice it in this house."

Chuckling, he shook his head. "I'm sorry. I know that wasn't very nice, but, well...she *was* behaving like an idiot."

Kasey bobbed her head, telling Adam that while she might agree, she wouldn't resort to name-calling. "That doesn't answer my question."

Somehow, he'd known she'd come back to that subject.

"Do you remember that night?"

Remember? If he lived to be a hundred, he'd never forget that night.

Kasey sighed. "Strange..."

"Why?"

"Because, in the overall scheme of things, it shouldn't have seemed like such a big deal to so many people. I'm surprised to learn any of you remembered what happened."

"'Any of you'?"

"I could tell Wade's recollection was as vivid as Marcy's and Carole's. And you..." She turned to shove a handful of silverware into the dishwasher basket. "Why, you looked as if you'd seen a ghost."

With good reason, he thought. Never in his wildest imaginings had he expected to meet up with Al Delaney's daughter, and not in a million years did he think he'd be this close to having her find out that he'd been involved in her father's death.

"So, how much do you remember?"

He chose his words carefully. "I remember enough."

She stood water goblets and iced tea tumblers upside down in the top rack. "I'm tougher than I look," she said over her shoulder. "I'd really like to hear it, from an outsider's point of view."

Outsider? As one of the guys who'd *caused* the accident, Adam would hardly call himself an outsider! "I remember reading the article in the *Sun* the morning after, seeing the photograph of your mom and dad and you." Suddenly, it felt like that same photograph, encased in clear plastic, was burning a hole through his jeans pocket. "You were pretty, even as a little girl."

Kasey blushed and rolled her eyes. "Men," she said, laughing softly. "You'll say just about anything to sidestep a difficult subject, won't you?"

What had he said or done to make her think he was sidestepping? To make her believe he saw the subject as "difficult"?

Everything, he thought. But if hearing the truth meant she'd hate him, Adam admitted silently, then yes, he'd say just about anything. And surely she would hate him. Probably had hated him, from afar, since learning about the prank that caused her father's fatal heart attack.

"Can I ask *you* a question?"

"Okay. Shoot."

Shooting's too good for me. "What did you think—what *do* you think...about those boys who made the dummy?"

She sighed, a long shaky sound that wrapped around Adam like an icy wind.

"At first, I despised them."

He flinched, and hoped she hadn't noticed.

"But after a while, after a little maturing and a whole lot of time, I realized it wasn't really their fault, what happened." She sighed again. "They were just having a little fun. They hadn't set out to hurt him. And besides, Dad had put a lot of effort into hiding his condition. There was no way they could have known he had a weak heart, no way they could have anticipated what might happen when that pumpkin-headed dummy hit the tracks."

Relief coursed through his veins upon hearing she hadn't spent all these years detesting them...detesting *him*. Still, it was all Adam could do to keep from hanging his head. "Like I said before, you're something else, Kasey Delaney."

She sent him a silly, lopsided grin. "Not really. Coming to that conclusion was easy."

"As compared to what?"

"The energy it takes to hate." She shrugged her dainty shoulders. "Hate is a lot of work. Besides, people said all sorts of ridiculous things, and even at my tender age I knew they were only speculating because they needed to blame somebody for what happened, when in reality, *fate* was more to blame than anything else."

He wished he could tell all those people they could have spared themselves the effort. He'd blamed himself enough to satisfy the lot of them. "What sorts of things did they say?"

"Oh, that the boys were juvenile delinquents, that their real purpose was to derail the train that night. That they weren't kids at all, but criminals who wanted to create a distraction while they robbed a bank.'' A funny little laugh popped from her lips. ''I think they were just kids, bored teenagers with no malicious intent, no evil plot. It was just a Halloween prank that went horribly, horribly wrong.''

Well, she'd hit the mark on that one, but Adam didn't dare admit it.

''I've prayed for them ever since I worked it out in my head.''

''Worked what out?''

''If they *were* decent kids, just goofing off that night— and I believe that's exactly what they were—it must have been terrible for them, hearing what happened because of their 'trick.' I imagine they've spent as many sleepless nights as I have.''

''How could you know a thing like that?'' he said without thinking, without caring that the question might well implicate him.

She poured soap powder into the receptacle in the dishwasher door. ''I've imagined what might have happened— but they were *there*.'' She snapped the door shut and adjusted the dial. ''I'd wager their consciences have taken quite a beating over the years.''

She'd hit the mark so well this time, it caused an ache in Adam's gut that he could only compare to the steel of a sucker punch.

''I'm glad I decided to serve dinner early,'' she said, after a moment of silence. ''The trick-or-treaters will start ringing the doorbell soon, and now I won't have any distractions.''

''Mind if I stay?''

''Won't it bore you silly?''

''Why would it bore me?''

''Well, for starters, you're a footloose, fancy-pants doctor." She shot him a teasing wink. "Carole is waiting for you...."

"Now, there's an enticement," he joked right back.

"Still, I'm sure you have more interesting things to do than drop lollipops and gumballs into trick-or-treat bags."

"None that I can think of," he said, and meant it.

Kasey headed for the front hall and grabbed her sweater. "I'm glad it isn't very cold."

"And the rain stopped."

She nodded. Then, opening the door, she glanced at Adam's corduroy shirt. "You gonna be warm enough in that?"

He shrugged. "I'll be fine."

Kasey left him standing alone in the doorway and poked around in the hall closet. "Will this do?" She held up a red and black Buffalo plaid jacket.

It was way too large to be hers, and he doubted a teenage girl would wear such a thing. Which meant it had belonged to Al Delaney. No way he could put it on. "Thanks, but I'll be fine."

"What, not your style?" she taunted.

"No, it's not that. I'm just... I'm afraid I'd rip a sleeve or something."

She looked from Adam's chest to the jacket. "You make a good point." Hanging it up, she said, "I have just the thing, and I know it'll fit."

Before he could protest, Kasey had disappeared. He could hear her, rummaging somewhere beyond the kitchen. When she returned, she carried the sweatsuit he'd loaned her.

"All washed and fluff-dried," she announced, tossing him the sweatshirt and hanging the pants over the banister.

As he slid it over his head, Adam inhaled the clean, fresh scent of detergent. Or fabric softener. Or both. His clothes had never smelled like that, though he took them to the best laundry in town. He was seriously considering never laundering them again, when the doorbell rang.

"Trick or treat!" a lop-eared bunny shouted.

"Trick or treat!" hollered his black cat companion.

"My, my, look at you!" Kasey said, grabbing a handful of candy from the overloaded bowl beside the door.

"Thanks," said the bunny, as a candy bar hit the bottom of his bag.

"Yeah, thanks, lady," said the cat.

"You be careful out there," Kasey called, as they ran down the porch steps. "And remember to look both ways when you cross the street."

She zipped up her jacket and grinned. "They're probably too excited to listen to reason."

"Which is why there oughta be a law—no trick-or-treating unless accompanied by a responsible adult."

Kasey led the way onto the porch, invited Adam to sit in the adirondack chair beside hers. "What was your favorite costume when you were a boy?"

He leaned back, rested his hands on the chair's wide wooden arms. "I was a monster, a soldier. Even dressed up as a superhero once."

"Only once?"

Chuckling, Adam shook his head. "Couldn't see through the eyeholes on that plastic mask. I'd only been to four or five houses when I tripped on my cape and fell flat on my face. Broke my nose and sprained my wrist, and spent Halloween in the emergency room."

"Oh, Adam, how terrible! How old were you?"

"Five, maybe six." He met her eyes, glittering like green gemstones in the porch light. "How 'bout you? What was your favorite costume?" He held up a hand. "No, wait. Let me guess. You were a princess, or a ballerina, or a nurse...."

She shook her head. "Actually, I preferred comfortable costumes to stuff like that."

"Comfortable?"

She nodded. "Too hard to manipulate your trick-or-treat bag wearing frilly dresses and tiaras, and carrying magic wands. Not to mention, you could freeze to death in the flimsy things! I liked going as a hobo, a private detective—self-made characters that didn't require one of those plastic masks and—"

"Private detective?"

"Yup. I'd wear one of my dad's white shirts, borrow a tie and a sports coat, and put on his old Sunday hat." She groaned softly. "But Mom wouldn't let me carry a toy gun—said it was bad enough her only daughter didn't want to put on makeup and a frou-frou outfit—"

"Frou-frou?"

"Y'know...gauzy, ruffly things." She lifted her chin. "I preferred sensible costumes. Much to Mom's dismay, I was a tomboy all the way."

Adam recalled the way she'd looked, all wet and windblown, on his cabin porch the night before. "Didn't look like a tomboy last night," he admitted.

"Are you for real? Jeans and hiking boots and—"

"—and all that gorgeous hair, those big beautiful eyes. You could put on full camouflage gear and not fool anyone into thinking you're a boy."

"I don't want to fool anyone into thinking I'm a boy. It's just that—"

Little Red Riding Hood and the Big Bad Wolf skipped up the steps, singsonging "Trick or treat!"

"—sensible," he finished, as she doled out the sweets. *One more reason to like you, my dear,* he thought.

"Hey, lady," said the Wolf, "the candle in your pumpkin blew out."

"Goodness," Kasey replied. "How terrible. I'll get right on it. Thanks for pointing it out."

The kids were on her neighbor's porch before she'd finished thanking them. "I'll be right back," she said, rising.

Adam grasped her wrist. "Where're you going?"

"To get a book of matches, of course."

It was clear how much she enjoyed watching the children parade in and out in their multicolored costumes, and it didn't seem fair that she might miss even one. "I'll get them," he said. "Just tell me where they are."

She sat down so quickly, he knew he'd made the right decision.

"In the drawer under the coffeepot, which is beside the refrigerator. You can't miss 'em."

He headed inside. "Don't sneak any gumballs while I'm gone."

"Wouldn't dream of it." She cupped a hand beside her mouth. "Peanut butter candies are my favorites."

On his way to the kitchen, Adam cut through the dining room, aglow with the soft light filtering in from the stove hood. Kasey had made several flower arrangements in here. Two flanked a cornucopia on the buffet, and one stood in the center of the gleaming cherry table. She'd woven some kind of twisted branches around the curtain rod, and topped off both corners of the window with dried flowers. He searched his memory for a word to describe the room. *Homey,* he decided, like the rest of the house. He could live like this...if he'd had the guts to tell Buddy to take a flying leap that night.

Adam all but stomped into the kitchen and pulled open the drawer under the coffeepot. It surprised him a bit to find the matches in a tidy row, strike-pads all facing the same direction. They reminded him of broad-shouldered paper soldiers, standing at attention. The organizer tray also held screwdrivers, pliers, a tape measure, assorted batteries, and a small jar of nails, tacks and screws. What would have been a jumble of this-and-that in most kitchens had been stored here with military precision.

Adam grabbed a book of matches, careful not to disturb the careful arrangement. Curiosity compelled him to open the cabinet above the coffeepot, to see if the same meticulousness continued there, as well. Sure enough, mugs and cups stood in straight lines; on the shelf above them, boxes of herbal tea and canisters of flavored coffees were stacked.

The next cabinet held plates, and there, too, attention had been given to the order in which things had been placed. Likewise, the silverware drawer, where spoons and forks nestled one atop the other, appearing at first glance to be one fat utensil rather than dozens of thin ones.

Yep, Adam told himself, *I could live like this.*

Still, he couldn't help but wonder *why* things were so perfect in the Delaney household. Had it been her way of reclaiming command of a world gone out of control?

"Took you long enough," she said, when he stepped onto the porch. "I was getting ready to send in search dogs!"

"Your jack-o'-lantern awaits, m'lady," he said, bowing low before handing her the matches.

She hurried down the steps, to where the carved pumpkin sat in the bowl of a concrete birdbath, then struck a match and held it to the candle's wick. "There!" she announced, as the flame frolicked in the breeze.

He'd seen the pumpkin earlier, as the foursome ascended the steps for dinner. "Did you carve it yourself?"

Kasey plopped down beside him, nodding. "Uh-huh. Well, not *all* by myself. Aleesha helped."

"Your adopted daughter."

"One and the same. But we never say 'adopted' around here. She needs all the assurances she can get that I love her like crazy, even if she isn't my flesh-and-blood kid."

He understood, and admired her attitude. "Where is she, out trick-or-treating?"

"No, she considers herself much too mature and sophisticated for such childish nonsense." Kasey laughed. "Which is why she's at the church, doing her best *not* to enjoy the costume parade and contest the youth group is sponsoring."

"I forget...how old is she?"

"Seventeen. I adopted her on her sixteenth birthday."

"And she was what, thirteen or fourteen when you met, right?"

"Right."

"You're something else, Kasey."

"You keep saying that—I'm going to need a carpenter."

"For what?"

"To make keyhole shapes out of all my doorways, so I can fit my big head through the openings!"

Chuckling, Adam said, "You can't blame me. I don't know another person who's adopted a struggling inner-city kid."

"And isn't that a shame? There are so many children out there, yearning for parents." Kasey blew a stream of air through her teeth. "Everybody wants newborns, though I don't for the life of me understand why."

"Maybe because they're not secure enough to take on a kid who already has opinions and mind-sets of their own." He shrugged. "Get a brand-new baby, you get a blank slate and unofficial permission to write on it whatever makes you comfortable."

She sat forward to meet his eyes. "I never thought of it

that way before.'' Grinning mischievously, she added, ''Very philosophical. *You're* something else, Dr. Adam Thorne.''

He was about to protest when half a dozen giggling and shouting boys stormed the porch. ''Trick or treat!'' they bellowed.

Adam recognized the usual comic book and TV characters. But one youngster's costume puzzled him. ''What're you supposed to be?''

The kid adjusted a wide-brimmed hat, then tugged at the Windsor knot of a too-long tie. Extending a half-filled bag with one hand, he plopped the chubby fist of the other on his hip. ''I'm an undercover FBI agent,'' he said, rolling his big brown eyes. He looked at his pals as if to say, *What's this guy, a moron?*

''I thought maybe you were a private detective,'' Adam explained, winking at Kasey, ''or a newspaper reporter. But an FBI agent. Wow. You had me going for a minute there.''

''Private detective? Who ever heard of being a private detective for Halloween?'' The boy and his buddies snickered, as if it was the most ridiculous idea they'd ever heard. ''Thanks for the candy, lady,'' the FBI agent said. ''And didja know the light's out in your pumpkin?''

''I had no idea!''

Adam thought he heard a trace of disappointment in her voice. Because the candle was out again? Or because the boy made fun of her favorite costume? When the kids were out of earshot, he said, ''If I was that boy's dad, I'd teach him to be respectful of his elders.''

''You would?''

''You betcha. Especially beautiful, shapely elders who're handing out free candy!''

The sound of his own voice sounded alien in his ears. Adam couldn't recall the last time he'd cracked a joke, deliberately or accidentally. Couldn't remember a time when he'd enjoyed himself so completely. His life, it seemed, had had two purposes: help his patients, and help the Delaneys. Fun was for others, who hadn't destroyed a man's life, and in the process, the man's family.

Uncomfortable with the newfound emotions, Adam coughed. "Say, I have an idea...."

Kasey tilted her head.

"To keep the light in your pumpkin from going out again. Well, from *blowing* out again, anyway."

"I'm all ears."

"When I got the matches from the kitchen drawer, I saw a flashlight. Plenty of batteries, too. Why not take out the candle, replace it with the flashlight?"

If it was possible for an entire body to smile, Kasey accomplished it. She got to her feet and clapped her hands, reminding him of an excitable, enthusiastic girl. *And she calls herself a tomboy,* he thought, grinning. She didn't overdo the jewelry or the makeup, and didn't seem to fuss much with that gorgeous mane of reddish curls. But Kasey Delaney was all woman, a fact she couldn't hide under hiking boots and blue jeans. She couldn't hide it under that bulky fisherman's knit sweater, either.

"That's a terrific idea, Adam," she said, half running toward the front door. "While I'm inside, can I get you anything? Soda? Iced tea?"

She could get him a guilt-free conscience; maybe then he could *really* enjoy his time with her, make some plans for the future, start living like a normal guy. "Nah. I'm fine. But thanks."

"How about if I put on the teakettle? We could sip hot chocolate while we wait for more kids to show up."

He hadn't known her long, but so far it seemed to Adam that Kasey was happiest when doing for others. Hot choc-

olate had never been one of his favorite beverages; he kept
the instant stuff at the cabin for people who used the place
on the weekends he didn't, for friends who joined him
when he did. But he said, "Sure. That'd be great."

"I'll just be a minute."

"Take your time. I'll hold down the fort."

"Okay, but don't eat any gumdrops while I'm gone."

"Not a chance. Peanut butter candies are my favorite."

A full minute after she was out of sight, her musical
giggle still echoed in his ears. And, oh, how he delighted
in the sound of it! Fact was, he liked everything about her,
from her orderly cabinets to her genuine delight in seeing
the costumed youngsters. She brought out the best in him,
made him feel good and decent...something he hadn't felt
in a decade and a half. Made him feel that maybe, somehow, there was a way he could live a normal life, if she
was at the center of it.

The only way that could happen was if he was willing
to 'fess up, about everything. The very thought sent a chill
snaking up his spine. Yes, she deserved to know what kind
of guy she was getting involved with, but Adam didn't
know if he had what it took to be that honest.

A lot of what she'd said earlier about him and the other
boys was true. Buddy's gang had been a bunch of rowdy,
attention-seeking mutts who'd created mischief and may-
hem everywhere they went. But they'd never hurt anyone.
At least, not before that Halloween.

Buddy would likely always be Buddy, but Wade and
Luke and Travis often pointed out that Adam had been
solely responsible for the choices they'd made after that
night: his determination to right the wrong committed on
the tracks had given them all the courage to grow up and
go straight.

He'd always denied it, but in his heart of hearts he'd

known it was true, that they *had* listened to him back then. If he'd been able to muster the backbone to stand up to Buddy...

Well, he hadn't, and because he hadn't, the lot of them would live with the part they'd played in Al Delaney's death, forever. Didn't matter, here and now, that they'd changed a lot, that *he'd* changed a lot, had walked the straight and narrow for fifteen years. Kasey Delaney was the only thing that mattered. She deserved only the best life had to offer.

And from where Adam sat, that surely wasn't him.

"How many costumes did I miss?" she asked when she returned.

"None."

"Must be the threat of rain. Or the chill in the air. Some years, we get a hundred kids." She glanced at the deep candy bowl that sat on the board floor between their feet. "We'll be lucky to get two dozen this year."

He couldn't bear to hear the disappointment in her voice, couldn't stand to see it in her eyes. "You want me to go home, come back in my scrubs? I've got this neat pleated mask, though I don't know if I have a proper trick-or-treat bag...."

Kasey laughed, gave his shoulder a playful shove. "You nut. 'Course I don't want that." Her smile faded as she added, "I'm having a perfectly wonderful time, even without a throng of kids."

She leaned forward. Did she mean to kiss him? Should he let her? No, he should do the kinder, more honest thing, and sit back. No point dragging this thing out; better to put an end to it before it started, for both their sakes.

The kiss never happened, because the teapot's whistle split the quiet night. Kasey leaped up. "Hot chocolate or tea?" she asked, clasping her hands beneath her chin.

If he had any decency, if he was any kind of man at all, he'd get to his feet and walk away from here. He wouldn't look back, and he wouldn't *come* back. But Adam knew better than anyone that he wasn't decent. Hadn't he proved that, fifteen years ago? "Hot chocolate, I guess," he said at last.

She combed the fingers of her left hand through his hair, held her right palm against his cheek. It was a moment, a tick in time. A simple, mean-nothing gesture.

But if it meant nothing, why did it touch him like nothing before?

"Your face is cold," she said softly, pocketing her hands. "Maybe we should close up shop, go inside and—"

"Not on your life. There are more kids coming. I'm sure of it."

"You think so?"

He relished the hopeful note in her voice, the sweet smile on her face. "I know so."

"You're sure you don't want to borrow—"

Al's jacket? No way! "I'm sure."

He hadn't seen it coming; if he had, Adam might have done something to prevent it, to protect her from getting any more involved with the likes of him....

Kasey leaned down and pressed a soft kiss to his forehead. And closing his eyes, Adam did his best to memorize how the heat of it felt against his October-chilled skin, to imprint the sweet flowery scent of her breath on his brain. Because after tonight, he wouldn't be seeing her anymore, for her own good, for his good, too.

"Back in a jiff."

"I'm countin' on it."

"The hot chocolate should take the chill off."

He nodded, knowing full well it wasn't the drink that would warm him.

Chapter Five

It was nearly ten o'clock when the pastor's wife dropped Kasey's mother off.

"Thanks for the ride, Rose."

"Anytime, Patricia."

Pat Delaney waved goodbye as the aging station wagon drove off, then climbed the porch steps. "So were there many trick-or-treaters?" she asked. "They didn't soap our windows, I hope, or overturn our—" The moment she noticed Adam, sitting in the shadows of the big pine beside the house, she stopped talking.

"Everything's fine, Mom. There weren't as many kids as usual, but we managed to give away most of the candy." Kasey turned her attention to Adam, who'd stood and pocketed his hands. "Pat Delaney, Dr. Thorne. He's the man I told you about?"

Pat gave Adam a quick once-over. "Well, as I live and breathe, a flesh-and-blood hero, right here on my front porch." She leaned against the white-picket railing. "I'm so glad to have a chance to thank you for taking such good care of my girl last night."

"Mrs. Delaney. It's nice to meet you."

Kasey thought she detected a slight tremor when Adam extended his hand, but chalked it up to the chill breeze. It wasn't so easy explaining the shudder in his voice. If she didn't know better, Kasey would have said he was afraid of her mother, which was ridiculous: Pat Delaney was a lot of things, but intimidating? Never!

As if to prove her wrong, Pat gave her daughter a playful shove. "Kasey, what kind of hostess makes a handsome young guest sit outside in the cold? It can't be thirty degrees!"

She started to defend herself, but Adam beat her to it. "I'm afraid this was my idea," he said. "Before long, the winter will have us confined to quarters, like it or not, so I thought we may as well enjoy the fresh air while we can."

"*Frozen* air you mean!" Pat said, laughing. "Now then..." She rubbed her hands together. "If I know my girl, there's a teapot of hot water on the stove, just begging to be turned into cocoa."

A silent second ticked by, then two.

When neither Kasey nor Adam made a move, she held open the door. "Well?"

"I—I really should get a move on," Adam said. He faced Kasey. "Dinner was delicious. Thanks for inviting—"

"At least come in and let Kasey fix you a plate to take home."

"Thanks, but I—"

Pat leaned toward Adam and, in a loud whisper, said, "You'll be doing Aleesha and me a huge favor if you do. I've never known Kasey to make 'just enough' lasagna. If you don't take some with you, we'll be eating it for the next week!"

He held up a hand as if to defend himself. "Thanks," he said again, "but I really ought to—"

"I might be known for a steady supply of tea water and a tendency to cook too much food," Kasey interrupted, "but Patricia Delaney's claim to fame is stubbornness." She kissed her mother's cheek. "Trust me, Adam. If you don't do what you're told, right now, you'll still be standing here at midnight, going back and forth this way."

Pat folded her hands and looked at the porch ceiling. "Arrgh! So this is what I get for having my only child at forty-six."

A wood-paneled station wagon parked at the curb, commanding their attention. "Aleesha's home," Kasey told Adam. "I was hoping you'd get a chance to meet her."

He only nodded, a thin-lipped smile on his face. He'd said earlier it would be nice to meet Aleesha. Kasey had believed him then. Now, she wasn't so sure.

A lanky man assisted a chubby black girl from the front passenger seat. "Hi, Mom!" she called. "I had a great time. Pastor Hill put me in charge of all the li'l kids, *again*."

"That's only because you're so good with them," he said.

Kasey hurried down the walk to meet them halfway. "Thanks for picking her up and dropping her off, John. You're a peach."

The reverend gently knuckled the top of Aleesha's head. "What a silly *pair* Mrs. Hill and I make—a peach married to a Rose."

Kasey groaned. "I take it back. You're a nut!"

Aleesha giggled. "Very punny, you two."

"G'night, Kase," he said, slamming the passenger door. "See you tomorrow, Leesh." He waved toward the porch. "Rose got you home in one piece, eh, Pat?"

"Yes, and ten minutes ahead of schedule, to boot," she called, as he climbed into the driver's seat. "Drive safely, John." And to the rest of them she added, "The lot of you can stand out here blabbing in the cold if you want to, but I'm going inside where it's warm!"

She did, too, and slammed the door behind her.

"Uh-oh," Aleesha said. "Is Gramma in a bad mood?"

"No, sweetie. She's just tired." She slung an arm over the girl's shoulders as they walked up the sidewalk. "I'll bet you're tired, too."

Aleesha pointed. "Who's that?"

Kasey looked up, saw Adam standing on the edge of the porch, shoulders hunched into the wind, hands deep in his pockets. "Gramma's right, it's cold out here. Let's go inside, and I'll make proper introductions."

Aleesha aimed a suspicious glance at Adam as she headed inside. "He gonna be over here all the time like that crazy man from across the street?"

"Mr. Mauvais isn't crazy," Kasey whispered. She wished for a little more light, so she could see Adam's reaction to Aleesha's mention of Buddy. "And it isn't nice to talk that way about grown-ups."

While Kasey closed the front door, Aleesha hung her jacket on the hall tree and studied Adam more deliberately. "This the man who let you sleep on his couch last night?"

"Yes. Dr. Adam Thorne, this is my daughter, Aleesha."

Adam held out his hand. "Pleased to meet you, Aleesha."

The girl grasped it, gave it a quick shake. "What kind of doctor are you?"

"Cardiologist."

She nodded. "So all your patients have bad hearts." Another nod. "Interestin'."

Adam chuckled. "It's a living."

She glanced at Kasey, then met Adam's eyes. "She told you I'm adopted, right?"

"I believe her exact words were 'My daughter's name is Aleesha, and I love her like crazy.'"

"You said that? To a complete stranger?" Beaming, the girl wrapped her mother in an affectionate hug.

Chin resting on Aleesha's head, Kasey looked at Adam. *My hee-roe,* she mouthed, grinning.

"I've made a big pot of hot chocolate," Pat called from the kitchen. "Not that powdery stuff in envelopes, either, but real made-from-scratch cocoa."

Aleesha broke free of Kasey's hug. "I'll be in the kitchen, Mom." To Adam she said, "Gramma makes some of the best cocoa I ever drank, and I'm gettin' some even if she *is* in a bad mood!" With that, she hurried down the hall.

"She's right, you know." Kasey rubbed her palms over her upper arms. "You owe it to yourself to have just one cup."

He took a step closer. "You're cold?"

"I'll warm up, soon as I get some of Mom's cocoa into my stomach. You'll join us, right?"

He winced slightly, then glanced at the face of the grand-father clock.

"If you have early surgery or something—"

"Fact is, I'm off tomorrow."

Kasey noted his smile didn't quite make it to his eyes. "All right, then. One cup, and yer outta here, mister," she said, aiming a thumb at the front door.

"Deal."

The four of them sat around the kitchen table, listening to Pat and Aleesha describe their evenings. Half an hour later, Kasey's mother decided to head upstairs, blaming creaking bones for her weariness. "Good meeting you, Dr.

Thorne,'' she said from the doorway. ''Hope to see you again soon.''

''Call me Adam, please,'' he said. ''And the pleasure was all mine.''

Something in the way he'd said it made Kasey believe he didn't plan on seeing any of them soon…maybe at all….

''Aleesha,'' Pat interjected, ''you help your mother with those dishes before you go up to bed, you hear?'' She shook an arthritic forefinger in the girl's direction.

''I love you, too, Gramma.'' Her dark eyes twinkled with mischief as she blew a kiss in the older woman's direction.

''Oh, you're such a caution!'' Pat said. But she came back into the room for no purpose other than to kiss Aleesha's coffee-colored forehead. ''G'night, and don't let the bedbugs bite.''

''She say that when you were a girl?'' Aleesha asked, once Pat was out of earshot.

''What? 'Don't let the bedbugs bite'?''

''No, that 'caution' thing.'' The girl rolled her big eyes. ''She's been sayin' it since I came here to live, but I ain't figured out yet what it means!''

''It means she thinks you hung the moon,'' Adam said as Aleesha stooped to unbuckle her leg braces.

''Oooh,'' she sighed, ''sure does feel good to get those things off.'' She shot Adam a half grin. ''So 'you're a caution' and 'you hung the moon' means…?''

He chuckled. '''You're one terrific kid.'''

She seemed to like that. Smiling, she started collecting mugs and teaspoons.

But Kasey stopped her. ''I'll get those, sweetie. You run on up to bed. You have a big day tomorrow, don't forget.''

Aleesha threw back her shoulders and lifted her chin. ''I'm singin' a solo at the Sunday service,'' she explained to Adam.

"You don't say. Which tune?"

She giggled. "'Amazing Grace.' And it ain't a tune, it's a hymn." She looked at the ceiling. "Old people say the strangest things."

"Good night," Kasey said. "I'll be up soon to tuck you in."

Again she rolled her eyes. "Hey, Dr. Thorne, you got a pill for mothers who treat their kids like babies for*ever?*"

"'Fraid not, kiddo. Guess you're just going to have to learn how to deal with a mom who loves you like crazy, huh?"

"I guess." She hugged Kasey's neck. "I love you like crazy, too."

"That's some kid," Adam said when she'd left the room.

"Yeah. Some kid."

"Why does she wear braces on her legs?"

"Malnourishment when she was an infant stunted her bone growth. That's also why she's not quite on a par with other kids her age—intellectually, I mean." She sighed. "She handles it like a champ, though."

"There's a very good reason for that. She's got you for a mother."

She took a deep breath. "Honestly, Adam. You have to stop saying things like that."

"Why?"

Sadness had turned down the corners of his eyes, reminding her of the way he'd looked over dinner, when the subject of her father's death came up. "Because I don't want to become one of those conceited, self-centered women who—"

"Not a chance."

She did her best Bullwinkle impersonation. "Oh, **you** know me so well, do you?"

Evidently, her silly expression and goofy voice weren't

proof enough to him that she'd only been teasing, because the gloom in his eyes deepened.

"I know enough."

He sat quietly for a moment or two, thumbnail absently picking at a nub on the tablecloth. Then, without warning, he stood so abruptly that his chair legs squealed across the polished tiles. "Let me help you with this mess," he said, grabbing two mugs in each hand, "and then I'll get out of your hair."

She didn't have the foggiest notion what had caused his sudden melancholy, but at the moment, it didn't matter. What *did* matter was comforting him. "Adam," she whispered, wrapping her fingers around his wrists, "I don't want you out of my hair. Haven't you figured that out by now?"

He blinked a few times before crossing the kitchen to put the mugs into the sink. Then, leaning both palms on the counter's edge, he hung his head. "Kasey, there are things about me you should know...."

His voice, barely more than a broken growl, echoed the unhappiness she'd seen in his eyes.

"...things that, if you *did* know..." He blew a stream of air through his teeth.

Kasey went to him, gave him a sideways hug. "Whatever it is, it can't be *that* bad," she said, stroking his back. "Seriously, it isn't like you killed a man or anything!"

But the instant the words were out, she felt his muscles tense under her palm. Surely he hadn't killed anyone! If only she could get him to talk to her, so she could convince him that no matter what sin he believed he'd committed, he was loved. Something made her silently tack on *loved by God, that is.*

"You know, folks say I'm a pretty good listener."

He looked at her then and, tucking in one corner of his

mouth, shook his head. "Seems you're pretty good at a lot of things." Brown eyes blazing, lips trembling, he added, "Wonder how good you are at forgiveness."

Forgiveness? What in the world could a man this good, this decent, have done to feel unworthy of forgiveness?

While she stood there trying to decipher his comment, Adam grasped her upper arms and squeezed his eyes shut. "How much do you know about me?" he demanded, his voice raspy and ragged. "How much do you *know?*"

Kasey had never seen a man look more tortured, more troubled. She felt helpless, inept, unable to put a stop to his misery. And so she did what she'd always done in times of trouble, and turned to God.

Lord, she prayed, *guide me. Help me know what Adam needs to hear right now.*

Ten seconds passed, twenty, yet no comforting message came to mind, no words of wisdom. The complete quiet, punctuated only by the ticking of the clock and Adam's irregular breathing, enveloped them.

Slowly, Kasey realized what God was trying to tell her with His silence: Adam didn't need *words* now, he needed the quiet assurance of friendship. And so she slid her arms around him, and simply held him.

Two days passed, and it had taken every ounce of strength Adam could muster to keep from picking up the phone and calling her. He'd almost blurted out the truth, standing there at her sink that night.

It had brought tears to his eyes when she'd wrapped her arms around him and pressed her cheek to his chest. Only the sob aching in his throat had kept him from confessing everything; shameful as it had been, his moment of weakness had saved him.

"I don't want you out of my hair," she'd said. *"Haven't you figured that out by now?"*

Yeah, he supposed he had figured it out. Had figured it out when he'd blocked her fall into the hearth and they'd kissed.

Now, Adam forced himself to focus on the patient file open on his desk blotter. His patient, Mitchell Gardner, who was getting dressed after his examination, would be in to discuss the results of his most recent tests at any moment, and the elderly gentleman deserved Adam's full attention. He took a swig of cold black coffee, frowning as he swished the bitter liquid around in his mouth.

The door opened, and Wade poked his head in. "Got a minute?"

Since he had a nagging suspicion that his partner intended to give him the third-degree about Kasey, Adam had been avoiding Wade since dinner at her place. "Yeah, but that's about all."

Closing the door, Wade looked at Adam. "So…?"

"So *what?*" He knew perfectly well what Wade was getting at, but maybe, if he stalled, Mr. Gardner would knock on the door and Adam wouldn't have to go into it.

Wade sat in one of the chrome-and-tweed chairs in front of Adam's desk and propped an ankle on his knee. "So, what gives with the Delaney girl?"

Frowning, Adam read and re-read Mr. Gardner's home address. "I don't know what you're talking abou—"

"Don't give me that. You've been dodging me for days to avoid talking about it."

He met Wade's hazel eyes. True, but he sure wasn't about to admit it. "I've been busy," Adam said. Equally true. But not so busy that he couldn't have taken a moment to discuss Kasey with Wade.

Wade leaned forward. "We're in this as deep as you are, pal."

Yeah, right, Adam thought angrily. "We?"

"Luke and Travis and me…we wanna know what she knows."

He aimed a hard stare at his lifelong friend. "The three of you have been discussing this? Behind my back?"

Wade leaped to his feet, began pacing back and forth in front of the door. He stopped at the corner of Adam's desk, then said, "You bet your sweet sports car we've been discussing this. We have as much to lose as you do. Now lay it on the line, Adam. Are we gonna need to hire a lawyer? What's she planning?"

"Nothing. At least, I don't think so."

Wade looked toward the ceiling, loosed a loud breath. "You don't think so. You don't *think* so…." He walked to the door and, one hand on the knob, said, "You'd better find out what she knows, pal. Pretty Miss Green Eyes could be setting us all up for—"

Adam got to his feet and tossed the file onto his desk, spilling the pages onto the floor. "That's ridiculous. Kasey isn't like that. She's—"

"Oh, it's 'Kasey,' is it?" Wade stomped back to Adam's desk, flattened one palm on the blotter. "You want some advice?" he demanded.

"No," Adam shot back, "but I have a feeling I'm gonna get some, anyway."

"We were idiots that night. What we did was wrong. No gettin' around that. But with the exception of Buddy, we've all made amends, we've all taken the straight and narrow ever since." He straightened and, slapping a hand to the back of his neck, added, "I didn't spend the past fifteen years keeping my nose clean so some curvy little gal could waltz in and—"

A soft knock interrupted his tirade.

"Dr. Thorne?" his nurse called. "Mr. Gardner is ready to see you."

Adam jerked open the door. "Give me a minute," he said, gesturing to the mess he'd made of the file. Grinning sheepishly, he added, "I seem to be all thumbs today."

She looked from the paper-strewn floor to Wade to Adam. The strained smile on her face told Adam that while she didn't know what the altercation had been about, she was definitely aware there had been a dispute.

Her gaze returned to the file. "You want me to tidy that up for you?"

"Nah, I'll take care of it. Just give me a minute," he repeated.

Her expression reminded Adam of Mrs. Anderson, his seventh-grade English teacher, who had a certain way of saying, with little more than a glare, *You're behaving like kindergartners*. The instant she closed the door, Adam stooped and began gathering up the papers that made up Mr. Gardner's file. "Trust me, Wade," he said from the floor, "even if she knows something—and I'd stake my life that she doesn't—she's not planning to sue anybody. Kasey isn't like that."

He heard the door open, heard Wade say from the hall, "I don't know how you can be so sure, but I hope you're right."

Adam flopped onto his chair and began replacing pages in order by date.

He took a deep, shaky breath. "Me, too," he whispered. "Me, too."

"Are you sure it's all right?"

The secretary nodded. "Absolutely! Dr. Thorne has had back-to-back patients all morning. He'll appreciate a friendly visit." She waved Kasey toward the hall leading to the partners' offices. "His door is the second one on the right." With that, she went back to filling out insurance forms.

With an "if you say so" shrug, Kasey headed for Adam's office. His door was slightly ajar, and as she lifted her hand to knock, she heard him say, "I don't have time for this, Wade. I'm telling you, she won't sue." He gave an exasperated sigh. "Why don't you do something productive with your time?"

Clearly, he was angry with Wade. *Strange,* Kasey thought. Hadn't they told her at supper the other night that they'd been friends since childhood?

"See if you can wrangle a tee time out of the receptionist at Hobbit's Glen," he continued, "and let me handle this K—"

"May I help you?"

The suddenness of the woman's voice made Kasey lurch, and she nearly dropped her packages. "Goodness!" she gasped, readjusting her grip on things.

"Sorry. Didn't mean to scare you," the nurse said.

"I—I'm here to see Dr. Thorne. His secretary said it would be all right...."

She gave Kasey a wary smile, then shoved Adam's door open. "Expecting anyone, Adam?"

He'd had his back to the door, feet propped on the windowsill. Both feet dropped to the floor with a solid *thump* and he swiveled his chair to face them. A bright smile flashed across his face when he spotted Kasey.

She would have said he seemed genuinely pleased to see her, if not for the fact that he immediately shielded his eyes with one hand.

"I'll get back to you on that," Adam barked, then hung up the phone.

With a protective nod, his nurse backed into the hall and closed the door.

Adam stood. "Kasey."

He sounded pleased to see her, too.

And yet there was something written on that handsome face. She would have named that "something" *guilt*. Did it have something to do with what he'd said the other night—that there were things she needed to know about him…?

"What a nice surprise," he said, gesturing to one of the chairs facing his desk. "What brings you here?"

Kasey took a seat, draping her coat over the arm of the chair beside hers. She slid a blue-lidded plastic container onto his desk. "You forgot your lasagna the other night." Plopping a brown grocery bag beside it, she added, "And your sweatpants. They were hanging on the banister, remember?"

"Yeah, I do."

I do?

Chances were slim to none that she'd hear those words spoken on an altar, echoed by her own vow. Shaking off the silly thought, Kasey feigned a laugh. "Maybe we could both do with a dose of that memory-booster herb."

"I don't put any stock in that kind of bunk." He frowned, waving her suggestion away.

What had put him in such a grumpy mood all of a sudden? she wondered. "Well," she began, matching his tone, note for gruff note, "I'm not surprised to hear you say that. Doctors rarely put stock in anything but medical science."

Adam's smile tightened. "Name me one other thing *worth* putting your faith in."

Several times since he'd left on Halloween night, Kasey had wondered about the condition of his soul, about his relationship with God…if indeed he had a relationship with

God. Adam seemed like a good and decent man, but experience had taught her that a man's behavior was no barometer of Christianity.

"How about God?" she blurted.

She'd touched a nerve, mentioning Buddy in Adam's cabin. She'd touched another just now, as evidenced by the furrow between his brows and the narrowing of his brown eyes.

So much for wondering where he stood on the Christian issue. His expression made her want to dig deeper, to explore his attitude further. But as the verse in Ecclesiastes said, there was a time for everything under heaven.

This, common sense told her, was not the time.

She forced a bright smile. "Aleesha wanted me to be sure to tell you the lasagna is best with fresh-grated Parmesan cheese." She shrugged. "I would've brought some, but we're all out."

He glanced at the covered dish and sat back in his overstuffed black leather chair. "Nice of you to come all the way over here to bring it. You didn't have to do that."

Kasey laughed. "Oh, but I did! Aleesha and Mom have been nagging me since I got up yesterday morning to get this over here." She tucked an annoying wayward curl behind her ear. "Besides, I was in the neighborhood, delivering an arrangeme—"

"Really?"

Calmly, he folded his hands on the desktop. Too calmly? Kasey wondered.

"Where's your client?"

"Right here in your building, actually. A plastic surgeon on the fifth floor."

"Ah, that'd be Dr. Kantor." Adam chuckled. "Well, if anybody can afford flowers for his waiting room, it's Bill."

He pulled the bag closer. "Let me guess. He ordered an arrangement with lots of roses in it, right?"

She tilted her head. At least his mood seemed to have improved. "What makes you say that?"

He shrugged, opening the paper sack. "Most of his patients are women." He met her eyes. "And don't all women prefer roses?"

Kasey narrowed her eyes. "They're pretty enough, but they're not my favorite flowers."

He stuck his face into the bag and inhaled, making Kasey wonder if maybe the big secret he'd been hiding had something to do with his sanity.

"Smells great," he said. Adam glanced at the clock on his wall, then back at her. "Say, have you eaten yet?"

"No."

He got to his feet again. This was the perfect opportunity to pump her for information. By the time she'd downed the last morsel of her lunch, he'd know for sure whether or not she'd dropped into his life calculatingly…or like manna from heaven.

If he were a betting man, he'd put his money on the manna. "There's a terrific little café, walking distance from here. I could buy you—"

"Adam, really. I couldn't. I owe you so much already."

Ignoring her comment, he grabbed his sports coat from a peg behind the door and nodded at the boxed lasagna. "Does it need to be refrigerated?" He didn't wait for her to answer. "Dorothy," he called to his secretary, "we're going to Mi Casa." He picked up Kasey's coat with one hand, the food dish with the other. "Could you put this in the fridge, please?"

Dorothy relieved him of the container. "Mi Casa, eh?"

"That's the plan."

"I'll do it on one condition."

Adam rolled his eyes. "Conditions. Don't you gals ever do anything with no strings attached?" He was only half kidding.

But Dorothy blundered on. "...if you'll bring me back an order of sugar-fried dough."

He held up Kasey's jacket. "Deal."

Slipping into it, Kasey said, "Olé."

He hesitated. "Olé?"

"You did look a little bit like a bullfighter, standing there holding her wrap," Dorothy injected.

"Seems fitting," Kasey said. "Somehow, I find myself on my way to lunch, and I don't recall saying *sì* or *hambriento*." She shot Adam a teasing look. "And something tells me that even if I had said 'yes', or 'I'm hungry', we'd be halfway there, anyway."

"Why do you say that?"

"Because," she said, slinging her purse strap over her shoulder, "I have a feeling you're more like Ferdinand the bull than the bullfighter."

"Ferdinand?"

"The bull. *Stubborn* like a—"

Dorothy's laughter bounced up and down the hall. "Oh, I like her, Doc. You don't wanna let this one get away!"

He liked this one, too. But he had a sinking feeling that Kasey wasn't going to *get* away so much as he was likely to *drive* her away.

Unless he could keep her from finding out the truth about him....

Kasey liked the way Adam put himself on the street side of the walk as they strolled to Mi Casa. It was an old-fashioned, chivalrous action that reminded her of her father, who had always held doors, pulled out chairs, and helped Kasey's mother into her coat.

In the restaurant, the hostess suggested a spot near the door, near a table of rowdy teenagers. Politely, he suggested a table closer to the kitchen, where they could enjoy the soft beat of Mexican music that flowed from the overhead speakers.

He pulled out Kasey's chair, then handed her a menu.

"So what're you in the mood for?" Adam asked, sitting across from her.

She studied the lunch offerings. "Maybe a nice crispy salad."

"Rabbit food? Nah, get something that'll stick to your ribs, something with meat in it!"

"There's ground sirloin in the taco salad...."

"They make a mean *chimichanga* here," he tempted.

The waitress stepped up to the table. "What can I get you folks to drink?"

"Two iced teas," Adam said, his tone businesslike yet cordial. "You still serve that terrific salsa with homemade tortilla chips as an appetizer?"

"We sure do."

His easy way with people—the waitress, his secretary, his nurse—told her something about Adam's character. His choice of restaurants said a lot about him, too: he was a simple man, with simple tastes.

Though she'd never much enjoyed it, Kasey had dined in Baltimore's best eating establishments—thanks to Buddy's "connections"—where tuxedoed waiters delivered meals on sterling silver serving carts. Here, cartoon chili peppers decorated the aprons of waitresses who balanced stainless flatware on plastic trays. Kasey knew there wouldn't be scented hand soaps and lotions in the ladies' room, or a strolling violinist to play romantic tunes beside a linen-cloaked table. Instead of velvet draperies, shiny-leafed philodendrons hung at Mi Casa's windows, and in place of brocade-upholstered furnishings, there were hard-wood chairs.

This was a family place, just the kind her father would have loved. Her dad, a solid, do-the-right-thing kind of guy who'd lived a down-to-earth life.

Was this place the reason Kasey felt completely and totally at ease…or was it her companion?

She looked across at Adam, prepared to thank him for introducing her to Mi Casa when their waitress returned, balancing a tray laden with mugs of steaming coffee and tall tumblers of iced tea. "You guys ready to order?" she asked, placing a basket of chips and a bowl of salsa in the center of the Formica-topped table.

"The lady will have the taco salad," Adam said, "and I'll take the beef *chimichanga*."

After scribbling their order on a blue-lined pad, the waitress nodded and moved to chat with the patrons at the next table.

He frowned suddenly, then grabbed her hand. "What have you done to yourself?" he asked, inspecting her forefinger.

"It's just a knick, one of the hazards of the trade, I'm afraid."

"I should have asked for a tour when I was at your house the other evening."

"Of the workshop, you mean?"

"I think what you do is fascinating. You're—"

She held up a hand to forestall yet another compliment. "It's a living," she said, reminding him of what he'd replied when Aleesha enquired about his profession. "You should stop by some time." Kasey paused, then added, "You know, other than Mom and Aleesha, I don't think anyone has ever seen it. Well, except for Buddy."

It surprised her that his cheeks reddened. In response to her invitation? Or because she'd said "Buddy"?

"Did someone mention my name?"

The suddenness of the loud voice made Kasey jump, and she nearly upset her glass. "Buddy! You nearly scared me out of my shoes!"

"Sorry, sweet cheeks," he said, bending to plant a kiss on Kasey's forehead. "Didn't mean to startle you, but it surprised me, seeing your pretty face when I came in, and—"

Either he hadn't noticed Adam earlier, or he had just now recognized him. "Thorne." He all but spat out the name. "I didn't know rich, successful doctors frequented places like this." Buddy's tone made it clear what he thought of "places like this."

"I like it," Kasey defended. "It's quaint. Charming, even."

Adam shot her a look that was either gratitude or amazement, then wrapped his big hand around his iced tea glass.

"Long time no see," Buddy said to Adam. "Didn't know you and Kasey were, uh…acquainted."

Anger sparked from Adam's usually gentle brown eyes. "Yeah. We're, uh…acquainted." He let a moment of silence punctuate his statement. "I'd invite you to join us, *Buddy,* but I know how busy you are."

Buddy's glare darkened his entire face. "Thanks," he all but snarled, "but you're right. I *am* busy."

Adam chuckled. "So what brings you to a 'place like this'?" he asked, drawing quote marks in the air. "Delivering jukeboxes? Picking up bets made at Pimlico?" He looked at Kasey, as if to underscore his blatant accusation that Buddy had more twists and turns than the Mississippi River.

Buddy's eyes narrowed. "Nothing that concerns you."

He turned his heated stare on Kasey. "I called your workshop, and the answering machine picked up. I figured you were out delivering one of your little flower arrangements." The glare riveted on Adam once more.

Kasey stiffened. She'd always hated it when Buddy referred to her work as "little arrangements," but out of gratitude to him for his generosity, she'd never told him so.

One hand on the back of her chair, the other on the table's edge, he leaned in and whispered, "In the future, you might want to check with me before…" Moving closer still, he said through clenched teeth, "You want to be more careful who you're seen with in public." He cleared his throat and stood up straight. "We'll talk, later."

Clearly, it was an order, one Kasey not only resented but intended to confront. She couldn't help but notice that Buddy's presence had commanded the attention of nearby diners; adding to their entertainment didn't appeal to her.

"You bet we'll talk later," she said in a quiet, matter-of-fact voice.

Whatever business had brought Buddy to Mi Casa never got concluded, because he stormed out the door, got into his sleek roadster and pealed out of the parking lot.

"Sorry," Adam said.

"*You're* sorry? For what?"

"For not taking you seriously the other night."

The waitress came to deliver their food. "Anything else, folks?" she asked.

Adam nodded. "Couple glasses of water would be nice."

"What do you mean?" Kasey asked when the waitress left.

"You said he'd asked you to marry him, that you hadn't given him an answer yet." Fiddling with his paper-encased drinking straw, he added, "Guess I misinterpreted our…

your..." He cleared his throat. "I didn't realize... If I had, I never would've..."

That night in his cabin, Kasey had asked Adam for information about Buddy, saying she needed to find out everything she could about him. "He's asked me to marry him," she'd said, "and I haven't given him an answer yet." Though he hadn't provided that information, she'd let him kiss her when he saved her from falling into the fire. Correction—she'd *wanted* him to kiss her. Evidently, Adam also counted that demonstration of affection when she'd tenderly kissed his forehead after their lasagna dinner, and summed up that she hadn't taken Buddy's proposal seriously.

What he must think of her now!

She reached across the table, gripped his wrist with both hands. "Adam, let me explain. This thing with Buddy and me, it isn't what it seems."

He picked up his fork. "Yeah, well, not that it's any of my business, but whatever 'it' is solves a lot of problems for me." He poked at his meal.

She'd known Buddy for years, had met Adam days ago. Buddy's outrageous behavior had sent the wrong message, one Kasey felt obliged to dispel. For a reason she couldn't explain, Adam's feelings—and his opinion of her—mattered...mattered very much.

"Better eat," he said, "before your food gets cold."

Maybe the best way to downplay Buddy's proprietary actions was to ignore them. As Adam took a drink of iced tea, she feigned a smile. "Taco salad is supposed to be cold."

But Adam never saw it, didn't react to her well-intentioned joke. Instead, he pulled back his shirtsleeve and glanced at his watch. "Wow. Look at the time. I'd better get back, before Dorothy sends a posse out after me."

He stood, slid his wallet from his back pocket and absently tossed a twenty and a five onto the table. "That should cover the tab." Finally, he met her eyes. "See ya around, Kase." And without another word, he dug his hands into his pockets and walked purposefully toward the door, shoving it open with one shoulder.

Kasey stared at the money, at his barely touched food, at her own uneaten lunch, then looked out at the parking lot. A familiar flash of silver caught her eye. Buddy's car? Of course it was—he'd special-ordered it from France, and there wasn't another vehicle like it in the tristate area.

She should have known he hadn't coincidentally run into her while conducting business at Mi Casa. Lovely as it was, the restaurant wasn't the kind of place Buddy—or his cronies—frequented. No, he'd *followed* her here with every intention of making Adam believe there was a wedding on the calendar.

Kasey rose slowly, and, trembling with anger, walked to the door. If Buddy's car was still in the lot when she stepped outside, she intended to have a word or two with him.

Chapter Six

Buddy didn't seem surprised when she opened the passenger door and slid onto the buttery leather seat.

"Hey, cutie," he said, leaning across the console for a kiss.

Kasey backed away. "What was all that about?"

"All what?"

"That...*scene* in the restaurant, that's what."

His pucker became a pout as he ran a hand through his dark hair. "Just lookin' out for my girl," he said, "makin' sure she's safe and sound."

She studied his olive-skinned face. If the spark in his eyes and his smile was any indication, his words had been sincere. Her attitude softened. "Buddy, I'm perfectly safe with Adam, and—"

"If you're smart," he interrupted, "you'll keep your distance from him."

How quickly his expression had turned from warm and protective to cold and uncaring! Instinct made her recoil. "Did you mean that to sound like a threat?"

One well-arched brow quirked as a corner of his mouth lifted in a wily grin. "You know me better than that."

She knew he was smooth. Kasey had known Buddy a long time, to be sure. He'd lived across the street for as long as she could remember. But what did she really know about this man sitting beside her? He'd never explained what he did for a living, never told her how his name had ended up on every Who's Who guest list from New York to Richmond, or why he seemed to have the ear of every politician in the Baltimore–Washington, D.C. area. In fact, Kasey realized, Buddy hadn't ever given her a straight answer to anything relating to his life, business *or* personal. She didn't know him "better than that."

"You haven't answered my question."

He reached out, tucked a wayward curl behind her ear. "Sorry," he said, his smirk becoming an impish smile, "but I don't remember the question."

Kasey fought the urge to swat his hand away. She'd never liked games, not the kind that came in boxes, and certainly not the type that tampered with people's lives. But that didn't mean she wouldn't give her all...*if* she'd decided to play.

"Well, then, Buddy, let me refresh your memory." She matched his innocent smile, tooth for tooth. "You said if I was smart, I'd keep away from Adam." She lifted her chin. "And I asked if you intended it to sound like a threat."

His expression gentled as he grasped her hand. "Kasey, sweetie," he said quietly, stroking her fingers, "of course it wasn't a threat. I'd never do anything to hurt you."

She remembered enough from her college English class to know it was a simple declarative sentence. Strangely, it came out sounding more like a plea. Kasey sighed, because if it had been Buddy who'd delivered money-filled envelopes, if *he* was her champion, how hardhearted and cold to accuse him of threatening her!

She was about to apologize for snapping at him, when he added, "Besides, what reason would I have to threaten you?"

It wasn't his follow-up so much as the instantaneous flash of fury that burned in his eyes that made her neck hairs bristle. Swallowing the lump of fear that now blocked her words, Kasey reached for the door handle. "I don't have time for this," she said, hoping he hadn't heard the flutter in her voice. "I have work to do."

"Don't go," Buddy implored, tightening his hold on her hand. "If I scared you, I'm sorry. I didn't mean to, honest."

Stiff as a statue, she stared straight ahead. *Please, God,* she prayed, *tell me what to do.* Holding her breath, Kasey waited, believing if she truly was in any danger, the Almighty would give her a sign of some kind.

A moment passed.

Two.

Nothing.

Exhaling, she shook her head. "I have to go," she said, opening the door. "My car's in the parking lot right down the street. I have two more…" The way he'd always called her work "little arrangements" echoed in Kasey's mind, but she refused to give in to feelings of petty resentment. Especially considering that Buddy was probably the man who'd made her business possible. "I have two more deliveries to make before I head home. And once I get there, I have to start working on the flowers for the Lauffer wedding. It's next weekend, you know." She was rambling and knew it, but seemed powerless to stop the rapid-fire flow of words.

"Close the door, Kasey."

Was she losing her mind? Paranoid? Because even that

simple request sounded hard-edged and icy...like a command. She looked at his face, searching for proof that he hadn't turned into a bullying brute.

Or had he always been exactly that, and gratitude had blinded her to it?

What she saw now was the plastic facade Buddy usually reserved for newspaper and TV cameramen, for glad-handing politicians and their always-nodding spouses. *"You know me better than that,"* he'd said a moment ago—but it wasn't true.

"Kasey?" He snapped his fingers. "You okay?"

She'd be fine, just fine, the minute she got out of this car, put some distance between herself and Buddy. Kasey gave the car door a push, swung her legs toward the opening, intending to do just that, when Buddy reached over her. One hand brought her knees back into the passenger seat as the other closed the door.

"Where's your car?" he asked, depressing the lock. "I'll drive you to it...when we're finished here."

Her cheeks and ears burned with humiliation. Her dad had taught her never to take any guff from anybody, for any reason. Yet here she sat, trembling like a frightened fawn, allowing Buddy to hold her against her will.

"You know very well where I parked," she snapped. "You followed me here, after all."

Buddy's narrowed eyes blazed into hers for a millisecond. Then, just like that, he laughed. He was near enough that she felt a burst of air when he did.

"You're such a li'l spitfire," he said, kissing the end of her nose. "Just one of the reasons I love ya t'death."

He hadn't denied her accusation, she noted while he leaned back in the driver's seat.

The diamond pinky ring on his right hand glittered in the afternoon sunlight as he turned the key in the ignition.

Instantly, the roadster's motor began to purr. After adjusting the rearview mirror, he slid a CD into a slot on the dash. "Buckle up," Buddy instructed. And in his reserved-for-public-speaking voice, he quoted the drivers' safety manual: "'It's a law we can live with.'" He put the car into drive, but kept his foot on the brake. Thumbs tapping the steering wheel in time to the music, he stared through the windshield and hummed under his breath, waiting, she knew, for her to obey.

Obey, indeed. *Dad would turn over in his grave!*

Gritting her teeth, Kasey unlocked and reopened her door, not minding at all when a look of shock widened his dark eyes. And knowing how he babied the car, she slammed the door and walked away.

It was a true test of her willpower to keep from looking over her shoulder; something told her that if she opened her compact, she'd see Buddy's startled image in its round mirror.

A twinge of guilt pricked her conscience. *That was a mean-spirited thing to think about the guy who likely saved your bacon.*

And on the heels of that thought came a question: Would a man who'd do something that generous and kind want to intimidate and control her, even in subtle ways?

Kasey didn't think so.

She stepped up her pace. Clearly, she had a lot to pray about.

"Good ole Buddy called while you were out," Aleesha said, the moment Kasey walked into the kitchen.

"Really." She tried not to let on about the altercation she'd had with him after lunch at Mi Casa several days earlier. Tried too, to ignore the sarcasm in Aleesha's voice. "Did he say what he wanted?"

The girl's thick, black cornrows bobbed as she shook her head. "Said he might stop by tonight, lucky us...." She pressed a fingertip to the end of her nose and, in a haughty British accent, added, "...*if* he isn't too awfully busy, that is."

Smiling, Kasey hugged her. "So what're you working on? Your Biology term paper?"

"Yeah, and I think I'm gonna ace this one. Nobody in class is doin' anything like it."

"Is that so?" Kasey asked, sliding a package of pork chops from the freezer. "What's the topic?"

"The human heart."

Distracted by supper preparations, Kasey only nodded.

"Dr. Thorne is helpin' me."

"Is that so?"

"Uh-huh. I called him," Aleesha announced, "to ask for his advice."

Wait. Had she heard correctly? Aleesha had called Adam? Stunned, Kasey froze. "Y-you called Dr. Thorne? When?"

"Day before yesterday," she said, hunched over her work.

Kasey hadn't seen or heard from Adam since their lunch, and that had been over a week ago.

"He said he'd be glad to help me." She riffled through the stack of papers next to her textbook. "He dropped this stuff by yesterday afternoon. Ain't it neat?"

Kasey put the chops on the counter and stood beside her daughter.

"See? He made me full-color slides to use on the overhead projector, and these color photocopies are to hand out to the rest of the class. Plus," she said, voice rising with enthusiasm, "he brought me—"

"He delivered all this? In person?"

"Yup. He called, and when I told him you were delivering that wedding stuff, he said he'd come right over."

"Where was Gramma?"

"In the family room, I guess, watchin' *Oprah* like always."

Kasey wondered why neither of them had mentioned that Adam had stopped by.

Aleesha opened a cardboard box and carefully removed a life-size reproduction of the human heart. "It opens up, see, to show all the arteries and stuff inside. Ain't it great?"

"Great. Yes." Several times since her lunch with Adam, she'd considered calling him. But Buddy had made her look like a mealymouthed little twit—and she'd let him. Embarrassed, she hadn't called.

Besides, the way he'd hotfooted it out of the restaurant made it pretty clear what Adam thought of her relationship with Buddy. Since then, she'd been hoping that in time she could figure out a way to explain, so he'd understand how things really were between her and Buddy.

The memory of the way he'd left the restaurant, looking stunned and hurt and confused, came to her mind. Well, she could try to explain things.

"...such a nice thing to do," Aleesha was saying.

Kasey blinked herself back into the present and focused on her daughter's words.

"I bet *Buddy* would never do anything like this for me."

Kasey felt it was her duty as a mother, as a *Christian* mother, to defend him. "Now, Aleesha. You don't know that. Have you ever asked him to do anything for you?"

"Well, no," Aleesha answered, returning the heart to its box. "Even if I liked him—which I do *not*—what could *he* do for me? What stuff could a guy like *that* teach me?" Grinning, she mimicked an anchorwoman's voice: "'And now a word from Buddy Mauvais on How to Tell Believable Lies.' No, wait!'' she said, giggling. '''I'm proud to introduce the author of *Con Jobs Made Easy*.'''

Suddenly, Aleesha was all business. She shook her head and said, ''Really, Mom, I don't know what you see in that guy.''

Rather than plumb the depths of explanations and excuses, Kasey relied on an age-old lecture. ''Remember what I've always told you....''

Aleesha sighed heavily. ''I know, I know'' came her bored monotone. ''The Golden Rule.'' She met Kasey's eyes. ''But I remember another rule you taught me, too.''

''Which is?''

''Respect is a two-way street. How am I supposed to respect a jerk like Buddy?''

''Aleesha! You know better than to say things like that. So be fair. Buddy has never been anything but nice to you.''

Aleesha pouted. ''That ain't true, exactly. He always talks like he thinks I'm stupid, like he thinks he's better'n me. Talks to Gramma and you the very same way, an' you know it's true.'' She folded her arms over her chest. ''He *ain't* better'n us, ain't better'n most folks, if you ask me.'' And huffing, she added, ''Ain't smarter'n us, either.''

The memory of the way Buddy had spoken to her in Mi Casa, and in his car afterward, echoed in her memory. There was some truth in Aleesha's words, more truth than Kasey cared to admit. ''We'll talk more about this after supper. Right now,'' she said, taking a baking dish out of the cabinet, ''I think you should concentrate on your report.'' She put the pork chops into the pan, poured half a cup of water over them.

''You know what?''

''What?'' Kasey asked, sliding the pan into the oven.

"Dr. Thorne told me I could call him Adam if I wanted to."

Kasey adjusted the temperature dial. "You don't want to?"

"'Course I do. But I'm hopin' if I call him Dr. Thorne, like I respect him—and I *do*—he'll want to spend more time around here."

She was about to ask why Aleesha wanted to spend more time with a man she'd so recently met, when the girl said, "Maybe if Dr. Thorne was here *more,* Buddy would be here *less.*"

Wiping her hands on a kitchen towel, Kasey cleared her throat. Even if she hadn't thought Buddy had been helping the family all these years, she'd have treated him with basic human kindness, as any good Christian would. Had her behavior been misinterpreted…as requited love?

Aleesha stood, limped over to the sink, and wrapped Kasey in a warm hug, saying, "I know I'm not as smart as the other kids. But I'm not so dumb that I don't understand grown-up things, like love and stuff."

Kasey prayed for a way to explain how she felt, but ended up relying on a cliché: "You're smart as a whip," she argued, kissing the top of her daughter's head.

The girl tightened her embrace. "I know some things. Like, for example, I don't know *why,* but you act like you owe Buddy something. And like, I know you have feelings for Dr. Thorne—like, maybe you're falling in love with him."

The word *love* reverberated in her mind. Kasey's heart thudded. Had her budding, confusing feelings about Adam been that easy to read?

Aleesha leaned back. "You're the best, Mom. The best mother, the best daughter, the best flower arranger ever. So you *deserve* the best, and that ole criminal across the street sure ain't it!''

Kasey grinned. ''Criminal! Buddy isn't a—''

''Just 'cause he ain't been caught yet don't mean he's a good guy.''

Pressing both palms to her daughter's cheeks, Kasey said, ''You know that isn't a very Christian thing to say, right?''

The girl returned to her homework. ''When I say my prayers,'' she began, ''I include Buddy, just like you said I should.'' Shrugging, she continued in a whisper-soft, uncertain voice, ''But every time I do, I get this creepy-crawly feeling, like God's trying to tell me Buddy needs prayers more'n just about anybody.'' Absentmindedly, she tapped her pencil eraser on the tablet and shook her head. ''I think we'd all be better off if ole Buddy would just up and move to…to Timbuktu or someplace.''

It was downright eerie the way Aleesha's words echoed her own feelings, especially lately.

The image returned of the shadowy, sinister stare he'd shot at her as they sat in the front seat of his car.

Like a shroud, a chill wrapped around her. Kasey found herself testing the lock on the window above the sink, then looking over her shoulder to see if the deadbolt was in place. It was small satisfaction to know that all the hatches were battened.

She hoped Buddy hadn't merely been making small talk when he told Aleesha he'd probably be too busy to stop by tonight.

Adam had gone home earlier than usual, changed into sweats and ordered an extra-large pizza, thinking to eat the leftovers for breakfast. Hopefully, an action-packed movie on TV would get his mind off Kasey and Buddy.

But distraction tactics hadn't worked last night, hadn't worked *any* night since he'd seen them together at Mi Casa—Buddy flexing his proprietary muscles, Kasey behaving a little too accustomed to it.

An old Second World War movie filled the screen. "Ironic," he said to himself, "but right on target."

When the doorbell rang, he fished his wallet out of the big wooden bowl on the foyer table, slid a twenty from it and threw open the door. He froze, one hand extending the money, the other on the doorknob. "What do you want?"

"Good to see you, too," Travis kidded, grinning.

"Yeah," Luke said, echoing Travis's tone.

Grinning, Wade looked at the cash crumpled in Adam's fist. "Doesn't surprise me you hafta pay people to come visit, not if you greet 'em *that* way."

Frowning around a grin, Adam stepped aside. "Thought you were the pizza."

"Pepperoni and sausage," Wade said to Travis and Luke. "Follow me." He sauntered into the foyer, then pumped Adam's arm up and down. "They call me the big cheese. Mind if we stick around a while?"

Laughing, the men headed for the family room.

"Whoa, I like what you've done with the place," Travis said, glancing at stacks of dog-eared magazines and an ankle-high pile of newspapers on the floor. He shoved a basket of unfolded laundry aside, flopped onto the couch and nodded approvingly. "Very lived-in. Very down-to-earth."

Luke removed a pair of running shoes from the seat cushion of an easy chair. "Yeah. What do you call this style?" he asked Wade. "Early Locker Room?"

"Good a guess as any. Only thing missing is the stink of sweaty socks." He elbowed Adam in the ribs.

Masculine laughter filled the room as the lifelong friends made themselves comfortable.

Only Adam remained standing. "You guys want a soda? I could put on a pot of coffee...." May as well be hospitable, he thought, since it appeared the guys would be here a while.

"Maybe later," Wade answered. "Have a seat, Adam." He gestured to the well-worn recliner. "Make yourself at home."

Perched on the edge of the chair, Adam rested his elbows on his knees and clasped his hands in the space between. He was almost afraid to ask "So what's up?"

Luke spoke first. "Wade here tells us you've been seeing a lot of Kasey Delaney. We're just lookin' for assurances that she's not out to even any old scores."

"Yeah," Travis put in. "There's nothing to stop her from filing a civil action, not if she's figured out who we are. There's no statute of limitations on a thing like that, y'know."

"Like I said in the office the other day," Wade added, "we've all got a lot to lose. If there's a lawsuit in the works, we gotta protect ourselves, and to do that, we oughta be considering legal—"

"Look," Adam interrupted, none too politely, "I've said it before, I'll say it again—Kasey isn't that kind of woman. But just to satisfy what appears to be contagious paranoia, let me amend that." He met each man's eyes in turn. "Far as I can tell, she doesn't have a clue who we are, or that any of us were involved in her father's death."

Was it his imagination, or had his friends simultaneously winced at the mention of the word *death*?

"I've sunk everything I have into our medical practice," Wade added.

Luke spoke up. "Yeah, and the Howard County fire marshal is retiring next spring. I'm on the shortlist of replacements.''

''I'd high-five you,'' Adam said, grinning, ''if I wasn't too lazy to come over there.''

Travis cleared his throat. ''And I'm going to make a run for police chief.''

''Congrats, Travis,'' Adam said. He focused on Luke. ''And good for you, man. The county needs guys like you at the helm.'' He stared at the floor, clenching and unclenching his jaw muscles. ''The three of you know me better than anyone, so you know I wouldn't feed you a line of bunk. Kasey's an okay gal. I'd stake my life on this. Even if she knew—'' he shrugged one shoulder ''—about *that,* she's not the type to file a lawsuit.''

Wade rubbed his jaw thoughtfully. ''Okay, pal, if you say so.''

''I say so.''

The moment of companionable silence was interrupted by the doorbell.

Luke headed for the door. ''Pizza, anybody?''

''Count me in,'' Travis said.

Wade hollered, ''It's on me.'' Then he hooked an arm around Adam's neck and playfully smacked his head. ''I hope you ordered extra large, 'cause it looks like our conversation gave the boys an appetite.''

''Only extra-large thing around here,'' Adam retorted, laughing as he reversed the hold on Wade, ''is your big yap.''

''Hey, Wade, you said the pizza's on you, right?''

Wade uttered a muffled ''Mmm-hmm.''

''Then, you owe me $17.57.'' Luke plopped the pizza box on the coffee table. ''Adam, where d'you keep the paper plates?''

"Kitchen," he growled, snickering as he struggled to maintain the half-nelson, "cupboard beside the sink."

Travis shook his head, feigned a weary, disgusted look as he took in his friends, wrestling on the family room carpet like a couple of rowdy pups. "The more things change, the more they stay the same, eh?"

How true, Adam thought, releasing Wade.

Wade had already taken a bite of pizza before Luke returned with the paper plates.

The more things change, he repeated mentally.

But was that a curse...or a blessing?

Kasey sat beside her mother, third row from the altar and on the center aisle, to assure herself a clear view when Aleesha got up to sing her choir solo. Heart pounding with maternal pride, she double-checked the camera. Yes, the flash was working, and no, she hadn't forgotten to load the film.

Pat leaned closer and whispered, "Easy, Kasey. She's going to do fine, just fine."

"I know, Mom," Kasey said, slinging an arm around the older woman's shoulders.

"You're not surprised by all this, are you?"

"Not really." Aleesha had done such a beautiful rendition of "Amazing Grace" that it would have surprised her more if Pastor Hill *hadn't* asked the girl to sing another solo.

"Is there room for one more in this row?" asked a familiar voice.

Kasey looked up, unable to believe her eyes. "Adam," she gasped. "What are you doing here?"

"Aleesha called yesterday, asked me to come hear what she called her 'very unique version' of 'I Believe.'" He smiled. "Couldn't very well refuse an invitation like that, now could I?"

Her gaze went directly to the altar, where Aleesha sat, waving. Waving at *Adam*, Kasey realized, a fact that made her smile.

"Scoot in a bit, Kasey," Pat instructed, sliding left on the wooden bench, "so Dr. Thorne can sit down."

"Adam," he gently corrected.

Pat returned his smile. "All right, then, Adam." She patted the empty space beside her. "We'd love it if you'd join us."

Gingerly, he stepped over Kasey's high-heeled shoes and took his place between mother and daughter.

"You look positively dashing in that tie," Pat said.

Kasey could almost feel the heat of his blush, though he'd made sure to leave a good six inches between her left thigh and his right one. She had to agree with her mother, though: Adam did look handsome in that slate-gray suit. But then, he'd looked gorgeous in sweats, in blue jeans...

"So, how have you been?" she asked him.

"Fine." He nodded emphatically. "Real good."

"Working too hard, though, I'll bet."

He leaned forward, just enough to look into her face. "What makes you say that?"

She'd noticed right away that he looked haggard, especially around the eyes. "Just a hunch."

"Adam," Pat said, tapping his shoulder, then pointing at the altar, "Aleesha is waving at you."

Smiling like a proud papa, he sent the girl a snappy salute.

"It was so nice of you to come all the way across town, just to hear her sing," Kasey's mother said. "I'm sure you have better things to do with your Sunday morning."

"It's only a ten-minute drive. Besides, I can't think of anyplace I'd rather be."

Either he'd meant it, or Hollywood was missing out on the greatest acting talent since Clark Gable, Kasey thought.

Just then, Edna O'Shea, seated on Pat's other side, said in what she believed to be a whisper, "Who's that man? Kasey's new boyfriend?"

Pat held her hands out in an "I'm not sure" gesture.

Edna patted her cotton-white hair. "The dude is a *hunk*."

Old Mrs. Madsen, who always arrived early enough to secure a seat in the front row, turned around and scowled at Pat and Edna. "Hush, you two." She clucked her tongue. "'Dude' and 'hunk', indeed! Ladies, act your age, why don't you!"

The instant Mrs. Madsen faced front again, Pat and Edna snickered. Kasey sat forward and, reaching around Adam, lay a hand on her mother's knee. "Do I have to take you girls outside and give you a good talking-to?" she said around a smile.

The women sat up straight and folded their hands.

"No, dear," Pat said.

And Edna added, "We'll behave."

Then the pair burst into another fit of girlish giggles.

Kasey looked at Adam, who expelled what she supposed he'd intended as a stern, fatherly sigh. She rolled her eyes, as if to say, *What am I going to do with her!*

Kasey looked so adorable that he didn't resist the impulse to reach out and take her hand. Its satiny warmth surprised him, made the breath catch in his throat.

For an instant, their eyes met and locked. Like an invisible current of electricity, the moment sizzled and popped, awakening a longing inside him like none he'd ever known. If only he'd mustered some courage that night fifteen years ago...!

Thankfully, strains of "Onward Christian Soldiers" throbbed from the church's ancient organ bellows. The quiet rustle of fabric and the soft creak of wood harmonized with the instrument's resonant notes, as congregants got to their feet.

All around him, paper crinkled as parishioners searched for the correct page in the hymnals. Throats cleared. A cough echoed from the tall stained-glass windows. Someone sneezed, and a whispered "Bless you" was punctuated by a quiet "Thanks!"

As the organist held onto a wailing C-chord—her signal that the first verse was about to begin—Adam regretfully let go of Kasey's hand.

If he'd known how hard it would be, seeing her again, he'd never have agreed to come here. Being this near her was downright painful, and frankly, he hadn't expected that. He'd spent a total of, what, twelve hours in her presence, so how much sense did these feelings make?

His memory did a quick rewind of Aleesha's request. Almost immediately, his mind started whirling with possible excuses and semi-believable reasons to decline her invitation. Trouble was, he genuinely liked the kid. Liked her mother, too, more than he cared to admit, and way more than was healthy...or smart. And so he'd mumbled an agreeable yeah, okay, sure, love to come to church, hear the song.

Adam ground his molars together, realizing he'd been born with one major character flaw: the inability to say no. If he'd had the guts to say it that Halloween night, long ago, there'd be no regrets about saying yes to listening to Aleesha's song.

And maybe he'd even have a chance at a future with the angelic beauty who stood beside him now, putting everything she had into her own off-key singing.

* * *

"So what did you think, Dr. Thorne?"

Kasey watched in quiet amazement as Adam tugged gently on one of Aleesha's thick braids.

"Y'done good, kiddo. Real good." He pulled her into a hug.

Seemed a shame, Kasey thought, for a man like that not to be a father; he had such a natural, easy way with children. She'd seen enough on Halloween night to know that was true.

"Thanks," Aleesha said, beaming. "I practiced for *hours.*"

"And it shows." Adam took what appeared to be a regretful step back. "So how's the report coming?"

"Finished. It's due tomorrow." She looked up at him, blinking expectantly. "Would you take a look at it? Make sure I got everything right?"

Adam winced, then ran a hand through his hair. "I, uh, well, I'm not sure." He held out his hands, palms up, in a helpless, awkward gesture. "I have patients at the hospital to check on, see, and paperwork that's piling up at the office...."

Kasey didn't get it. What had turned him from a calm, confident man into a bumbling, fidgeting wreck?

But Adam's ineffectual faltering didn't seem to have come across to Aleesha as rejection. Grinning, she grabbed his hand and changed the subject. "It's only a week-and-a-half until Thanksgiving!"

Adam shook his head. "I didn't realize the holiday was that close."

Did he realize how fatherly he looked, Kasey wondered, standing there with the girl's hands sandwiched between his own?

"Where you havin' turkey dinner?"

He shrugged. "Hadn't given it much thought."

"Don't you have any family in town?"

"I'm afraid not. Lost my father when I was a boy, and my mom is on a European cruise with her best friend."

"A European cruise!" Pat clasped her hands at her bosom. "What a wonderful treat."

"Treat?" Aleesha said.

"You paid for the trip, didn't you, Adam? What was the occasion? Mother's Day? Birthday?"

Blushing, he nodded. "Birthday. How'd you guess?"

"You just seem the type who'd give a gift as generous as that."

Generous.

The word reverberated in Kasey's head like a Chinese gong. He'd been so giving, so welcoming when she showed up at his cabin, dripping like a rusty faucet. He'd fixed her soup and a sandwich, fetched warm clothes for her, tried to give up his own bed so she'd be comfortable. After the lasagna dinner, he was the only one who'd insisted on staying to help with the dishes, and he'd stayed on even after that, mostly to keep her company as she doled out candy to the trick-or-treaters.

And what about the gentlemanly way he'd treated her before Buddy showed up at Mi Casa, like walking beside the curb to protect her from traffic, pulling out her chair, suggesting she get something more substantial than salad for lunch. She thought of all the trouble he'd gone to, helping Aleesha with her term paper, his chosen career....

This was the kind of man who might deliver envelopes of money in the dead of night—though she had yet to figure out *why* anyone would do such a thing for fifteen years— because everything about Adam shouted "hero"!

So what had made her think Buddy had been the Delaneys' benefactor?

It might have been as long as ten years ago when she'd asked Buddy, straight out, what he knew about the money deliveries. He'd been her only suspect back then, because from the time he was in junior high, he'd taunted the Delaneys as much or more than any family on Old Fence Court. Maybe a case of "guilty conscience," she'd thought, or pity upon learning about her father's death, had inspired the charitable donations. But in typical Buddy style, he'd neatly sidestepped the question, neither confirming nor denying.

She had another suspect now....

Get real, Kasey, she scolded herself. She hadn't known Adam back then, so even if, like Buddy, he, too, had been a juvenile delinquent, Adam would have had neighbors of his own to harass.

She looked at him, handsome and gentlemanly as he politely chatted with Pat and Aleesha. The very idea that he could ever have been anything but what he was now seemed comical!

"Kasey, you look like the cat that's swallowed the canary," Pat said. "What're you smiling about?"

Blinking, she snapped to attention. "Oh, just remembering Aleesha's beautiful song, I guess." *Nice save, Kase,* she told herself.

"So you're sure?" Adam asked. "You don't want me to bring anything?"

She swallowed. "Um, bring? To what?" Kasey felt a silly grin broadening her lips as a dim recollection surfaced in her mind. She'd nodded, hadn't she, in response to something Pat and Aleesha and Adam had been discussing, but for the life of her, she couldn't remember what, specifically.

Aleesha gave a teen-typical groan. "M-o-m," she said. "Thanksgiving dinner? You *said* he could come, just a second ago...."

Ah, so that was it! She'd agreed to include Adam in the Delaney Thanksgiving celebration, and he, in turn, must have offered to provide a pie, or rolls, or…something.

"Just bring yourself," she said, grinning to mask her embarrassment.

He looked as confused as she felt.

"Okay," Adam said, "if you're sure."

"Positively sure. Dinner is at three."

"But we like to start gathering by two," Pat added. "Kasey won't allow anyone to eat until they've thought of at least one reason to be thankful."

"First time I ate with them, before I became a real Delaney," Aleesha said, giggling, "I almost got a headache tryin' to think of something!" Turning her smiling face toward Kasey, she added, "It's easy to come up with stuff now." She reached for Kasey's hand. "Thanks to Mom."

Kasey's heart beat harder, partly in response to Aleesha's unabashed love, partly in response to the look of admiration shining in Adam's eyes.

They descended the church steps, single file. "So how many will there be this year, honey?" Pat asked.

"Let's see," Aleesha said in Kasey's stead. "There's the Pastor and Mrs. Hill and their two kids, Mr. Weiss next door and his grandson, Uncle Chuck and his family, my friends Susie and Noah—they go to my school—" that was her aside to Adam "—Gramma, Mom, me and Dr. Thorne. How many is that?"

"Eighteen," Pat said. "I think we need to round up two more mouths to feed, make it an even twenty!"

Adam whistled. "Wow. I've never eaten with that many people, except in restaurants."

The reverent tone in his voice revealed more than that he wasn't accustomed to big family get-togethers. It told Kasey that his life had been all but devoid of relatives, that he hungered for more than the food prepared for holiday gatherings.

"Kasey loves it," Pat explained. "'The more the merrier,' she always says."

Adam's look of admiration deepened. "I wouldn't miss it for the world."

And it sounded to Kasey as if he meant it.

Between now and then, she decided, she'd find out what his favorite dessert was, so he'd feel welcome, so he'd feel *special.* Kasey sensed he hadn't experienced much of that in his lifetime.

Without knowing it, he'd awakened all sorts of womanly emotions in her, like the need to pamper and take care of him, and despite the fact that he was a big strong guy, able to fend off foes, she wanted to protect him, too, to comfort him from all the world's woes.

If she had anything to say about it, "special" would become a routine feeling for Adam, starting this Thanksgiving.

And if it was in the Lord's plan for her life—and Kasey prayed that it was—Adam would be one of the things she would thank God for *next* year.

Chapter Seven

Adam thrust out his chin, hoping the knick he'd given himself shaving earlier wouldn't show when he peeled off the tiny wad of toilet paper. He ran a comb through his hair, adjusted his collar, examined his teeth.

Over his shoulder, he caught sight of his bed reflected in the mirror, and groaned. Piles of rumpled clothes were scattered across the comforter, evidence of the trouble he'd had deciding what to wear. In the end, he'd rejected the coat and tie idea, opting for a white knit shirt and blue slacks.

"You're losin' it, pal," he told the man in the mirror. "When was the last time you went kablooie over a...a *girl?*" Not since junior high, he acknowledged, grimacing—years before that nasty train business ever entered Buddy's head.

Enough, he thought, grabbing his bomber jacket. On his way to the door, he noticed that the plant his mom had given him "to warm the place up a bit" was in desperate need of a good watering. She'd put it on the foyer table, saying it would be an earthy welcome for guests.

Wilted branches and yellowing leaves told him it was

probably too late to save it, but he had to at least try. It would be the first thing his mother asked about when her cruise ship docked at the Baltimore harbor.

He hung the jacket on the front-door knob, stepped into the powder room and slid a paper cup from the wall dispenser. Realizing it would take ten trips with a vessel this small, he drank the water and tossed the cup into the trash can. He'd water the plant tonight, after he'd cleared off his bed.

Glancing around as he headed back into the foyer, he realized the whole place needed a thorough cleaning. He might not have noticed, if he didn't have such a clear memory of how tidy Kasey's place was. He smiled, because very soon, while he admired neat furniture arrangements and artfully placed knickknacks, he'd be surrounded by the scents of roasting turkey, baked yams, simmering gravy....

Licking his lips, Adam used his forefinger as a hook and slung the jacket over his shoulder, all but dancing out the front door. He hadn't felt this good since—

No point dwelling on that; it'd only spoil the mood.

He bolted the door and, whistling, he descended the porch steps. If he saw one of those street-corner flower vendors on his way to Kasey's, he might just stop, buy her a bouquet.

He was driving along, singing an old Thanksgiving tune that was on the car radio, when he spotted a peddler, doing a keep-warm two-step as he huddled in a white tent.

Walking up and down the narrow, grassy aisles, he remembered Kasey saying that while she thought roses were pretty enough, they'd never been her favorite flowers. But which *were?* he wondered, reading ID tags that hung from each blossom-filled pail. The carnations were pleasant enough. So were the asters and lilies. He saw out-of-season tulips and daffodils, chrysanthemums the size of volleyballs, and something called Bachelor's Buttons. One pot's label said Snapdragons; another, Impatiens. *He* was running out of patience!

The day before, he'd purchased a three-pound box of chocolates, but something told him Pat and Aleesha would get more enjoyment out of the gift than Kasey, what with her wasp-waist and all. He wanted to bring something just for *her*. But how harebrained was it, he chided himself, to so much as consider bringing posies to a woman who made flower arrangements for a living?

Groaning inwardly, Adam was about to give up, when he spotted a colorful bunch of blooms in the corner. "What're these called?" he asked the boy behind the counter.

"Wildflowers." The kid grinned and pointed at the individual buds in the assortment and rattled off their common names: "Black-Eyed Susan, Baby's Breath, Queen Anne's Lace, daisies…"

Something about that last grabbed Adam's attention. He thought the daisies were graceful and appealing in a simple yet elegant way…just like Kasey. "How much?"

"Ten bucks," said the teen, "or two for fifteen dollars."

Adam glanced around the tent-like stall. "You have another one like this?"

"Sure." The kid produced a second bouquet. He donned a proud expression. "But I don't know why y'want these, 'cause basically, they're just weeds." He gestured toward the long-stemmed red roses in the front row. "Girls *love* roses," he said, nodding.

"Not this girl," Adam said, acknowledging a pride all his own. He plunked a twenty-dollar bill on the counter.

The boy rang up the order, held out a five as change.

"You keep it," Adam told him. "You've been a big help."

Pride became pleasure as the kid pocketed his tip. "Thanks, sir. Happy Thanksgiving!"

"Same to you," Adam replied. But the boy hadn't heard him, for he'd already turned his attention to another customer.

Back in his car, Adam cranked up the heat and rubbed his hands together to fend of the chill, late-November wind. He'd be warm soon enough, because if he knew Kasey, there'd be a fire blazing in the hearth.

Blending into traffic, he smiled at the two paper cones that protected Kasey's wildflower bouquets. If he hadn't been so satisfied with his purchase, Adam might have noticed that a low-slung, silvery sports car was headed in the same direction.

"Somebody's here!" Aleesha shouted. As usual, she'd posted herself in the living room window half an hour earlier, determined to announce the guests as they arrived.

She parted the gauzy living room curtains. "Wrong. I heard a car door, but it's just somebody going to the Russells' house across the street."

Suddenly, Aleesha groaned. "Oh, man, who invited *him?*" Frowning, she turned from the window.

Kasey looked over her daughter's shoulder. "Who?"

"Jerk," the girl said, pointing at the man walking toward their house, "that's who."

"Aleesha, I've spoken to you about that...."

"I won't never say it to his *face.*" And under her breath, she muttered, "Much as I'd like to."

Kasey's heart knocked against her ribs as she watched Buddy approach. "Mom," she called over her shoulder, "did you invite Buddy to Thanksgiving dinner?"

"Yes, honey." Pat came into the room drying her hands on a red-and-white plaid dish towel. "I ran into him at the post office yesterday. He reminded me his folks will be in Florida until spring, asked what we were doing for the holiday. I couldn't very well tell him about our feast without inviting him. He looked so...so sad and so lonely.''

I'll just bet he did, Kasey thought, as Aleesha used her sleeve to buff a breathy vapor cloud from the polished glass. "Great," she muttered. "This is just great."

"What's wrong, Mom?"

Tidying the curtain, Kasey forced a bright note into her voice. "Nothing, sweetie. Everything's fine."

"No, it ain't. I can tell." Then Aleesha nodded. "Oh, I get it. Buddy and Dr. Thorne...they ain't exactly best friends, right?"

If there was an Understatement of the Year award, Aleesha would have won it with that one!

"Does Dr. Thorne know *he's* gonna be here?"

"No, sweetie. I'm afraid not."

"And Buddy, he doesn't know Dr. Thorne will be here?"

Kasey shook her head.

"Hoo-boy!" She slapped a hand over her eyes. "This is gonna be some interestin' meal!"

"You can say that again." *Lord,* Kasey prayed, *watch over us today especially.*

"Oh, honey," Pat said, wringing her hands. "I wasn't aware the two of them even knew each other, let alone..." She bit her lower lip. "If I'd known, why, I never would have—"

"It's okay, Mom." She gave her mom's hands a reassuring pat-pat-pat. "I'm sure they can get along for one afternoon."

Pat grabbed the doorknob. "Please, God, let that be true!"

She opened the door and smiled brightly. "Buddy. Do come in, won't you?"

"How you doin', Mrs. Delaney?" Buddy kissed her cheek.

"Let me take your coat," she said, "then you can—"

"No problem, Miz D. I know where it goes." He dug around in the hall closet for a hanger. "Mmm-mmm-mmm," he said, sniffing as he stuffed his jacket in with the others, "I smell pumpkin pie."

"Sweet potato," Aleesha corrected. "Gramma is allergic to pumpkin."

Only when he looked toward the girl's voice did he seem to notice Kasey, standing in the wide arch leading to the living room. "Hey, Kase. Good of you to invite me, considering…"

She didn't need to ask "considering what?" "No problem," she said. "There's a tray of vegetables and dip on the family room coffee table," she said, gesturing toward the hall. "I have a few last-minute things to do before everyone else gets here, but I'm sure there's a football game on somewhere, so make yourself at home."

He didn't go into the family room, but followed her into the kitchen, instead. "You want I should set the table? Peel potatoes? Take out the garbage?"

Kasey hoped he couldn't hear the nervousness in her laughter. "No, but thanks." She didn't dare let him lift a finger. He'd mowed the lawn a time or two, and dragged the trash cans to the end of the driveway once. Even if he had been the Secret Santa who'd visited the Delaneys all year long, it gave him no right to think of her as chattel.

After the holidays, she'd get to the bottom of that mystery, once and for all. She'd get out her calculator and find out exactly how much she owed…whomever, and somehow, she'd return every penny. As her dad used to say,

"You don't want to be beholden to anybody, ever, 'cause even if they *say* 'no strings attached,' there's always some kind of price to pay."

Smart man, that Al Delaney. Maybe someday, she'd start writing down all his sage advice, and give it to Aleesha as one of her college graduation gifts.

"You're sure there's nothing I can do?"

"Everything's under control. Now, how about some iced tea, maybe a soda?"

"Water'll be fine." He pocketed his hands. "I'm glad nobody else is here yet, Kase. I was hoping we'd have a couple minutes to talk, alone...."

She tied a blue terry-cloth apron around her waist. "Oh?"

"Yeah. I've been meaning to call, apologize for the way I behaved the other day. I feel like a heel. Can you ever forgive me?"

Maybe, she thought, grabbing a glass from the cupboard, if the scene in the Mi Casa parking lot had been the first time he'd let testosterone rule his actions. But Aleesha had hit the old nail square on the head when she'd pointed out that Buddy routinely treated the Delaney women as if they didn't have one functioning brain among them. A clumsy male attempt to protect the needy women around him? Kasey didn't think so.

"I'm going to set the table," she told him, tightening her apron. "You'd better take advantage of controlling the remote while you can."

"Why? Will there be other guys here?"

Her heart skipped a beat. "A few."

"Do I know 'em?"

She nodded, filled the tumbler with water from the pitcher in the fridge. "Yes, except for Aleesha's friend from school, I think you do."

"Who?"

There was an edge to his one-word question that told her he suspected Adam was on the guest list, too.

Kasey handed him the glass and walked into the family room. She turned on the TV and clicked through the channels until she found the Ravens game. Tossing him the remote, she grinned. "You'd better flick while the flickin's good," she teased, winking.

He didn't change the station. "Seriously, who else is gonna be here?"

She started a mental rundown of the males who'd be seated at her table, intending to mention Adam last, of course. But the doorbell rang.

Like a bloodhound, he seemed to sense her relief. "Saved by the bell?" he asked, cocking his head slightly.

"Yeah," she said over her shoulder. *Please, God, don't let it be Adam...just yet.*

Another prayer answered, Kasey realized, as the pastor and his brood filed into the house. Hugs were dispensed all around and coats were hung, before the Hills joined Buddy in the family room.

"Melvin," the young pastor said, raising and lowering Buddy's arm like a pump handle. "How good to see you." He grinned impishly, pushing his spectacles up his nose. "Missed you in church this morning...."

No one dared call him Melvin. Not even his parents. Kasey had a feeling the only reason John got away with it was that white collar around his neck.

Red-faced, Buddy's smile tightened. "I'll make you a deal, John—you call me Buddy, and I'll try and make it to more of your sermons."

The reverend grinned good-naturedly, then said, "Tell you what. You come to Sunday service this week, and I promise never to call you Melvin again." He let a moment pass, then added, "Deal?"

A vein bulged on Buddy's forehead as his brows drew together.

Unfazed by Buddy's ire, John nodded. "Melvin," he said, thoughtfully rubbing his chin. "Very unusual. Yes, very different. Certainly not a moniker you hear much, especially not these days."

"I'm named for my great-grandfather. He was a fighter pilot during World War Two...died saving half-a-dozen soldiers in his unit."

"You don't say! Well, praise the Lord," John said. "You should be proud to be named after a hero!"

Kasey stood, frozen with dread in the doorway, hands clasped under her chin. When Buddy met her eyes, it was as though a calming wind had blown over him. The crimson in his cheeks faded and the throbbing vein in his forehead disappeared. He sent her a sheepish grin, one she read as a silent apology for his prickly attitude.

He slouched into Pat's recliner and turned up the TV. "You a Ravens fan, John?"

The preacher sat on the edge of the couch. "I suppose I could be, if only I had more time. They're doing well this year, or so I hear."

Kasey sighed in relief, as Buddy brought John up to date on player stats and competitors' recent scores. To give him his due, Buddy had a good heart, and as she'd just witnessed, he could be a nice guy when he put his mind to it.

As she made her way back to the kitchen, she prayed he'd be even half as gracious when Adam arrived.

Kasey stopped stirring the gravy and inclined her ear toward the back door. Shaking her head, she went back to work. *Could have sworn I heard someone knocking,* she thought, frowning.

The tapping started up again, slightly louder this time. Parting the curtains, she saw Adam's handsome face on the other side of the glass.

"Adam," she said, when he stepped into the kitchen, "how long have you been standing out there in the cold?"

"Just a couple of minutes." One corner of his mouth lifted in a boyish grin. "You look gorgeous in that getup, by the way."

She couldn't help but laugh at that. Her apron was spattered with grease and grime, and unruly curls that had escaped her French braid had been driving her crazy for the past half-hour. No doubt she'd worn all her lipstick off by now, tasting things.

"Why didn't you come to the front door?" she asked, blushing as she tried to pat a stray wisp into place.

"Because I wanted to give you these," he said, bringing the bouquets from behind his back, "and I didn't want to make a big fuss."

Kasey pressed a palm to her chest and bit her lower lip. "Adam, they're gorgeous." She looked into his eyes. "But where did you find wildflowers this time of year?"

He shrugged one shoulder, looking every bit like a shy teenage boy.

"I'd better get them in water," she said. "They can thrive under the most horrible conditions in nature, but once they've been cut…" She pulled a big cut-glass vase from the cabinet under the sink. "They're a lot like human beings in that way, don't you think?"

Adam had no idea what she was talking about, but he was so happy to see her, he didn't admit it. "I guess," he said carefully.

"Well, left to their own devices, people can survive incredible odds. But take them out of their natural environment, deprive them of the things that protect and nurture them, and they'll wither on the vine.'' She giggled. ''If you'll pardon my very poor metaphor....''

Was she comparing herself to the flowers, saying, in essence, that outside influences had tampered with her world, and she'd grown up differently because of it? Because if she was, maybe Wade and the guys had been right. Maybe she *knew*.

He could count on one hand the things in life that truly scared him, and have fingers left over. Kasey finding out what he'd done as a boy was one of those things. Adam swallowed, hard.

''Thirsty?'' she asked. ''There's iced tea and cold water in the refrigerator.''

He remembered exactly where she kept the tumblers, because he'd poked through just about every cabinet in the kitchen on Halloween night. Remembered, too, that the glasses stood on the shelves in orderly rows, like glass soldiers standing at attention.

He helped himself to one, filled it with water from the pitcher in the fridge. ''Smells great in here,'' he said, hoping to change the subject. ''You must have gotten up at dawn.''

''Actually, I did most of the cooking yesterday,'' she said, arranging the flowers in the vase, tall ones in the middle and shorter ones surrounding them.

''Yesterday?'' He sipped the water, grateful she hadn't returned to the subject of what happens when something tampers with a living thing.

''All I had to do today, really, was set the table and put the turkey in the oven.'' She glanced at the clock. ''In half an hour or so, I'll mash the potatoes and pop the biscuits in, and *voilà!*, dinner is served.''

He watched as Kasey stood back, one hand on her hip, the other beneath her chin as she tilted her head this way and that to study her handiwork. Her delicate fingers moved so quickly they seemed like a blur as they repositioned flowers in the vase.

"There," she said, clasping her hands in front of her chest. "A Thanksgiving centerpiece!"

Did she have any idea how stunning she was with her coppery hair aglow under the overhead lights and her cheeks flushed from the steaming pots and pans? Did she realize that one glance from those sparkling emerald eyes was enough to steal the very breath from his lungs? Or that her mastery of everyday things, like flower arrangements and alphabetized spice cabinets, kindled in him every urge God ever gave a man?

Adam gulped the water until the glass was empty.

"Warm in here, isn't it?"

Nodding dumbly, he smiled awkwardly.

"Give me your jacket," she said, dainty hands extended.

When he handed it to her, Kasey stroked the brown leather. "Ooooh," she said, eyes closed as she hugged it to her, "soft."

In the week between their lunch and today's dinner, he'd done a fair-to-middlin' job of tamping down the feelings she'd stirred in him. One look into that pretty, wide-eyed face in the church the other day, and he'd had to stomp them down all over again. He had suspected the same thing might happen if he accepted this invitation, and yet he'd said a hearty, hasty yes.

Fool that he was, he'd told himself he could get through one dinner without waking the emotions yet again. But the instant those curtains parted earlier and he saw her lovely smile on the other side of that window...

Idiot, he upbraided himself as she hung his jacket on a

peg beside the back door before returning to the stove. *Blockhead.* He was in so deep, he'd need a rope and a ladder to haul him out. *Good thing one of your best friends is a firefighter,* he thought, *you spineless moron.*

Somewhere between his house and hers, Adam must have lost his mind. Why else would he have crossed the room in two long strides and taken her in his arms? What else explained the way he pressed a lingering kiss to her soft pink lips?

For an instant she stood, stiff with surprise, one hand still holding the stirring spoon, the other gripping the pot lid. Then a soft sigh—no, it was more like a purr of contentment—issued from her as she relaxed, leaning into him, wrapping her utensil-laden arms around his neck.

"Something's burning," he mumbled against her lips.

"Mmm," was her whispery reply. Taking a half step back, Kasey looked up into his face. "Think it's your lips, or mine?" she asked, before her dreamy expression morphed into a cheery smile.

Chuckling, he held her at arm's length. The range of emotions she brought out of him ran the gamut from passion to fear to blatant joy. "No, it's something on the stove, I think."

She pulled away from him, put the spoon and the lid on the counter and snapped off every burner. Then, hands on her hips, she faced him. "Well, are you happy? You've made me ruin the peas!"

He could tell by the spark of merriment in her big eyes that she was teasing. Such a small thing, really, but the intimacy of their little joke made him take a step closer, made him press a palm to each of her rosy cheeks. "No big loss," he said, "'cause I've never liked peas."

One delicate, well-arched brow lifted slightly, as did one corner of her recently kissed mouth. "Really...?"

Something happened in the second that ticked by as she stepped on the foot pedal of the trash can and unceremoniously disposed of the burnt vegetables. Now he had a name for what he'd been feeling, practically since he opened the cabin door and saw her standing on his porch, soaked to the skin.

From the sink, Kasey shot a flirty glance over her shoulder. "Cool," she said, "we both hate peas."

Heart thumping and pulse racing, he returned her affectionate smile. Yep, he had a name for it, all right.

God help him, it was love.

To give them their due, both Adam and Buddy had done a stellar job so far, avoiding topics that might cause an argument. Kasey doubted that anyone other than Pat and Aleesha noticed the deliberateness of their pleasant, if stilted, conversation, and she made a mental note to thank the men—separately, of course—when the day ended.

Moments after everyone had a full plate, Adam's beeper went off. Frowning, he stood. "Mind if I use your phone?"

"'Course not. Help yourself."

While Adam was in the kitchen, Buddy helped himself to another slice of turkey. "Any cranberry sauce left?"

Pat passed the bowl. "Another roll? Butter?" she asked from the head of the table.

"Why not," he said, laughing as he patted his flat stomach. "I can always move my belt up another notch, if I have to."

His joviality made her wonder if maybe he'd somehow orchestrated the call that would more than likely take Adam away from the celebration.

It hadn't escaped Kasey's notice that Buddy and Adam had chosen the seats beside her own at the other end of the table, a spot she preferred because of its proximity to the kitchen. But when had Buddy moved his chair closer to hers? she wondered. Probably when Adam leaned in to ask about borrowing the phone.

"Hey, Mom," Aleesha said. "When are we gonna start the 'why we're thankful' thing?"

There had been so much going on as they all sat down, that Kasey had all but forgotten to announce it. Then Pastor Hill said grace, and the napkins had started flapping, and well, she'd decided it would be just as effective with dessert.

"Soon as I clear some of these dishes and put out the pie, we'll do it. You'll remind me in case I forget?"

Beaming, the girl gave her word.

Adam returned on the heels of Aleesha's promise. "Sorry I'm going to miss that," he said, slipping into his jacket. "Sounds like fun."

"Where are you going?" Aleesha asked.

"One of my patients had surgery yesterday, and she's worried that one of her stitches might have popped."

"I told him to take that sewing class in high school," Buddy said, grinning, "but would he listen to me? Noooo."

Amid the good-natured laughter his joke inspired, Kasey rose and walked with Adam to the foyer. "I'm sorry you have to leave so soon, but I understand." Joining him on the porch, she closed the door behind them. "If the problem with your patient isn't too serious, maybe you can come back, have dessert with us."

"Maybe."

His smile reminded her of the shy little boy who'd been in her Sunday school class last year, stirring an urge to stroke his cheek. Instead, she stuffed her hand into her sweater pocket.

"But if you can't come back in time for dessert, maybe

you can make it later this evening.'' She lowered her voice. ''I'm sure everyone will be gone by seven....''

''Maybe,'' he said again.

She lay a hand on his forearm, absentmindedly fingering the supple leather sleeve. ''I'll pack some leftovers for you to take home. You have a microwave at the office, don't you?''

He nodded. ''Yeah.''

''Good. I'll box up enough for a few lunches, too.''

''Kasey, you don't have to go to all that trou—''

''It's no trouble, no trouble at all. You'd be doing me a huge favor, really. You saw what was on the table. If you don't take some off my hands, we'll be eating Thanksgiving dinner 'til Christmas!''

He chuckled and shook his head, causing a lock of hair to fall across his forehead. Without thinking, she stood on tiptoe and finger-combed it back into place. Almost as an afterthought, she pressed a quick kiss to his chin.

She felt the heat of his shuddering breath as she said, ''Now get going, before that poor woman has a panic attack.''

He started down the steps. ''Thanks, Kase.''

''No, thank *you*. The flowers are beautiful. I'm going to move them into the kitchen after dinner, so I can enjoy them even more.''

''See ya later,'' he said, climbing into his car.

She didn't know what possessed her to do it, but Kasey blew him a kiss. ''I hope so.''

She waved until he'd backed out of the driveway. Then, cupping her elbows in her palms, she watched as he drove away. For a long time, she just stood there, heart aching and barely breathing and staring at the spot where she'd last seen his car.

Sitting on the top porch step, she huddled into her cardigan and, blowing warm air into her folded hands, closed her eyes. *"Lord,"* she whispered, *"I don't know what You have in mind for my future, but I know that, as always, You have my best interests at heart. You know I'll willingly submit to Your will."* She opened her eyes, looked down the street and sighed. *"But there's something about Adam. I don't know what it is, but I'm sure that You do!"*

Suddenly, she remembered the painful edge to Adam's voice when he'd said, *"There are things you should know about me"*—things, his tone implied, that would make her want to keep her distance from him, permanently.

But how could that be?

Those moments in her kitchen earlier echoed in Kasey's memory, rousing hot tears that pricked at her eyelids. How could that be? she thought again, remembering the tenderness of his touch, the gentle way he looked into her eyes, the sweetness of his lingering kiss.

He seemed so good and decent, so compassionate and kind. Could a man like that really have done something so terrible, so awful, that the mere knowledge of it would make her turn away from him?

Sighing, Kasey admitted that she honestly didn't know.

But God knew.

She'd just have to trust Him to guide her.

"I want Adam in my life, Lord," she continued, *"and I'm praying with all my might that it's what You want for me, too."*

And if it isn't, she added silently, *then You'd better give me a deep well of strength.* Again she glanced down the street, where moments ago his car had been. If she missed him this badly already, how much more would it hurt if he was out of her life forever?

Drying her eyes on her sweater sleeves, Kasey slowly made her way back to the foyer. Leaning against the closed door, she shut her eyes. The grandfather clock against the opposite wall chimed, announcing four o'clock.

God willing, Adam would be back before the clock struck five.

She didn't even try to fight the silly half grin that turned up the corners of her mouth. *You've gone and fallen head-over-heels for a guy you barely know. You must be out of your ever-lovin' mind!*

Accent on the *ever-lovin',* she added, her grin broadening. Because the truth was, for a reason she couldn't explain, Kasey believed she *did* know Adam Thorne. When she looked into his warm brown eyes, it was as if she could see into his heart, as if she could read his soul, telling her he was more than good and decent, telling her he was honest and honorable, right down to the marrow of his bones!

Somehow, she had to get him to tell her about this guilty secret he'd been hiding in his heart. Because once the truth was out, she could prove to him—to *herself*—that nothing he'd done was unforgivable.

She gave a shaky sigh and peered into the mirror above the foyer table, hoping her eyes didn't show the telltale signs of her teary prayer.

"What's the matter," said a deep, grating voice. "Don't tell me you miss Romeo already?"

Chapter Eight

"Buddy, I'm going to have to put a bell around your neck if you keep sneaking up on me that way." Kasey pressed both palms to her chest, willing the action to calm her wildly drumming heart.

"Sorry." He leaned on the front door. "So what's the scoop? Old Thorne agree to come back for a little...dessert?"

She only stared at him.

"I'm just sayin' it took an awfully long time to say goodbye, especially for a doctor on his way to a hospital emergency."

The way to handle him, she hoped, was to ignore sarcastic comments like that. "Did you get enough to eat?" she asked cheerfully.

"You bet." He patted his belt. "One more notch, I would've been in big trouble."

"Remind me, when you leave, to pack some leftovers for you."

He grimaced. "You know I don't like reheated food."

She ignored the pout, too. "You might feel differently

at midnight when all the takeout places have closed.'' She breezed past him. ''Because if I know you, the only thing in your refrigerator is a six-pack of beer.''

Buddy caught up to her. ''Fat lot you know.'' He grinned. ''Last time I checked, there was a stale loaf of bread and some moldy cheese in there, too. Oh, and something in a plastic bowl that I'm scared to touch.''

''You realize, don't you, that you're making my point for me.''

He chuckled. ''Yeah. I guess you are.'' He slipped an arm around her shoulders, gave her a sideways hug. ''You're the best, Kase. I'm a lucky guy, havin' a woman like you lookin' out for me.'' He kissed her temple. ''Don't know what I'd do without you.''

His moods were like quicksilver, changing and reshaping in a heartbeat, without so much as the slightest warning. This latest mercurial shift, she hoped, was proof she'd succeeded in taking his mind off Adam.

She returned to her seat in the dining room, and sipped her water. Kasey had barely touched her meal—not unusual, considering she'd taste-tested every food item on the table before the meal. Watching the enjoyment of friends and relatives made all the cooking and cleaning and baking more than worthwhile. The contented feeling induced a gratified smile.

Buddy caught her eye. He must have thought the smile had been intended for him, for he sent her a teasing wink. Blinking nervously, she looked quickly away and blushed—exactly the wrong thing to do, as it turned out, for it encouraged another wink, punctuated by a tolerant grin.

If only she could come up with a good excuse to leave the room, even for a moment. But the baskets she'd placed at either end of the table brimmed with golden biscuits, and the deep bowls of mashed potatoes, gravy and mixed vegetables still steamed aplenty. Kasey reached for the water pitcher, but even before she grasped its silvery handle, condensation on the jug's rounded sides told her it didn't need refilling.

"Would you pass the butter, Kase?"

Buddy sat, both hands flat on the table, blinking innocently at her.

Kasey handed him the covered, ornate stoneware plate, and when he took it from her, he grazed her skin with a lingering fingertip. The fact that he didn't seem to mind when she snatched back her hand and hid it in her lap told her the touch had been calculated, deliberate.

Exasperation began building inside her. She tried to concentrate, instead, on the quiet dinner conversation. But there were half-a-dozen discussions going on simultaneously: whether or not the Ravens would make the playoffs, would Cal Ripkin play another season for the Orioles, was the gravy homemade or the stuff from a jar?

The soft notes of classical music wafting from the stereo speakers was oddly in sync with the *clink* of silverware against china. Somehow, over the din, Kasey heard the hushed *swish-swish* of the pendulum as it swayed to and fro in the mahogany body of her grandfather clock, and above that sound, the hollow *tock-tock-tock* of its mechanical timepiece.

And in the middle of all this controlled commotion, she thought of Adam, tall and strong, with an air of self-assurance that calmed everyone within reach of the sound of his manly voice. Oh, how she wished she could hear that voice now!

She wondered if he'd made it to the hospital yet. Kasey said a quick prayer, asking God to see to it there was nothing serious wrong with his patient—not only for the woman's sake, but also so Adam would be able to return before dinner was over.

A picture of him formed in her mind: stethoscope draped around the collar of his white lab coat, nodding in a caring yet professional way, assuring his patient that all was well. The image might have made her smile...if she hadn't looked up just then and caught Buddy staring at her.

Turning away quickly, Kasey smoothed the napkin on her lap, shoved a bite of turkey back and forth through the gravy pond in her mashed potatoes, picked at a nub on the tablecloth...until she remembered that was exactly what Adam had done at her kitchen table on Halloween night. Folding her hands in her lap, she recalled that moments later, he'd delivered his warning. *Don't judge a book by its cover,* he seemed to be saying, *because this one is nothing but a list of disappointing surprises.* He'd sounded so miserable that she'd hugged him, and the way he'd held her— tightly, holding his breath as his muscles tensed—made it clear how very much he needed a friend.

Kasey sighed. Oh, for a moment alone!

There were pots soaking in the sink. She could go into the kitchen right now and scrub them. But how polite would it be for the hostess to leave her guests while she performed dishwashing duties?

Peripheral vision told her Buddy was paying careful attention to her every move. What *was* it with him, anyway? For the past few years, she'd had a distant, edgy perception, like somehow he'd slipped a collar around her neck with every intention of keeping a tight hold on her leash. Nothing too obvious, of course—that wasn't Buddy's way—but the feeling had been plain enough.

And it was getting plainer by the day.

Did he actually believe that a few thousand dollars could *buy* her, like a puppy in a shopping mall pet store?

The question stopped her cold.

She'd done the math, enough times to know that the total donated by her anonymous gift-giver over the years added up to more like a *hundred*—not a few—thousand dollars. Maybe she'd implied, by *using* that money, that she was, indeed, for sale.

She couldn't have given the money back because it had always arrived just when they'd needed it most!

You didn't have to spend it, she chided herself for the millionth time. *You could have donated it to charity.*

Then Pat laughed, a carefree, comfortable sound, and Kasey remembered how many times that same money had paid the mortgage, or bought groceries or kept the electric company from turning off their power. Aleesha's animated face and gestures echoed Pat's contentment, reminding Kasey that there were reasons why the courts had let her adopt the girl: Kasey owned this house outright, her business was thriving. Neither of which would be true if she *hadn't* put that money in the bank.

Hundreds of times, she'd tried to uncover the identity of her mysterious caretaker. Back and forth through darkened rooms she'd pace, stopping at every window to peer out into the black night, staring at each silhouette, studying even the slightest movement of branch and bush and tree in the hope she'd catch him tiptoeing to or from the mailbox.

But he'd been too stealthy, too secretive. Like the night shadows that blanketed the Delaney house, he managed to slip in and out without making a sound, without leaving a trace…not even the slightest footprint.

"Pickles, Kasey?"

Buddy's harsh, abrasive whisper slammed into her thoughts like a hammer. Again, she jumped, nearly upsetting the pickle dish.

"Sorry. Didn't mean to scare you."

But his sneaking up on her—figuratively and literally—was getting to be a habit, and not a good one, either. She leaned in close and hissed through clenched teeth, "If I didn't know better, I'd say you do that on purpose, that you *like* frightening me."

He blinked, eyebrows raised. One hand on his chest, he said, "Kasey, you break my heart talkin' like that. I love ya like crazy."

She sat back, thankful no one else had heard their quick, quiet exchange.

This time, it was Buddy who leaned close. "Like I've said before, what reason would I have to hurt you? Hmm?"

They were nose to nose. Near enough to kiss, close enough for Kasey to believe the spark in his dark eyes was put there by spite. She reared back and cleared her throat, wishing the meal would just end, that everyone would just go home.

Because it was all she could do to keep from holding her head in her hands and screaming.

He stretched out on the cushions of the brown tweed couch in the doctors' lounge, fingers linked under his head and feet hanging over the worn sofa arms, and groaned.

Wade flopped onto the matching chair across the room. "You're makin' old man noises, Adam." He propped his feet on the coffee table. "Keep that up, and pretty soon you'll be belting your trousers up under your armpits."

"Tell you the truth," Adam said around a yawn, "all I care about right now is getting five minutes of sleep."

Wade stretched. "Thanks for taking care of that popped stitch for me. I never would've made it all the way around the beltway in time to keep the next one from going."

Shaking his head, Adam closed his eyes. Popped stitch,

ha! What should have been a ten-minute quick-fix turned into a four-hour ordeal. The elderly woman who'd popped a stitch worked herself into such a frenzy over it that she disconnected her monitor wires and her feeding tubes, and tore out the staples securing her bypass, as well.

"You're supposed to say, 'No problem, pal. You'd do the same for me.'"

"No problem. You'd do the same for me."

Chuckling, Wade said, "You forgot 'pal.'"

"No," Adam said, grinning as he opened one eye, "I didn't."

Wade wadded up a paper napkin that someone had left on the table and tossed it at Adam, who didn't even flinch when it landed beside his head. The only movement was the steady rise and fall of his chest.

"Man, you must be pooped. You're not even tempted to throw it back?"

"Sure. Put it in a safe place and I'll get around to it when I wake up. Or at the turn of the century, whichever comes first."

"So how was dinner?"

Scrubbing his face with both hands, Adam shook his head. That kiss in her kitchen was the only thing he could recall. "Delicious," he said, grinning to himself.

"She's a good cook, huh?"

I have no idea, Adam thought, *but she's a good kisser....* "How 'bout your dinner?" he felt obliged to ask. "Did your sister make her famous sausage stuffing?"

"Yeah."

"Did you bring Marcy?"

"Nah."

In response to the downhearted tone in his friend's voice, Adam sat up. "What did you do, take Carole, instead?"

Wade grimaced. "You've gotta be kiddin'."

Adam wasn't surprised. The blond gum-snapper would have been to a Cameron family celebration what an alligator would be to a baby nursery.

"Who did you take?"

"Nobody."

"Why not?"

In place of Wade's usual mischievous grin, there was a tight-lipped scowl. "Mom's got…she was diagnosed with breast cancer a couple weeks back."

Adam winced. He'd spent almost as much time in the Cameron house growing up as in his own. Despite the nasty divorce when Adam and Wade were ten that forced Mrs. Cameron to take a full-time job, she'd found time to bandage Adam's skinned knees, to stitch the rips in his football jersey, to teach him to waltz before his junior prom.

"Sorry to hear that," he said. A tight knot formed in his stomach as he wondered why things like that happened to people like Mrs. Cameron.

"Have they done a biopsy yet?"

Nodding, Wade said, "Yeah."

It didn't sound good. Not good at all. "So they've scheduled surgery?"

He nodded again. "Yeah. Next week."

Adam didn't have to ask if the doctors would perform a radical mastectomy; Wade's tone made that clear enough.

"How long have you known?"

"Since day before yesterday." Wade leaned his elbows on his knees, pressed his palms to the sides of his head. "She insisted on a quiet no-guests-allowed dinner. Wouldn't say why. The rest of us thought maybe early senility was startin' to set in, 'cause you know how Mom loves big family gatherings." His voice broke slightly when he added, "Now we know why—"

"How is your sister taking it?"

"'Bout the same as me, I guess, putting on a brave face for Mom...."

...and falling apart when she isn't around, Adam finished silently.

Wade got to his feet and stared at the ceiling. "I've got a bad feelin' about this, pal. A real bad feelin'."

Adam stood, too, and walked over to his friend. "No reason to think that way," he said, dropping a brotherly hand on Wade's shoulder. "They're working miracles in oncology these days." He gave the shoulder a slight shake. "Look, if there's anything I can do—take some of your patients, do follow-up exams, make hospital rounds—"

Wade nodded. "I might take you up on some of that. Thanks." He held Adam's eyes. "She asked me to tell her 'unofficial son' that he's the only non-Cameron allowed at the hospital that day."

Her unofficial son.

That's what she'd been calling Adam since he and Wade met in Mr. Beazley's fifth-grade classroom. From the moment Adam had first set foot in her galley kitchen, Mrs. Cameron had made him feel like a member of the family. Years later, on one of the many nights he'd spent on her living room sofa, she'd caught him sneaking back into that tiny kitchen, and somehow coaxed a tearful confession out of him...about the Halloween prank, about the extra part-time job he'd taken to earn money for the Delaneys. After that, there was nothing he couldn't tell her; after that, she was every bit as much a friend to Adam as anyone he'd ever known, as anyone he ever *would* know.

How could something like cancer be happening to a woman as kind, as giving, as Mrs. Cameron? If he lost her...

Adam shook off the horrible thought of a world without Jaina Cameron.

Being a doctor should have made accepting things like that easier.

It didn't.

The lounge was so quiet that Adam could hear melting water pecking the refrigerator's drip pan. A lump formed in his throat, and he swallowed to keep a sob at bay. Wade needed him to be strong now, needed his support. He pocketed his hands. "I'll give her a call first thing tomorrow, get the particulars, clean up my schedule so I can be there."

"She'll like that." Wade gave a halfhearted, grating chuckle. "Guess it takes something like this to put things in perspective, eh?"

Perspective?

"All that worrying about what Kasey Delaney knows, about her maybe taking us to court, suing us for everything we have to get even for what we did...." Wade rubbed his eyes and gave a heavy sigh. "Compared to what Mom's about to go through, none of that seems very important." His eyes challenged Adam. "Does it."

Adam could have repeated his belief that Kasey had a heart as big as her head, that even if she knew about their part in her father's death, she wasn't the vindictive type. But that wasn't the kind of assurance Wade needed at the moment.

If he thought for even a minute that God would answer the prayers of someone like him, Adam would have fallen to his knees in an eye-blink. But he knew better, of course, and so he said, "Only thing that's important right now is making sure your mom gets through this, safe and sound."

"Yeah." Wade shuffled toward the door. "Listen, thanks, man."

Adam held up a hand. "Hey, it's all in a day's work."

"I wasn't talking about what you did in the O.R."

Somehow, Adam had known that. "Get some sleep. You need it."

"Look who's talkin'. You look like something the dog dragged in."

"Ha-ha," Adam said, smiling humorously.

Wade walked into the hall and pressed the elevator down button. The doors parted and he stepped inside. For a moment, he just stood there, looking back at Adam. And then he said, "Sure would be nice to be able to count on a bona fide miracle once in a while, wouldn't it?"

"Yeah," Adam whispered as the doors hissed shut. "It sure would."

"I don't get it," Kasey said. "Why all the secrecy?"

"Because," Buddy answered, "if I told you where we were going, it would spoil the surprise."

She sighed. He'd shown up, unexpected as usual, and laid such a guilt trip on her about the tense way they'd parted on Thanksgiving night that she'd agreed to take a ride with him. But they'd been driving for nearly half an hour.

"Easy," he said, "we're almost there."

"Good. Because I have twenty-four 'little arrangements' to make for the grand opening of the Arundel Mall."

If he heard the sarcasm in her voice, Buddy didn't show it. He steered the sports car between two towering brick pillars that flanked the entrance to a tree-lined drive. As he maneuvered the mile-long ribbon of black asphalt, Kasey noticed a tennis court and a pond in the distance, a guest house beyond the barn.

"So what do you think?"

"It's gorgeous." She counted six horses in the white-fenced paddock. "Who lives here?"

"I do. Well, I *will,* once all the papers are signed, sealed and delivered."

"*You?*"

He frowned slightly. "Why do you sound surprised?"

Kasey shrugged. "It's just... How many acres?"

"Twenty-five. Eighteen are wooded."

As if to punctuate his answer, the house came into view. The facade was three stories high and built of solid brick, with no fewer than three dozen many-paned windows. Like brawny arms, a chimney hugged each side of the mansion; beside them, thick, gnarling oaks that had likely been standing guard for centuries.

Buddy parked on the circular drive, facing the mansion, and climbed out of the car. "C'mon," he said, waving at her through the windshield. "Don't you want to see the inside?"

"Sure," Kasey said, joining him, "I'm game."

Side by side, they climbed the curving multitiered brick steps. Once he'd unlocked the double-high, double-wide black doors, he took her hand and led her inside.

"Wow," she whispered, her voice echoing from the black-and-white marble floor, "the foyer is bigger than my whole downstairs!"

"You think this is something, wait 'til you see the kitchen."

He'd been right, she realized the moment they set foot in the room. All white, from floor to ceiling, the kitchen boasted every appliance known to modern man...and a few she didn't recognize. "Wow," she said again. "It's beautiful."

He half ran up the plushly carpeted, curved staircase and beckoned her to follow. On the landing, he stood at the tall, arched window. "You can see the Gunpowder River from up here. Gorgeous, isn't it?"

Kasey nodded. It was gorgeous, all right. With pines and meadow grasses as far as the eye could see, the lawn stretched out before them like a hilly, verdant blanket. Clumps of graceful white birches dotted the landscape. A grouping of grapevines here, a cluster of leaf-bare fruit trees there. "It's like something out of a movie," she said, as he continued upstairs, taking the steps two at a time.

He showed her a library, an office, and a bathroom bigger than any she'd ever seen. In the master bedroom, he opened the doors to twin closets, each larger than the room she called her own at home. There were shelves for sweaters and pegs for belts and scarves, and a built-in padded bench in the center, where, she supposed, the lady of the manor could sit to slip into the shoes she'd chosen from one of several dozen cubbies.

She threw open the French doors and stepped onto the balcony. "Buddy," she said, peering onto the back lawn, "what's a bachelor like you going to *do* with all this space?"

He grasped her hands and looked meaningfully into her eyes. "I'm gonna fill it up with kids—yours and mine— that's what."

Kasey felt her jaw drop. Kids? Hers and…*his?*

She licked her lips, swallowed, cleared her throat. Surely he didn't mean—

He reached into his jacket pocket and withdrew an elegant black velvet box. When he lifted the small, creaking lid, sunlight glinted from the biggest solitaire she'd ever seen.

"Buddy," she whispered, "what're—"

He got down on one knee and slid the diamond ring from its satiny pillow. Balancing her left hand on his right palm, he held the ring between the thumb and forefinger of his free hand. "Kasey," he said, "will you do me the honor of becoming my wife?"

She wanted to tell him to get up and brush the dust from the knee of his trousers. Wanted to tell him to put that enormous diamond back into its fancy little box. *Don't put that thing onto my finger!* she wanted to say.

Turning from him, she rested both palms on the polished wood banister. Why had he put her in such an awkward position? How was she supposed to ride all the way back to Ellicott City from—she didn't even know which Baltimore suburb this was!—after rejecting his proposal?

"Kasey," he whispered, standing beside her now, "you don't have to answer right away. Give it some time. Think about it for a couple of days, let it sink in." With a grand sweep of his arm, he gestured toward the lawn. "This could all be yours, Kase...yours and mine and our kids'...."

What shady deal had he struck to get the money for a place like this? she wondered. What poor fool had he snookered, what lies had he told? She'd always suspected that his commercial wheelings and dealings were less than honest, that the individuals he 'wheeled and dealed' with were less than reputable. But she'd shrugged it all off, thinking it wasn't any of her business. How he earned a living was between Buddy and God.

Well, he'd made it her business by popping that question, and she wasn't the least bit happy about it. "Would you take me home now?" she said quietly, voice trembling.

"Okay," he said, and she couldn't help but notice that his voice was shaking, too. "But on one condition."

She blew out a heavy breath. "What."

"That you won't give me an answer now. That you'll promise to think about it, at least?"

Kasey counted that as two conditions, but she didn't say

so out loud. If pretending to agree with his stipulations would get her out of here, away from this place...

She nodded. "Okay," she said, then started walking.

She moved quickly out of the master bedroom, through the wide, high-ceilinged hall, down the expansive mahogany-railed staircase. And, heels clicking as she ran across the marble foyer floor, she made her way to the front door, onto the porch, to his fancy one-of-a-kind car.

Kasey could almost picture him up there, stuffing the ring back into its satin slot, snapping the box shut and pulling the French doors to, with an angry *thump*.

As if to prove her right, he slammed the big doors shut with a *bang*, locked them with a flourish and stomped toward the car. "What's wrong with you?" he demanded, palms flat on the driver's side fender. "Why did you run off like that and leave me up there, all by myself?"

She shook her head, avoiding his eyes. "I needed air," she said. And it was true. His proposal had stunned her, scared her, taken her breath away. Even out here, with twenty-five acres around her, Kasey felt stifled.

But she reminded herself it would be a long, difficult ride back home if she didn't cooperate...or at least give the appearance of cooperation.

"I-It was a lot to absorb. I never expected... I'm surprised and..." Finally, she mustered the courage to look up. "I don't know what to say, Buddy." Not entirely true, but not a lie, either, because she knew what she *wouldn't* say. She wouldn't say "yes," not now, not ever.

His angry look dissipated, melted into an expression she could only call "understanding."

"Oh, I get it now," he said, smiling. "Well, okay, in that case, I'll be patient." He gave the fender a gentle knock, then opened the driver's door and slid behind the wheel. "I did this for you, remember."

Kasey pretended she hadn't heard that, as she got into the passenger seat.

"Buckle up," he said, starting the engine.

Somehow, even with the seat belt securely fastened across her chest, she didn't feel safe, didn't feel the least bit secure. Somehow, Kasey knew that even though she'd told Buddy what he'd wanted to hear—for now, anyway— it was going to be a long, *long* ride home.

The answering machine was blinking when she got into the house. Fortunately, Buddy had dropped her off in the driveway, apologizing for not being able to come inside— saying he had "some paperwork to take care of"—because the call was from Adam and one thing she didn't need was Buddy's jealousy right now.

"Hi, Kase," came his pleasant, masculine voice. "Sorry I didn't stop by last night. Had an emergency, and a—" the usually smooth voice faltered "—and a friend with a big problem." Adam cleared his throat. "I, uh, wondered if maybe it's... I was hoping it isn't too late. You said something about leftovers, from Thanksgiving dinner, and well, I, uh..." She heard his frustrated sigh. "Just gimme a call when you get in, will ya? I hate talking to these machines...."

Hugging herself, Kasey slumped to the floor, right there in the foyer, beside the telephone table. If only she could be hugging *him*, maybe this whole Buddy fiasco would seem less oppressive, more manageable.

Well, Adam wasn't there to make everything feel all right. Aleesha would be home from school soon, and Pat from whatever Ladies Auxiliary planning meeting she'd attended today. And as she'd always done, Kasey had to pull herself together, quickly, or be forced to explain why she was a trembling, teary-eyed mess.

Gathering her strength, she got to her feet and went into the kitchen. She'd start a pot of stew for supper, then head out to the workshop to get busy on those arrangements for the new mall. Losing herself in work, experience had taught her, was the best diversion of all.

A message awaited her on the office line, too. Pushing the blinking red button, Kasey sat at her desk, pen poised to write down the name and number of the caller.

"Hey, Kase..."

Adam.

Despite the last few Buddy-induced tension-filled hours, she smiled.

"I left a message at the house. Thought maybe I'd see if you were in the shop, working." There was a pause, then, "Sorry I missed you."

"So am I," Kasey whispered. "So am I."

She slid the pen back into the leather-bound cup Aleesha had made her for Mother's Day and rolled her desk chair away from the desk. Hand resting on the telephone, she debated about calling him back. She wanted to, but because she wanted it so *much,* Kasey decided it wasn't such a good idea. Later, maybe, after she'd knocked off a couple of those arrangements. Or after the supper dishes were done, and Aleesha and her mother had gone to bed.

After Buddy called back, demanding to know if she'd made up her mind yet about marrying him....

The thought stopped her cold, and she leaned forward to rest her forehead on the desk blotter. *Aw, Dad,* she muttered mentally, *I sure could use some of your good old-fashioned homespun advice right about now....*

It didn't matter that more than fifteen years had passed since he'd left them; Kasey knew she'd miss her father 'til she drew her last breath.

"Enough self-pity," she said, getting to her feet. And

perched on the stool at her workbench, she pulled out a drawer, grabbed a clump of florist's clay and pressed it to the bottom of a widemouthed ceramic urn. One by one, wildflowers and corkscrewed grapevines mingled with dried thistles and palm leaves. An hour later, with two of the twenty-some mall's arrangements standing side by side on the table, she assembled the products for a third.

Headlights panned the wall in front of her. Aleesha's ride? Or Pat's return? Kasey wondered. She'd finish this vase, then call it a day. The clock on her desk told her it was nearly suppertime, anyway.

There was a soft knock. "Come in," she called.

"Hi."

Kasey swiveled around to face the door. "Adam," she said, doing her best to control the width of her smile. "I got your messages. I was planning to call you when things settled down for the night." A nervous laugh punctuated her fib. "But then, around here, that could mean never!"

Chuckling, he moved closer. "Nice job," he said, nodding at the flowers.

"Three down and twenty-one to go."

"Wow. That's quite an order."

She shrugged. "Perfect timing, too. The orthodontist says Aleesha's braces have to stay on a while longer."

"So," he said, and she heard the tentativeness in his voice, "how've you been?"

"Good." She hopped off the stool. "And you?" Why were they standing there, talking like strangers, she wondered, when three times, locked in one another's embrace, they'd shared some of the most romantic moments in her life!

"Fine," he said, nodding like one of those back-of-the-car doggies. "Fine."

"Good," she said, mirroring the nod. "Good."

"So…"

"Buttons."

His brows rose. "Buttons?"

She grinned. "Sew? Buttons? Get it?"

"Oh. Yeah." He chuckled again. "Sew."

"So…have you eaten supper?"

"No."

"I made beef stew. If you can hang around 'til I wash up, I'll whip us up some dumplings."

That induced a smile. "I'd like that."

Maybe, Kasey hoped, with Pat and Aleesha around, she and Adam would find a way to knock down this…this wall of uncomfortableness that seemed to have built up between them.

She led the way to the door, and when he joined her, she snapped off the lights and locked up. "So," she said as they walked toward the house, "how's your patient?"

"Turned out it was one of Wade's patients." He explained how the woman's agitation had caused all kinds of internal damage, gave her a quick rundown of how he'd repaired things.

"Must be a good feeling," she said, once they were in the kitchen, "knowing that what you do for a living makes real differences in people's lives, that what you do actually *saves* lives."

"Sometimes," he said, helping himself to a glass of water, "and sometimes not."

Win a few, lose a few? she wondered. That couldn't be easy to cope with.

"Sometimes," he continued, sitting at the table, "it's just tough, because, let's face it, sometimes, doctors are just plain powerless."

Kasey got out a mixing bowl, started assembling the ingredients to make dumplings. "You're not invincible," she said matter-of-factly. "No one expects perfection *all* the time."

"*I* expect it."

She could tell by his tone that he meant it. "But Adam," Kasey said, stirring the batter, "that's impossible. Nobody is perfect."

He nodded. "I know," he said quietly. "But confound it, doctors oughta be. People put all their faith, all their trust, in us. We're supposed to *know* things, supposed to have the education and the experience to *fix* things, y'know?"

As he nodded, Kasey sighed. She wondered what else had happened at the hospital to upset him. "That's a terrible burden." She glanced over her shoulder. "Must be why they pay you the big bucks." She smiled to make sure he knew she'd only been teasing.

Adam smiled back. "Yeah. Big bucks."

Something told her he hadn't become a cardiologist for the money. Maybe someday, he'd tell her why he had.

"Remind me when you leave that I still have Thanksgiving leftovers to give you."

"Great," he said, grinning, "I just got here and already you're planning my departure."

Kasey blushed. "I didn't mean it that way!"

He nodded. "I know. Just pullin' your leg, is all."

She dropped the dumpling mix onto the bubbling stew, one tablespoon at a time.

"Can't recall the last time I've had stew 'n' dumplin's."

"Nice rib-stickin' meat meal, eh?" she said, hoping to remind him he'd suggested meat at their Mi Casa lunch.

"So," he said, leaning back in the chair, "where's Aleesha and Pat?"

She glanced at the clock. "They'll be home soon. Aleesha had play rehearsal after school, and Mom is working on the White Elephant sale for the church." She paused. "It's this Saturday, you know. Wanna come?"

Adam shrugged. "Hmm," he said, "I'm afraid I have one too many white elephants already."

Laughing, Kasey put the lid on the stew pot. "So have I. But I'm going, anyway. Other people's junk fascinates me. And sometimes, I find things that work in my arrangements."

"Cool."

"Yeah. Cool beans."

He took a gulp of the water. "So, what've you been up to?"

What would he say? she wondered, if she said something like, *Oh, nothing much…just turning down marriage proposals, mostly.* Kasey looked at the bare ring finger of her left hand and thought it had never looked better.

"Seen Buddy lately?"

Her heart thudded. Had Adam read her mind? "As a matter of fact, I saw him this afternoon."

His smile vanished. "Is that so?"

"Yup. He wanted to show me the property he's going to buy. Someplace way out in horse country. Twenty-five acres and a mansion that makes the White House look like a cottage."

Adam whistled. "Well, that's Buddy for ya—if you're gonna do a thing, do it big."

She pictured the diamond, thinking *If only you knew!*

"If I was a betting man," Adam began, "which I'm not—I'd bet ole Buddy hasn't given up on you."

Really? she thought. Buddy's proposal echoed in her mind. The other day, she'd considered giving Aleesha the Understatement of the Year award. Maybe, she thought, Adam deserved it more.

"Can't think of any other reason he'd want to show off a grand estate to you."

I can think of one, was Kasey's silent response, *He wants me to be lady of the manor.*

Heart pounding, she forced the idea from her head.

She could avoid it for now, but sooner or later, she knew, Buddy was going to show up and demand an answer. It'd be nice, she mused, if that answer was *Sorry, Buddy, but I've already agreed to marry Adam.*

Now there's *an idea I can live with,* she decided, smiling.

Aleesha burst through the door, bubbling with information about her school day. Practically on her heels, Pat came into the room and started telling them about the plans for the White Elephant sale.

They both behaved as if it was perfectly natural, perfectly normal, for Adam to be sitting in the kitchen, nonchalantly sipping water, while Kasey set the table. In fact, they acted like his presence was an expected part of their family ritual.

Kasey decided right then and there not to wait for Buddy to command a decision. First chance she got, she'd call him, and as delicately—but firmly—as possible, tell him no.

Because if there was so much as a remote chance for her and Adam to have a future together, she didn't want anything standing in the way of it.

Chapter Nine

Hands on her hips, Pat said, "You haven't been yourself for weeks. What's wrong?"

Kasey continued loading flower baskets into her car. "Nothing's wrong, Mom. I'm just flustered. You know that Christmas is my busiest time of the year." She slammed the trunk.

"Nonsense. You thrive on 'busy.' But lately, you're as nervous as a mouse in a maze, always looking over your shoulder, like you're a fugitive from the law!"

Fugitive? Well, she *had* been running...from facing Buddy. She needed time to sort things out, to pray about what would be best for everyone concerned. As she waited for a sign from God, Kasey tried her best not to jump every time the phone rang, lurch at the sound of the doorbell.

Pat's concern was proof she hadn't tried hard enough.

If she'd just followed her heart, there on the balcony of that exquisite mansion, she wouldn't have needed a list of legitimate excuses to dodge Buddy. But for as long as she could remember, she'd sidestepped confrontation—giving up sandbox toys, handing over lunchbox treats, playing games—anything but risk sparking even the most minor dispute. After all he'd done for her family—and she couldn't think of anyone else it might be—refusing him without giving the question careful, prayerful thought would have been unkind, un-Christian, ungrateful, to say the least. Maybe after the holidays, when things didn't seem so rush-rush, she'd have the courage to face the issue.

The thought made her feel a certain kinship with a lion tamer. But at least the khaki-clad circus performer was allowed to bring a whip and a chair for protection against the beast's rage.

"Are you listening to a word I'm saying?" Pat asked. "Where *is* your mind lately! Seriously, Kasey," her mother said, "you're beginning to worry me."

"Sorry, Mom," Kasey said into the trunk. "But honest, there's nothing to worry about. I'm fine. I promise."

Pat scowled. "Tell that to the vein in your temple."

Instinct made her put a hand to her head. "Vein? What vein?"

"The one pounding like a bass drum. Ever since you were a toddler, it's how I could tell when you were trying to hide something."

Kasey sat on the car's rear bumper, rested her palms on her thighs. This was a lose-lose proposition, and she knew it, because once Pat got an idea into her head, she could be like a puppy with a bone: there'd be no peace until Kasey told her what she wanted to hear.

Pat was as hale and hearty as any seventy-three-year-old. Still, Kasey didn't like the idea of worrying her mother any more than she looked forward to listening to more of Pat's enquiries. "Buddy asked me to marry him," she blurted.

Pat gasped. "He…he *wh*—?"

Nodding, Kasey sighed. "Yup. He bought himself a huge

estate in northern Baltimore County. 'This can all be yours,' he said."

Grabbing Kasey's hand, Pat started for the back porch. "You're coming with me, and you're going to tell me everything. Do you understand?" She shook a warning finger under Kasey's nose. "And if you dare leave out a single detail," she said, grinning as they walked along the flagstone path, "you'll go to bed without supper!"

"Okay," Kasey promised, "I'll give you a blow-by-blow description."

In the kitchen, Pat poured them each a cup of coffee, then sat at the table. "Aleesha won't be home for hours yet." She pointed at the seat across from hers. "Start talkin'." She folded her hands on the place mat, waiting.

"Well," Kasey began, hanging her jacket on the back of her chair, "a couple days after Thanksgiving, he asked me to take a ride with him, said he had something to show me. A surprise. We ended up at this twenty-five-acre grand estate that looked like something out of *Gone With the Wind*. He told me there were just a few minor details to iron out before it would all be his." Kasey frowned. "And mine...if I'd marry him."

"Oh, Kasey." Pat held her head in her hands.

"Mom," she said, forcing a smile, "relax. He proposed, that's all. Last I heard, it wasn't a death sentence."

She came out of hiding and pursed her lips. Kasey got the distinct feeling that her mother was preparing to tell her that marriage to Buddy was exactly that.

"So where is this...plantation?" Pat asked, instead.

Glad to change the subject—and the mood—Kasey said, "Near the Maryland–Pennsylvania line, in a little town off I-83 called Freeland. It used to be exclusively a farming community, but according to Buddy, it's built up quite a lot in the past few years.'' She hesitated. ''The house is gorgeous, and more than two hundred years old.''

Pat sipped her coffee. ''And...?''

''And what?''

''And what did you tell him?'' She looked at Kasey as if to say, *Are you trying to drive me crazy?*

''I didn't tell him anything.''

The heavy ceramic cup hit the table with a *clunk*.

Kasey shrugged.

''You didn't say no?''

Another shrug.

''Well, you didn't say *yes*, did you?''

''It's a long, long ride from Freeland to Ellicott City, Mom.''

Pat didn't say a word, but Kasey knew that *look*. When Kasey was a girl, the expression accompanied Pat's stiff-backed, arms-crossed posture, and was usually the precursor to ''I know what you've been up to, young lady.''

''So,'' Pat said, ''to keep the peace, you let him think you might say yes.''

Exactly! Kasey thought.

''Do you think that was wise?''

''Probably not.''

''When will you tell him?''

Kasey sighed. ''I don't know.''

An exasperated groan prefaced her mother's question: ''You *are* going to say no, aren't you?''

She shrugged, just one shoulder this time.

''You mean to say you're actually thinking of *accepting?*''

Actually, it had crossed Kasey's mind. Half a dozen times, if not more.

For years, Buddy had been setting the stage to run for public office. In the past year, he'd set his sights on a Senate seat. In a few years, he'd confided, he'd be eligible for the governor's mansion. "Only thing missing is a house, a wife and two-point-five kids." If he'd said it once, he'd said it a hundred times. And how many times had she heard, "You're good for me, Kase. You make me look respectable."

The plain and simple truth of the matter was, Buddy needed her. And after all he'd done for her family, Kasey felt she owed it to him to at least give the proposal serious consideration.

Besides, Pat wasn't getting any younger. Every couple of months, it seemed, the doctors were prescribing additional medications to control high blood pressure, high cholesterol, hiatal hernia. And Aleesha had a whole laundry list of things wrong with her; only God knew what would crop up next. If Kasey had only herself to take care of, Fleur Élégance would have generated more than enough cash for a comfortable lifestyle. But Aleesha's everchanging condition was costly, and insurance usually didn't cover nearly enough of the medical bills. Kasey would rather die than let even one of the girl's symptoms go untreated.

Several times since the adoption, a pile-up of medical emergencies had put their little family in such financial straits that Kasey had started hunting for part-time jobs. But just when all seemed hopeless, she'd find an envelope in the mailbox....

It wasn't a great leap, going from "Buddy has been taking care of us" to "Buddy will *keep on* taking care of us."

"If I married Buddy," she said quietly, picking at a hangnail on her thumb, "we'd never have to worry about money again."

When she looked up, Kasey was surprised to see tears swimming in her mother's eyes.

"Don't do it, Kasey. Don't settle." She accented the last two words—*slap-slap* on the tabletop.

Kasey reached out and blanketed her mother's hands with her own. "Mom, what choice do I—?"

"We've always landed on our feet. Where's your faith, Kasey?"

In the mailbox, in a plain white envelope, was Kasey's miserable thought.

"If I sit here and let you make the same mistake I made without even trying to talk you out of it, I'd never forgive myself."

There was a haunting, heartbroken note in her mother's voice when she said "mistake."

"When I was a young woman, I wanted to be married so badly!" Pat began. "I wanted children and a house, a husband to pamper...the whole nine yards." Blotting her eyes with a paper napkin, she sniffed. "I was in my twenties, all my girlfriends were married, some even had a couple of kids. I wanted that life, too, so much that I..."

She swallowed a gulp of coffee. "Now, don't get me wrong," she continued, "your father was a good man, a good provider, and God rest his soul, I loved him. But..."

But? How could there be a "but" when Al Delaney was the most wonderful man in the world?

Pat bit her lower lip. "...but I was never *in love* with him."

Kasey felt her mouth drop open, and snapped it shut again. Frowning, she put her hands in her lap. It was all she could do to keep from leaping up, stomping out of the house, away from this conversation.

"After your dad popped the question," her mother said, "I told him about my dream. He promised we'd have kids, dozens of them if that's what I wanted, soon as we could afford them.

"Well, a year went by, then two, and I started nagging him, demanding to know when we could start our family. But every time I brought it up, he had a hundred reasons why he thought we weren't ready yet, why we should wait...."

Ever since Kasey was old enough to speculate, she'd wondered why her parents had waited until they were in their mid-forties to start a family.

Pat sighed, blew her nose. "After a while, I realized he didn't think we'd *ever* be ready. I began to understand he didn't want children, that he probably never had wanted them, that he'd only said what I wanted to hear because his mother thought it was high time he got married and out on his own. I thought I'd grow calluses on my knees, praying for God to change his mind."

But her dad had been such a loving, doting parent! Kasey didn't understand. She looked at her watch, ran her hands through her hair, crossed her legs, then uncrossed them. She wanted out of here, now, before she found out her father's love had only been an act...his way of telling her what she needed to hear.

Pat stared at the wall above the sink. "I remember once," she said, her voice soft and thoughtful, "when we'd been married about twenty years. I'd been spring cleaning. Your father came in and saw the leather jacket I'd bought him for our first anniversary in the trash bin. He'd put on a few pounds and hadn't been able to wear it in a decade or more, but, oh, what a scolding I got for trying to throw that ratty old thing away!"

Pat held her arms out to her sides. "'I cherish that coat!'" she hollered, mimicking him. "'You cherish a *coat?* I yelled right back at him. 'Well, *I* would have cherished our *children!*'"

Kasey turned sideways in her chair, ready to walk away

from the table, to exit the house. To her way of thinking, Al Delaney had been perfect in every way...the perfect father, the perfect provider, the perfect neighbor, a perfect friend to everyone who knew him. She didn't like anyone— not even her mother—tampering with that memory.

"We never had a honeymoon," Pat continued, "never took a vacation. And I didn't complain, because I kept thinking, 'Look how much money we're saving by not gallivanting around.' Kept hoping and praying he'd finally say we had enough in the bank to..."

She wrapped her hands around the coffee mug. "And as I live and breathe I still don't know why—but he came home from work one day and announced he was taking me to Niagara Falls to celebrate our twenty-fifth anniversary. It was all a very big deal, and we planned that trip for months...."

She focused on the wide gold band she still wore on the third finger of her left hand. "He took me to a restaurant and paid extra for a seat near the windows, so we could see the Falls. Then, over dessert, he gave this to me. I cried like a baby, in front of all those people, because it was the first and only thing he ever gave me that I didn't *need*." An impish grin turned up the corners of her mouth as she added, "But I had a little surprise for him, too."

"'Al,' I said, 'you're going to be a father.' He didn't speak to me for days. In fact, he barely said a word the whole nine months."

It nearly broke Kasey's heart, hearing that, because she'd always believed her father loved her more than life itself. If the news had made him angry with her mother...

A dreamy smile sparkled in Pat's eyes. "But once you arrived, oh, did he change his tune! He loved you like crazy. And more than once, he told me if he'd known how wonderful fatherhood could be, he would have let me have that dozen kids.''

Pat took another sip of her coffee. "After that, we tried to get you a baby brother or sister." A faraway look distracted her for a moment. "But after a few years of trying, we gave up. The doctors said we'd waited too long. By then, it was too late, and I was just plain too old to—''

Enough! Kasey thought, getting to her feet. She'd convinced herself her mother's frail health had been the reason she'd had just one child. To find out she could have grown up in a noisy house, with pushing-shoving-giggling-yelling siblings, if not for Al's fear, or greed, or—at this point, it didn't matter *what* he'd been feeling—hurt. She slipped into her jacket. "I have deliveries to make," she said, grabbing the doorknob.

She was on the porch, ready to pull the door shut behind her, when her mother said, "Kasey?"

Shut the door, she told herself. *Just close it and get away from here before she tells you something else you don't want to hear.* "What."

"Are you in love with Buddy?"

Love?

Until that moment, she hadn't seriously thought about it. Buddy was nice enough, but while he seemed mulish about maintaining a fast-lane public image, he kept his private life a closely guarded secret. Could she spend a lifetime beside him?

Maybe…

Could she give her heart to a man like that?

No!

Because the guy she gave her heart to would have to be strong and dependable, caring and trustworthy…

Like Adam.

And, Kasey added mentally, he'd have to love the Lord

at least as much as she did. She didn't know what kind of relationship Adam had with God, but could he be that good, that decent, and *not* be a Christian?

Kasey didn't think so.

"Well, do you?"

"No."

"Then, you can't marry him. Wouldn't be fair to either of you."

She respected her mother too much to say, "Mind your own business." But the real reason Kasey didn't tell her to butt out was that deep down, she knew Pat was *right*.

She placed a soft kiss on Pat's cheek. "I'll be home by suppertime. We'll order pizza." She gave her a quick hug, then said, "Now, close the door before you catch a chill."

"I love you, honey."

"Love you, too, Mom. I won't be long."

"You be careful out there, honey. People drive like maniacs this time of day, you know."

She smiled. "Did you take your blood pressure pills?"

"Yes, but thanks for reminding me."

"You're missing *Oprah*...."

"It's probably a re-run, anyway."

She'd almost clicked the door shut, when Pat yanked it open again. "Don't do it, Kasey," she said, grabbing her daughter's arm. "You'll be miserable. Marriage is tough even when you love each other with all your heart and soul. But without it..."

Kasey looked into her mother's tear-reddened eyes.

"Remember the plaque that used to hang above my sewing machine?"

Kasey nodded, recalling the many times she'd heard her mother whisper its sentiments while folding towels, ironing tablecloths, pulling weeds from her flower beds. As a girl, Kasey had memorized it, in the hope that as she chanted the words, their meaning would become clear. But even after hundreds of recitations, the verse might as well have been printed in hieroglyphics, for all the sense they made.

Closing her eyes, she quoted it now. "'Life is like a shell game. In our desire to choose the things that will add value to our lives, we often choose badly, then blame ourselves for our lack of wisdom. But we should not, for the true value is in the choosing as well as in the choice.'"

It reminded her of a similar adage: Be careful when you're wishing, she paraphrased, because your wish might just come true. *At least I have the freedom to wish,* Kasey thought, as understanding dawned.

The days passed like a blur for Adam as he rearranged his schedule to be available to the Camerons. Lately, meals consisted of whatever he could find in the hospital vending machines, and relaxation came in the form of sitting at his desk to read patient files. And if he slept at all, tormenting dreams of cemeteries and lightning-streaked night skies woke him.

He tried to ignore the exhaustion that painted dark circles under his eyes, that had him yawning between duties. The only time he paid any serious attention to how he felt was when between rounds at Ellicott General and Greater Baltimore Medical Center, he'd tried to phone Kasey. Every time he heard her lovely voice, singsonging the greeting on her answering machine, disappointment loomed large in his heart.

He was bone tired. Of looking for ways to stay busy so he wouldn't have time to think about his out-of-control feelings for Kasey, about how powerless he was to help Mrs. Cameron. Maybe, when—if—she recuperated, he'd meet with Kasey and get the whole nasty secret out in the open, once and for all.

Sitting at a red light, Kasey's gorgeous face popped into his mind, and he watched it go from smiling and serene before his confession, to disillusioned and embittered afterward. The change made his stomach lurch.

No maybes about it. He didn't have the heart to do that to her.

Another truth bubbled just beneath that one, and Adam admitted his silence was as much for himself as for Kasey. Because guilt—and every negative emotion that went hand-in-hand with it—would be far easier to live with than what she'd think of him once she knew everything.

Why couldn't he have it all?

Why couldn't he have Kasey, and conceal his past, too? If he could learn to do that—

The car behind him honked, alerting him that the light had turned green. "Okay, all right," he grumbled, pulling partway into the intersection. "Hold your horses. You'd think there was a fire or—"

He braked when an ambulance careened around cars in the intersection. Lights flashing and siren screaming, it was a vicious reminder that despite good intentions, rigorous training and state-of-the-art equipment, paramedics couldn't save every accident victim. His own father's death was proof of that.

As the emergency vehicle sped up the street, Adam said a quick prayer for its crew, its passenger and their families. The night his dad died, he'd learned about the delicate balance between life and death. A tough lesson for a twelve-year-old.

Adam had a sudden urge to check on Kasey, make sure she was all right. At the next red light, he picked up his cell phone, dialed her number. "Hey, Kase," he said to her machine. "I'm on my way to Sinai, to see Wade's mom before her surgery." He hesitated, uncertain how to conclude the message. "Call you later"? "Gimme a ring"? "Lord knows I miss you."

"Talk to you soon," he said, and hung up.

He could only hope he would hear from her soon, because he missed her more than was reasonable, more than was smart, more than was safe.

Adam stopped at a nearby grocery store to pick up some flowers for Wade's mom, to brighten her bedside table after she left the recovery room. He was trying to decide between a bundle of carnations and a pot of roses, when someone touched his arm.

"Adam, it's so good to see you."

He turned toward the familiar voice. "Hey, Pat," he said, smiling. "Good to see you, too."

"You look horrible," she said, frowning up into his face.

He chuckled. "You sure know how to flatter a guy."

She ignored his teasing. "What have you been doing to yourself? Looks as though you haven't had a decent night's sleep in a month."

Hasn't been that bad, Adam thought, *but it's been close.* "Funny I should run into you," he said. "I left a message for Kasey, not five minutes ago."

Pat's left eyebrow lifted. "You don't say…"

If she meant to send some kind of secret message of her own with that expression, he wasn't alert enough to decode it.

"How's she doin'? I haven't talked to her in…" *In too long,* he thought unhappily.

"She's fine." Pat clucked her tongue, then looked around them like a spy who suspected she was being followed. "Considering," she added.

Adam's heart thumped. "Considering? She isn't sick or anything, is she?"

"No, no." Pat gave another cursory glance left, then right. "At least, not in a physical way."

What was it with women, he wondered, that made them talk in riddles? If there was something wrong, why didn't Pat just spit it out?

"I do believe the girl has lost her mind."

Adam frowned. Kasey was one of the most sensible, feet-on-the-ground women he'd ever had the pleasure of knowing. "Why do you say that?"

"Because…" She gave the area around them another look-see.

He tucked in one corner of his mouth, trying to summon the patience to pay attention, until Pat doled out the rest of her puzzle.

"That Buddy. He took her to some estate, way up in Baltimore County. Said he was buying it for…for her."

Adam was all ears *now*.

She clucked her tongue again. Rolled her eyes and sighed heavily. "I have never liked that man. He was trouble with a capital *T* when he was a boy, and just because the law hasn't caught up with him yet doesn't mean he isn't trouble now."

If only Pat would come to the point! He peered at his watch. "I hate to be rude, Pat, but I have to get to the hospital…."

She lay a hand on his forearm. "Goodness gracious sakes alive. Of course you do. How inconsiderate of me." She patted her mostly-white perm. "You get some sleep, you hear? Have a decent meal once in a while, too, why don't you. And don't work so hard. You can't help your patients if you keel over from exhaustion!"

Realizing she meant to walk off without telling him anything, Adam cleared his throat in frustration. "So what's up with Kasey?" He said it a little more harshly than he'd intended, and covered it up with a grating laugh that sounded foreign to his ears. "Buddy didn't harm her in any way, did he?" *Because if he did,* Adam thought, clenching his fists, *I'll—*

"He asked her to marry him!" Pat blurted.

Adam made a concerted effort not to swallow his tongue. "He...*what?*"

"I know," she said, shaking her head. "Isn't it just awful!"

"Awful" didn't come close to describing what he felt. "What— She— He— But—" He felt like an old phonograph record, stuck in the same groove. Shuffling his feet, he started again. "And what did Kasey say?"

"I wish I knew!" Pat huffed. "The girl is a passel of secrets these days. I have no idea what's in her head. For all I know, she's planning to elope, just to save our bacon."

Adam remembered the way Kasey had felt in his arms, the way she'd returned his kisses in the cabin that night, on her porch on Halloween, in front of her stove on Thanksgiving day. Surely she wouldn't have responded to him like that if she had feelings for Buddy...if she was seriously considering his marriage proposal.

Would she?

But wait, Pat had said "to save our bacon." So Kasey was considering marriage to Buddy because money was tight? Adam realized that, for one reason or another, he hadn't dropped off an envelope since the week before he'd met her.

"Between you and me," Pat said conspiratorially, "I was kind of hoping something would spark between *you* two." She grinned up at him. "Think how nice it'd be for me, bragging to all my ladyfriends about my son-in-law the doctor!" She giggled girlishly.

Son-in-law?

Kasey's husband.

Adam had to admit, the concept wasn't entirely new to him. Appealing as the idea was, he couldn't pursue it. Not with that secret hanging between them. Unconsciously, his fingers clamped tighter, crinkling the cellophane around the flowers and reminded him why he'd come to the store's flower department in the first place.

Wade's mom, the operation, his promise to be there, before she went into the O.R. "I'd better go," he said.

"Those are pretty," Pat said, pointing at the bouquet. "Who're they for?"

His mind felt like a yo-yo, and fearing he didn't have the presence of mind to construct a coherent explanation, he simply said, "A friend." It was true, after all. Mrs. Cameron had been one of his closest, dearest friends, for years.

"Is that so?"

Her expression made it clear she believed the flowers were for a *girl*friend. Well, Adam didn't have time to set her straight right now. As it was, he'd be lucky to make it to the hospital before they started the anesthesia....

"Good to see you," he said, tipping an imaginary hat as he backpedaled toward the registers. "Tell Kasey I said..." Tell Kasey *what?* he wondered.

"Bye, Pat. Take care."

He didn't remember paying for the flowers. Didn't recall driving to Sinai. But when he found himself in the hospital parking lot, staring at his steering wheel, he prayed for the first time in...he couldn't remember how long.

"Lord," he whispered, eyes closed, *"don't let Kasey do it."*

Maybe, he thought, climbing out of the car, God would listen.

A guy can hope, he thought, heading for the hospital lobby.

Wade was in the hall outside Pre-Op, pacing.

"If you're trying to wear a path in the linoleum," said Adam as he approached, "you're goin' about it the right way."

His friend stopped walking, clapped a hand on Adam's shoulder. "Thanks for comin', Adam." He gave the shoulder a slight squeeze. "She's been asking for you."

"She has?"

A faint grin lifted one corner of Wade's mouth. "Says she wants all her family around her." He added, "Gotta warn you, though, she doesn't look good."

Adam read the fear in his friend's eyes. "You and I both know that things can look downright bleak, then turn themselves around."

Nodding, Wade sighed. "Better get in there. They're about to administer the anesthesia."

Heart pounding, Adam put on his practiced "doctor" smile and walked up to Mrs. Cameron's bed. Wade stood on the other side. She looked pale and thin, older than her fifty-some years. "I can think of better ways to get a chance to sleep in," Adam said, kissing her forehead.

She opened her eyes and smiled. "Adam." Then she noticed the flowers. "For me?"

Grinning, Adam held up the bouquet. "These? Nah. They're for the first pretty gal I spot." He patted his shirt pocket. "Gotta keep my little black book fat and happy, y'know."

"Oh, you," she said, laughing softly. "You've always been such a tease. Soon as they dope me up for the operation, maybe you can hunt down one of those hideous green plastic pitchers to use as a makeshift vase." She winked.

"I'd hate for the flowers to wilt while you're waiting for that pretty girl to saunter by."

He lay the bouquet on the table beside the bed, then rested a palm on either side of her slight torso. "You're gonna be fine, just fine. You know that, don't you?"

Her smile faded. She held up her hand and, biting her lower lip, rested forefinger atop index finger.

Adam grabbed the crossed fingers. "You don't need luck, 'cause you've got a ton of people praying for you."

A shimmering tear sparkled in the corner of her eye, and she lay an ashen palm against his cheek. "You've always been the sweetest boy. I'm sure going to miss—"

"Ma," Wade interrupted, "don't talk like that. You're gonna come through this like a champ. You'll see. You've got the best team in Baltimore in there, scrubbing up." A film of tears gleamed in her son's eyes. "Tell her, Adam."

Adam wanted to choose his words well, for they'd be lifting Mrs. Cameron's spirits...and Wade's, too. *Lord*, he prayed, surprised to be beseeching the Creator so soon again, *it's okay by me if You put words in my mouth.*

With one hand, he grabbed the bouquet. "Only thing you have to worry about is which nurse is gonna try and take these flowers home." With the other hand, he lovingly brushed a wispy strand of graying brown locks from her forehead. "Wade's right. You've got the best in the business." *If they can't save you,* he thought dismally, *nobody can.*

Mrs. Cameron nodded, a mischievous glint in her eyes.

Wade and Adam exchanged a puzzled glance before she explained, "Isn't a woman entitled to a moment, at least, of attention-getting self-pity?"

Self-pity? Adam had always thought of Mrs. Cameron as the strongest, most selfless individual he'd ever met...until Kasey.

Straightening, Adam looked across the bed, into his friend's reddened eyes. "What do you say, Wade? Wanna throw your mom a pity party?"

Wade brightened slightly. "Sure. Why not."

Adam recalled how when they were boys, if he or Wade felt sorry for themselves, Mrs. Cameron would sit cross-legged on her kitchen floor, holding her head in her hands, wailing. "Waaa-waaa-waaa," she'd whine, "the world's not all rosy-red and perfect for my little men. Oh, what're we gonna do? Waaa-waaa-waaa." In minutes, whatever had caused their downheartedness was forgotten, and after scrounging through coat pockets and under sofa cushions for loose change, they'd celebrate with a trip to the local ice cream parlor for hot fudge sundaes.

Wade took his mother's right hand, Adam took her left, and the threesome smiled at the fond memory. How many more would there be? Adam wondered.

The squeaking wheels of an IV pole interrupted his thought. "Sorry to break up the party," the anesthesiologist said.

Mrs. Cameron sniffed, wiped a tear away with the back of her hand.

"Now, now, Mrs. Cameron," the man said, "no need to cry. You'll be—"

She nodded at the fat bags of clear liquid swaying to and fro on the pole's hooks. "People with sharp needles and sleeping potions are not welcome at *this* party!"

The doctor must have figured out that he'd walked in on a private joke, for he held up his hands like a man under arrest. Then he said to Wade, "You're welcome to stay, but it's time..."

Side by side, the almost-brothers stood, watching, waiting, praying. At least, Adam suspected Wade was praying.

Why wouldn't he be? He had a lot to lose with a mom like that!

Adam thought of his own mother, who by now was frolicking on a cruise ship somewhere in the North Atlantic. He'd shelled out the extra dough to provide her with her own private state room. "One with two portholes," he'd told the travel agent. She'd been a good mother, all things considered, and Adam loved her for all he was worth. Even as a little kid, he had tried never to compare his mom with Wade's, because somehow, he'd known the comparison was a recipe for resentment. Not every woman could be like Mrs. Cameron, who virtually teemed with vitality and bubbled with energy. Despite having a full-time job and an eight-room house and yard to take care of, she made time to bake cookies and chaperon field trips, hostess all-night, old-movie parties and coach her kids' county softball teams.

A question surfaced in Adam's mind: Why, after all she'd given throughout her life, did she have to suffer, even for a moment? He said a prayer of thanks for his own mother's good health.

Mrs. Cameron's surgeon walked into the cubicle then, dressed in drab green scrubs. "Ready?" he asked, patting his patient's hand.

She took a deep breath. "Ready as I'll ever be, I guess."

The orderly released the bed's brake and started rolling Mrs. Cameron toward the surgical suites.

"I'll find you soon as there's anything to tell," the surgeon told Wade. "Could be a while."

Adam and Wade had been in the man's shoes enough times to know what that meant. "A while" could be an hour...or it could be half a day.

"We'll be in the doctors' lounge," was Wade's stoic reply.

Heads down, the friends headed for the doctors' lounge. On the way, they passed the hospital chapel. Adam stopped in the yellow-walled hall, where a hollow *ping-ping-ping* was followed by "Doctor Buford, you have a call on line six," where elevator doors groaned open and hissed shut, and where the staff's crepe-soled shoes squeaked across the polished tiles. "What say we step inside for a minute?"

Brows knitted in a serious frown, Wade said, "Couldn't hurt."

As the door closed, they were surrounded by an incredible hush, a world so silent and serene that Adam could hear his own heart's rhythmic beats.

Adam sat in the back row, while Wade knelt at the altar. Even from this distance, Adam could smell the faint scent wafting from baskets of colorful flowers that stood in pots and vases on the red carpet. On either side of the oaken altar, tiers of candles flickered in garnet cups, like the twinkling red lights of Christmas. And above it, Jesus, hung from a rough-hewn wooden cross.

Adam stared at the face, painstakingly carved to show the Savior's suffering, then lowered his head, remembering what his third-grade Sunday school teachers had said: "Jesus died for all men so their sins would be forgiven." The Savior may have died for others, eight-year-old Adam had thought, but what had *he* ever done to earn a sacrifice like that!

He was full-grown now, with a man's duties and responsibilities…and a man's shame. He felt less worthy of Christ's gift now than when he'd been a runny-nosed kid. It was why he rarely prayed; why when he did pray, it was for others, not himself.

Since this plea was for Wade, for Mrs. Cameron, Adam believed God would listen: *Lord, I don't know anyone more worthy of a miracle than Mrs. Cameron.* The woman had devoted her entire life to making others feel loved and wanted, making her own children feel like the most important things in her world.

Kasey was a lot like that, Adam thought. She'd dedicated herself to taking care of her mother and adopted daughter. If she was considering marriage to Buddy, that same selflessness had motivated the decision.

Okay, so he knew two people worthy of God's mercy and love. But right now, one needed his prayers far more than the other.

Save Mrs. Cameron, Lord. Make her whole and healthy again.

If he could, he'd trade his life for Mrs. Cameron's. She had everything to live for…a daughter whose love for her mother was so great that it spilled out through her own husband and children…a son whose family would do the same, someday.

And what did Adam have? Nothing but a boatload of grief and guilt, and the incredible sorrow induced by having met the woman of his dreams, only to realize that his past sins made him undeserving of her.

Humbled, Adam looked away from the Cross, and silently wept.

Chapter Ten

Adam woke with a start, then said a gruff "Hullo?" into the phone.

"Adam, she's asking for you."

He sat up, plunked both feet on the floor and brushed the hair from his eyes. Even in this sleepy state, there was no mistaking the misery in his friend's voice. Mrs. Cameron was dying, and Adam intended to be there for her, for Wade, for Anna. "I'm on my way," he said. "Can I bring you anything?"

A shuddering sigh wafted through the earpiece. "No, thanks."

Adam glanced at the clock. At three in the morning, beltway traffic snarls were unlikely. "See you in twenty minutes," he said before hanging up.

Ever since Mrs. Cameron's surgery, Adam had slept on top of the covers, wearing a sweatsuit and socks, so he'd be ready at the drop of a hat in case the dreaded phone call came in the middle of the night. Now, perched on the edge of the bed, he laced up his running shoes, thankful for whatever had given him the idea.

Was it You, God?

If so, He'd planted the idea for the Camerons, not for Adam.

Every minute counted now, every second was precious. Grabbing his keys, Adam plopped a battered Orioles baseball cap onto his uncombed hair and dashed out of the house without bothering to shave or brush his teeth. Halfway to Sinai, he wondered if he'd remembered to lock the front door. Not that it mattered. What did he have worth stealing, anyway?

He made the drive in record time and headed straight for Mrs. Cameron's room. How odd, he thought as his shoes *squeak-squawked* down the hall. How still the hospital seemed. During the day, it was a beehive of activity, buzzing with patients leaning on the arms of therapists; the low murmur of visitors; doctors rushing from room to room, lab coats flapping behind them; nurses hotfooting it to see why the lights above doors were lit. The commotion ground to a near standstill once the lights were dimmed, reminding Adam of a play at intermission: a lot went on behind the quiet curtain of darkness, but only the unlucky ones saw those performances.

When Adam rounded the corner, he found Wade on one side of Mrs. Cameron's bed, his sister on the other. "Hey," he whispered, standing beside Anna.

"Hey, yourself," Wade said.

"Where's your better half?" Adam asked Anna.

"Home," she said with a soft smile, "with the kids."

Adam nodded, understanding. Many times, he'd sent patients' family members home with the admonition to take care of themselves, because, what good would they be to anyone if they became patients, too?

Anna was two years older than Wade and Adam, yet

they'd always treated her like a kid sister. "How you doin'?" he asked, wrapping an arm around her waist.

"Hangin' in there." She kissed his cheek. "But *you* look like you've just been run over by a truck. What'd you do, give up eating and sleeping?"

He was about to defend himself when Mrs. Cameron opened her eyes. "Adam," she breathed. And smiling weakly, she held out her hand.

He closed his fingers around hers and tried not to react to the chill in her thin bones. Not knowing what to say, Adam just stood there, nodding.

"You look awful," she told him.

He managed a quiet chuckle. "Why are all the women in my life saying that these days?"

"What women?" Anna asked.

"My secretary, the nurses, you guys, even Kasey's mom," he said.

"Kasey?" Anna wiggled her eyebrows. "Who's Kasey?"

Adam's heart thumped. *She's everything,* he wanted to say. *She's it.*

"Just some girl he's seeing," Wade offered.

"Girl?" Anna echoed, playfully elbowing him in the ribs. "Aren't you a bit long in the tooth to be seeing a 'girl'?"

"Your brother," Adam said, glad to be part of the family banter that was keeping everyone's mind off the inevitable, "thinks of all females under sixty as girls. Believe me," he added, smirking, "Kasey is all woman." Not that it mattered....

"Wade," his mother said, "take Anna down to the cafeteria, buy her something to eat."

"It's okay, Mom. I'm not hungry."

"She just ate half an hour ago," Wade added.

Mrs. Cameron silenced her children with a maternal stare. "I'd like to have a moment alone with Adam, okay?"

Wade headed for the door. "Okay," he said, holding his hand out to Anna.

The instant Wade and Anna were out the door, Mrs. Cameron reached for Adam's hand.

"Sit down," she began. "There's something I need to talk to you about."

He slid the chair closer to her bed, then sandwiched her hand between his own. "I'd say 'shoot,' but after the evil eye you just gave those two, something tells me that wouldn't be smart."

She smiled, looking a little more like the beautifully vibrant woman he'd come to think of as a second mother.

"You're safe," she said. "The doctor made me leave my .357 Magnum home."

Adam couldn't imagine what she'd want to discuss with him...alone. But knowing Mrs. Cameron, he wouldn't have to wonder for long. He began a mental countdown: Ten seconds, nine, eight—

"Wade told me you met Kasey."

Pulse pounding, he nodded.

"Tell me about her."

"I was at the cabin, last weekend in October. One of my typical hideaway weekends, y'know?"

She gave a weak nod, urging him to continue.

"This terrible storm brewed up, and blew her right in my door. Literally."

"Is she as pretty as Wade says she is?"

Adam smiled. "Prettier." He held a palm parallel to the floor, sliced it through the air until it rested against his chest. "She's this tall, with a riot of copper-colored curls and eyes as big as saucers...eyes as green as that emerald your mother left you. Every time she laughs, I'm reminded of those wind chimes outside your kitchen window.''

''The ones that scared you, made you walk into the door frame the night I caught you sneaking back into the house?''

Laughing softly, he said, ''Yeah. That'd be the ones.'' He gave her hand an affectionate squeeze. ''I sported that black eye for nearly a week.''

''Serves you right,'' she teased. Then she said, ''But what's she *like,* Adam? What kind of person is she?''

He told her how Kasey had been caring for her mother, how she'd adopted a handicapped inner-city orphan.

''Sounds like she'll be good for you.''

What an understatement! ''She's good to the bone. But...'' Grinding his molars together, he looked away.

''But what?''

''There's no future for Kasey and me.''

''What makes you say that? From what Wade says, she's nuts about you.''

The very thought made his heart skip a beat. If he could believe that...

No. He couldn't *afford* to believe, because the letdown would kill him. ''Did Wade tell you who she is?''

''Yes.''

''Then, you know exactly why there's no hope for a future with her.''

''Must be the pain,'' she said, pointing to her temple, '''cause I don't get it.''

For all Adam knew, these could be Mrs. Cameron's last moments on earth. He didn't want to waste them whining about his lovesick, foolish dreams. ''So,'' he said, rubbing his hands together, ''when are they gonna let you out of this place? I bet Mouser is meowing up a storm, missing her mama.''

"I imagine she is." She sighed, a forlorn, trembly sound. "I miss her, too. Unfortunately, she's going to have to adjust, like the rest of you are." She paused, looked deep into his eyes. "You know as well as I do that I'm not going home."

Adam frowned. He'd read her chart. At best, she had a one-percent chance of beating this thing. Still, he clung to hope. "Hey, is that any way to talk?"

"Sure is," she said matter-of-factly. "You've always been a tell-it-like-it-is kind of guy. Why the change?"

He took a breath, swallowed the hot, hard lump aching in his throat. She needed him to be strong, to cope with the unavoidable reality like a true medical professional. But God help him, he didn't *want* to accept those facts!

She gave his hand a gentle shake. "It's really not so bad, going this way. Fast is better. Take it from me."

He wished she hadn't sent Wade and Anna away. If they were here now, he could poke fun at one of them, crack a joke, do *something* to change the subject.

"You're wondering why I asked the kids to leave, aren't you?"

She'd always had a knack for reading his mind, his expressions and his tone of voice. The truth was, she knew him far better than his own mother ever had. The silent admission threatened the tight control he'd been holding on his emotions. *Get a grip, Thorne. There'll be plenty of time for—*

"I sent them away because I'm just about out of time. If I can't convince you tonight..."

A note of defeat rang loud in her voice. "Convince me of what?"

"Let it *go*, Adam. Just let it go."

Let what go? He didn't care. All he cared about was making her comfortable. Keeping her happy. Adam got to his feet. "You thirsty? Want me to get some juice from the nurses' station?"

Shaking her head, she rolled her eyes. "No, sweetie, I don't want any juice."

He hesitated.

"Humor this sick old woman, why don't you."

The twinkle in her eye made him want to hug the stuffings out of her. He would have, too, if she hadn't added, "Consider it my dying wish, then."

The words stopped him, like a hard left to the jaw. "Good grief," he said, wincing around a grin, "could you maybe *pretend* to beat around the bush? Just this once?"

"You know what the doctors say about my prognosis?"

He nodded.

"They say I might have a week...if I'm lucky. But I know different. If I'm lucky I'll be gone by morning."

His wince became a grimace.

"Oh, don't look so sad. It's my time, and I'm okay with that."

Well, *he* wasn't okay with that!

"C'mere." She held out her arms. "I need a hug."

Adam wrapped her in a warm embrace, careful not to squeeze her frail body too hard.

"I'd really like to go to Jesus, Adam," she whispered into his ear. "The cancer is everywhere, and I don't mind telling you, there isn't a place on me that doesn't hurt like crazy." She pushed him away, just enough so that she could look into his face. "Sweetie," she said, "you remember how you used to do little favors for me?"

Yeah, he remembered. Running to the convenience store, helping Wade rake the leaves, mowing the lawn when Wade was working his way through med school at Yale....

"I need you to do me one more favor."

He blinked, hoping to keep the stinging tears at bay.

Adam stroked her hand. "Your wish is my command, m'lady," he croaked out.

"Let it *go*."

He quirked an eyebrow. "Let what go?"

"The guilt. The shame. Whatever it is that's keeping you from turning to God, from turning to Kasey."

"This is stupid," he said again. Adam fluffed her pillow. Poured water into the green plastic cup on the nightstand beside her bed.

"What's stupid—" she interrupted his fussing "—is your blaming yourself for something that happened a lifetime ago."

He licked his lips.

"Oh, Adam, you're all grown up now, but in so many ways you're still that same foolish young boy!"

"Talk like this is a waste of time," he said, "especially now. We should be talking about you. About what we're gonna do to celebrate when you get outta this place."

"When I get outta this place," she repeated in a dull monotone, "it'll be in a pine box."

He bowed his head. "Aw, please, don't..." he rasped.

"Your specialty is cardiology, not oncology, but you know the signs when you see them."

As usual, she was right. Adam found himself fighting an urge to punch a hole in the wall. Kick that bleeping, blinking monitor into the hall. Shout at the top of his lungs about the unfairness of it all. But Adam sat quietly, his breaths coming in ragged gasps, summoning the strength to tough this thing out, the way she would if the shoe were on the other foot.

"I have something for you." She nodded at the nightstand.

Adam opened the drawer and immediately thought there

must be some mistake, because the only thing in there was her well-worn leather Bible.

"I want you to have it," she said. "It's brought me such peace over the years. And you could use a healthy dose of that right now!" she said on a sigh.

Except for the service Aleesha had invited him to, Adam hadn't been to church in years. Bibles were for good Christians, for people who had earned God's ear. "I—I don't deserve this. It should go to Wade or Anna, or one of the grandkids—"

"Oh, save it for somebody who's in the market for a line of malarkey."

Adam searched her face. "Malarkey?"

She twisted this way and that, struggling to sit up. "Help me get upright," she demanded, "so I can look you in the eye while I'm scolding you."

Ever so gently, Adam adjusted her pillows, then tidied the covers over her spindly legs.

"That's much better." She folded the sheet over the blanket, smoothed it into place. "Thanks."

"You're welcome."

"Now sit right back down there, you big goof, while I give you a piece of my mind."

Without hesitation, Adam did as instructed.

"You've been using that train fiasco like a crutch for so long, it's crippled your mind. Well, enough, already! You're no more to blame for what happened to that man than I am."

"But—"

"But nothing. You were a rowdy, pinheaded boy, same as my Wade, same as Luke and Travis and—" she rolled her eyes "—and even Buddy. Al Delaney had a long history of heart disease. For all we know, he was in the middle of a coronary when you kids threw that dummy onto the tracks.''

''Yeah, well, we'll never know for sure, now, will we?''

She pursed her lips. ''Self-pity, Adam, is not an attractive character trait.''

Stunned and hurt, Adam sat back. ''Self-pity?''

''You heard me. You've been using what happened that night as a shield. It protects you from everything. From relationships. From commitments. From planning for your future. As long as you're behind it, you think you're safe from the world…and it's safe from you.''

She lay a hand alongside his face. ''I know you're scared that Kasey might hate you when she finds out you were there the night her father died. But *everyone* is afraid of the unknown.''

Not when *Kasey finds out,* he thought, *but* if. Adam shook his head. ''We shouldn't be talking about this. It's only getting you all riled up and—''

''*Not* letting me talk about this is what'll rile me. If you don't let me get this off my chest, I swear, I'll get out of this bed and hunt for the biggest paddle I can find.''

He met her eyes, saw the spark. ''You wouldn't,'' he said, forcing a grin.

Grinning back, she said, ''Try me.''

They'd had a similar conversation twenty-plus years ago, when he'd tried to walk home, alone in the dark, after an argument with Wade. She'd won then, and something told Adam she'd win again tonight.

''Give me that Bible,'' she demanded.

He handed it to her.

''See all these little blue page markers?''

''Yeah…''

''These are so you'll know where to find the verses with *forgiveness* in them.''

He sat, slack-jawed. She wanted him to read Bible verses so she could go to her grave knowing he'd been forgiven. What had he ever done in his miserable life, Adam wondered, to deserve a friend like this!

"I want you to read them. All of them." She folded her arms over her chest.

"Now?"

Unfolding her arms, she clasped her hands in her lap. "Answer a question for me."

"If I can...."

"Do you think I'm a good person? That I'll go to heaven when I die?"

The mention of death wasn't softened, not even by the knowledge she'd end up in Paradise. "'Course you will. You're a...you're a living saint!"

Laughing, she touched her fingertips to her chest and opened her eyes wide. "Me? No!"

The moment of merriment contorted her face with pain. "Whew," she said once it passed, "that was a bad one." She sipped from the straw Adam held near her lips, then waved the cup away. "Like I said, every breath is torture, but I can't meet my Maker, not 'til I know you'll be okay."

Adam didn't want her to leave. But then again, he didn't want her to stay...not if staying caused her such agony.

She wagged a finger under his nose, then pointed at the Bible. "Start readin', mister."

Adam scooted his chair nearer the bed and faced his dear friend, then opened the Good Book to the first marked passage. With slow deliberation, he began reciting from Psalms. "'But there is forgiveness with thee, that thou mayest be feared....'" His back was to the door, so he couldn't see Kasey standing just outside the room.

But Mrs. Cameron saw her.

Kasey felt rooted to the floor under the weight of the

riveting and strangely meaningful eye contact. When the older woman looked away, Kasey shuddered involuntarily, as if a chill wind had whipped up the hushed hospital hallway.

"'Look upon my affliction and my pain, and forgive all my sins....'"

Mrs. Cameron grabbed Adam's wrist, gave it a slight shake. "Promise me something?"

Silenced by her sudden interruption, Adam studied her haggard face. "Anything. Anything at all."

She was dying, right before his eyes, and he was powerless to do anything to prevent it.

"How's about a hug?" she said.

Adam understood only too well why her weak, bony fingertips pressed insistently into his skin: she wanted to say goodbye. As his arms went around her, he thought of the hundreds of times he'd embraced this dear, sweet woman over the past two decades...hiya and thank-you hugs, you're-such-a-nut hugs and see-you-later hugs, but never *ever* goodbye....

She gave his shoulder a feeble pat. "Take care of Wade and Anna. They've always looked up to you."

He nodded, though he'd never quite understood why the Cameron kids had looked to him for counsel, consolation, even censure.

He leaned back slightly, looked deep into her eyes. Hand trembling, he brushed gossamer strands from her face, wishing he could smooth the furrows from her brow. "Sure, sure," he soothed, "'course I'll look out for 'em." He grinned a bit. "Always have, haven't I?"

"Yes, you most certainly have."

Her once-lovely features relaxed, as if his simple, heartfelt oath had soothed her torment. Such a small request, and yet the Almighty had heard...and responded. Humbled, Adam sent a silent prayer of thanks heavenward.

"One more thing, Adam?" The faintest smile lifted one corner of her mouth. "Let's call it my last request."

Every muscle in him tensed.

"I want you to promise me something."

"Anything," he said, and meant it.

She looked over his shoulder, toward the door, focused on something in the hall. One brow arched, she pursed her lips and lifted her chin. He was about to turn around, to see what had so completely captured her attention, when Mrs. Cameron faced him again.

"Tell Kasey the truth. If she's even half as good and decent as you say she is, she'll understand. She'll forgive you, like *God* forgave you a long, long time ago." She lay back, spent, and a tremor coursed through her. "Promise me you'll tell her."

Adam blinked. Swallowed. Cleared his throat. Did she realize what she was asking of him? If he made a confession like that, well, any chance he might have had with Kasey was gone.

"If she's everything you described," Mrs. Cameron said again, "she'll understand."

Her gaze drifted toward the door and she smiled warmly, as if she'd seen a long-lost friend. *Must be Wade or Anna,* he thought, twisting his upper body to tell them to hurry to their mother's bedside.

But her hand on his arm stopped him. "Is it cold in here, or is it just me?"

Must be a hundred degrees in here, Adam thought. He'd taken off his jacket and baseball cap an hour ago, had tossed the sweatshirt aside soon after. If she was cold in this makeshift oven, it could only mean one thing.

He eased the blankets up under her chin, then slid his

arms around her, gently brought her upright and held her close. "What a sneaky way to get another hug," he said, forcing a cheerfulness into his voice that he didn't feel.

His little joke made her laugh, and that warmed *him*.

She clung to him with a strength that belied her condition. "I'm glad it's you who's with me now," she whispered. "I prayed and prayed the kids wouldn't have to watch—"

Adam felt her hot tears seeping through his white T-shirt; until that moment, he hadn't realized Mrs. Cameron was crying. He searched his mind for something comforting to say, something profound and significant. As usual, she beat him to the punch.

"I'm proud to have known you, Adam Thorne."

He tried to echo the sentiment, but found it impossible to speak past the sob aching in his throat. Knowing there'd be plenty of time for tears later, Adam held his breath and grit his teeth, determined to keep his emotions in check.

From out of nowhere, it seemed, a long-forgotten Bible verse from I Corinthians 15:52 echoed in his mind.

"'And lo, I will tell you a mystery,'" Adam recited in a broken voice, "'in the twinkling of an eye, the trumpet will sound...'"

"'And the dead will be raised imperishable...'" Mrs. Cameron quoted.

"'...and we will be changed,'" they said in unison.

A moment of peaceful silence elapsed.

When she went limp, he knew her spirit had left her. "Not as proud as I've been to know you," he said, gently settling her back onto the pillows. "Not nearly as proud."

Like lava erupting from a long-silent volcano, the pent-up grief and anguish he'd been hiding as Mrs. Cameron wasted away boiled to the surface. Because she had no roommate to disturb, no next of kin to distress, he loosed his sorrow, one harsh, hacking sob at a time.

Kasey had never felt more like an interloper. Part of her wanted to go to him, to offer some kind of comfort; part of her sensed he needed this time alone with his dear friend.

Fingers pressed to her lips, she blinked back hot tears and fled silently down the hall. She looked up at the elevator numbers...seven, six, five...remembering, as the quiet *pings* counted the floors, the three o'clock phone call from Mrs. Cameron. "Come right away," she'd said. "There's something you need to know." She'd sounded so desolate, so inconsolable—how could Kasey refuse?

The woman had been a member of Kasey's church for years, and these past few Sundays, Pastor Hill had led the congregation in prayer for Mrs. Cameron's sudden illness, for her strength when the doctors said "terminal."

Life's daily responsibilities had prevented Kasey from getting to know the woman as anything more than a passing acquaintance. But what she'd witnessed just now, as Mrs. Cameron gave herself over to the Lord and Adam's very presence had gentled the brutal grip of death, spelled out exactly what kind of stuff Adam Thorne was made of.

Driving from her house to Sinai earlier, Kasey had wondered why the woman wanted to see her at a time like this. It hadn't taken long to get an answer. The purposeful *look* made it clear she'd been summoned for no reason other than to hear Mrs. Cameron's "Tell Kasey the truth and she'll forgive you" speech.

But...*forgive him for what?* And how could *she* be involved in the incident that had painted his face with such grief, slumped his shoulders with such burdensome guilt? Had the "what" prompted him to say peculiar things like *"There are things you should know about me, Kasey..."*?

Pulling her coat tighter around her, Kasey hurried toward her car. Her breaths puffed into the cold night air, each one a foggy trace of evidence that she was alive and healthy. The acknowledgment made her picture Mrs. Cameron, pale and lifeless in Adam's strong arms.

She got into the car and sat shivering behind the steering wheel, waiting for the motor to warm up. Soft music wafted from the car radio, and she shook her head. Adam had obviously been a friend—a very good one—to Mrs. Cameron, and she to him. Why else would she have said, flat out, that she was grateful to be with him at the end?

Kasey put the car into reverse and backed out of the parking space. As the tires hissed over frosty pavement, Mrs. Cameron's lecture reverberated in her mind. Like a migraine it thumped, demanding answers to questions as yet unformed.

Kasey would be only too glad to get home. Home, where her mother and Aleesha were sleeping peacefully, snug and safe beneath downy quilts. *"Thank You, Lord,"* she prayed, grateful for that small comfort on this bleak night.

The image of Adam, shoulders lurching with each grief-induced sob, haunted her mind.

Nothing happens without a reason, she thought; it hadn't been an accident that she'd arrived precisely as Mrs. Cameron was delivering her mercy sermon.

It was like a riddle with no solution, the *why* of the woman's loving yet stern tongue-lashing.

Kasey sighed with frustration.

Maybe Adam's secret was nothing more than some insignificant transgression, and his shame and guilt were the result of letting too many recriminations blow the thing all out of proportion.

Because, for the life of her, Kasey couldn't convince herself Adam could be capable of doing anything sinful.

Even if he had, the deed had been done somewhere in his dim, distant past. And if that was the case, didn't he deserve the same comfort and compassion he'd so tenderly and lovingly doled out to Mrs. Cameron?

"*Sweet Jesus*," Kasey whispered, "*help me figure out how to help him.*"

And when I hear what he's been hiding, she added silently, biting her lower lip, *please, please, please, give me the strength to listen with a forgiving heart.*

It was a gray December day when they buried Mrs. Cameron.

She hadn't been a member of the Ladies Auxiliary, had never joined parish committees, hadn't belonged to any of the church's many ministries, yet a hundred people braved winter's icy winds to huddle around her rose-blanketed casket.

Anna, her husband and children, and Wade sat in the front row, shivering despite the tartan blanket covering their knees. Beside them, just outside the protective canvas awning, stood Adam.

From her place in the last row, Kasey watched as he closed his eyes, rested his chin on the tidy knot of his dark blue tie, clasped black-gloved hands behind his back. His broad shoulders slumped despite the pads sewn into his calf-length trench coat, and his mouth, set in a grim, thin-lipped line, trembled as Pastor Hill's soothing tenor read God's Word:

"We find many references to death in the Good Book. '...for dust thou art, and unto dust shalt thou return...' 'the last enemy that is destroyed is death...' '...a time to be born, and a time to die...' to name a few."

After reading some more comforting passages from the Bible, the reverend closed it, then scanned the quiet, contemplative crowd. And nodding, he smiled, lifted his arms high and looked up. "Yes, it's true that our dear friend has passed from our sight," he said, forefinger pointing toward heaven, "but God is looking at her now." His sigh rolled over those gathered, as he held the Good Book to his chest. "Yes, *God* has welcomed her home."

Hushed "amens" mingled with soft sobs. One by one, the friends of Mrs. Cameron walked slowly past her coffin, some dabbing their eyes with white tissues, others shaking their heads as if to say, *What a shame, what a loss.*

When Anna stepped up, she slid a rose from the enormous cross-shaped arrangement, and leaned into her husband, who then led her and the children away.

Wade, too, took a flower. He stood a moment beside the shiny mahogany box, traced a finger over a gleaming brass handle, then quickly walked away.

The sounds were all too familiar to Kasey, who, at twelve, had consciously memorized the way mourners' footsteps crunched over the gravel walkway; words of comfort, murmured as they passed the sleek black limo that had delivered the family from the funeral parlor; the quiet *thump* of closing car doors; engines revving and tires hissing over damp asphalt....

Adam hadn't left with the Camerons, Kasey noticed, and it surprised her, because he'd seemed so much a part of their family. Instead, he remained exactly where he'd been throughout the service...until he believed everyone had gone.

She saw him glance right, then left, before taking those few plodding steps closer to the coffin. He wanted a rose, too, Kasey presumed when he reached out a trembling hand.

But he didn't take a flower. Rather, Adam plucked a single petal from the bouquet, brought it to his lips and gave it a lingering kiss. Encasing it in his fist, he touched a knuckle to his forehead and dropped to his knees. Now Kasey understood that he'd hung back for a chance to say one last goodbye to his friend.

As the sky turned to slate, the wind set the tent's scalloped trim to flapping against its aluminum support poles, rustled the ferns tucked among the roses. Winter-brown grass underfoot whispered, and the tree boughs overhead creaked and popped. A scrap of carelessly discarded paper floated around her ankles, and Kasey bent to retrieve it.

"I didn't expect to see you here," Adam said, his voice foggy and deep with grief.

That night at the hospital, not wanting to intrude, she hadn't given in to the urge to offer a touch, a word of comfort. She probably would have left him to the privacy of his sadness today, too…if he hadn't seen her.

Kasey stood behind him, lay a hand upon his shoulder. "I'm so sorry, Adam. Is there anything I can do?"

He blanketed her hand with his. "No," he said before getting to his feet. "Didn't realize you knew her."

She hesitated. Should she tell him that Mrs. Cameron had summoned her to the hospital? That the visit helped her understand how great a loss he'd just experienced? That she'd come here today in case *he* needed her support? One look into his red-rimmed eyes was her answer.

"Mrs. Cameron called me on the night she died."

His brows drew together slightly.

Kasey shrugged. "I didn't understand why, either. I knew her from church, but—"

When she shivered, Adam slid an arm around her, started walking toward the road. "Let's talk in my car, get out of this wind."

Earlier, she'd overheard people asking for directions to

the daughter's house. "I thought you'd be going to Anna's."

He slowed his pace. "Yeah. I owe it to Wade and Anna to be there." Adam stopped and faced her. "Why don't you join me?"

"Because it's a gathering for friends and family." She shook her head. "I don't belong there."

Adam reached out, tucked a windblown hair behind her ear, then pressed the butter-soft palm of his leather glove to her cheek. "You're *my* friend."

Oh, Adam, she thought, heart thumping against her rib cage, *I'd like to be so much more than that.*

He narrowed one eye and cocked his head. "Hey, wait just a minute here. Didn't Aleesha say that she and Pat would be in Pennsylvania with the church youth group all weekend?"

"Christmas shopping at the outlet malls." But what did that have to do with his invitation?

"So there's no one depending on you tonight...."

True enough, but Kasey would feel like an intruder, horning in on a function meant for those who'd known and loved Mrs. Cameron. She was about to suggest he stop at her house for coffee after leaving Anna's, when he added, "...except me."

Did it mean he'd like to be more than just friends, too? Kasey's already hard-beating heart pumped faster still at the possibility.

Mrs. Cameron's lecture rang in her ears. *"Tell Kasey the truth..."* And his own warning, *"Kasey, if only you knew..."* There wasn't a doubt in her mind that the two were connected, somehow. But an after-funeral reception was hardly the time or place to quell her curiosity.

Adam offered his elbow, and she took it.

"I'll follow you home," he said, steering her toward her car, "and we can ride over to Anna's together."

"Then you'd have the bother of driving me back again."

Adam stepped in front of her, put both hands on her shoulders. "Trust me, it'd be no bother." He gave her a gentle shake. "In fact, you'd be doing me a favor."

Wade had been his friend since childhood, and from what she'd seen in that hospital room, Kasey could only surmise the same was true of Mrs. Cameron. "Why?"

He frowned, shook his head. "I'm not very good with words at a time like this. Having you there would..." He shifted from one foot to the other. "It sure would take the edge off."

It took no more than a millisecond to read the sincerity on his handsome, careworn face. *This* was something she could do. "Okay, I'll go."

"Whew," he said. "You had me worried there for a minute." Then he wrapped his arms around her and pulled her close. For several moments, he stood there, stiff and silent as a statue, face buried in her hair and palms pressed to the small of her back. "Thanks, Kase," he said at last.

"No thanks necessa—"

His sad, shaky sigh silenced her, then he bracketed her face with both leather-gloved hands, lifted her chin and pressed a soft kiss to her forehead. "Maybe not, but I'm grateful as all getout, just the same."

She had a lot of things to learn about him, among them, the carefully guarded secret he'd been keeping for...for God only knew how long.

Did she have the strength to hear it?

You're in a heap of trouble if you don't, Kasey told herself.

Because, God help her, she loved the big guy.

Chapter Eleven

During the weeks following Mrs. Cameron's funeral, Adam's sorrow gradually ebbed. He knew full well that he owed his newfound peace to the passages she'd marked for him in her dog-eared Bible. She'd steadfastly insisted that once Adam opened his heart to God's love, mercy would rush over him like river waters.

Mrs. Cameron had also predicted that when Kasey learned he'd taken part in her father's death, she'd forgive him.

A guy can hope, Adam thought.

Several times, he'd almost bared his soul to her, but something always seemed to get in the way...like the good-night kiss after the reception at Anna's....

Now, as he sat with the Bible in his lap, Adam remembered how Kasey's very presence had helped him get through the polite banter with Mrs. Cameron's friends and relatives. Gratitude had made him want to hug her, tell her how much easier the whole ordeal had been, simply because she'd been there beside him.

So he'd wrapped his arms around her and kissed her

tenderly. A short while later she'd disappeared, then returned with a food-laden plate…and a gentle "you need something solid in your stomach" attitude.

Adam closed the Bible. Closed his eyes, too. He didn't even try to pretend he understood the feelings she'd roused with her caring ministrations. All he knew for sure was that he wanted her beside him now, too, because this time it wouldn't surprise him when he cradled her pretty face in his hands; *this* time he'd do it with calm deliberation.

Laying the Good Book on the table beside his recliner, Adam rubbed his eyes, wondering how his "thanks for being there, kiddo" gesture had morphed into a heartfelt kiss. Was he supposed to blame her long-lashed eyes for the wild drumming of his heart? The way she'd gently stroked the dark circles under his eyes and scolded him for not taking better care of himself? Or maybe the warm sighs she'd whispered when his lips touched hers could explain why he hadn't been able to breathe normally since last night.

Thinking about the way she'd responded to him had Adam tossing and turning until the bedclothes were a tangled mess. Surely Kasey wouldn't have responded to him that way if she loved Buddy. And if that was the case, she'd considered marrying the no-good bum only because she felt obliged to him.

Right?

That night at the cabin, she'd called Buddy her "generous benefactor." Adam frowned, telling himself Mauvais had put that idea into her pretty head. If he were a betting man, Adam would have bet that Buddy had never tried to convince her otherwise.

In the months since the raging thunderstorm blew her into his world, Adam had come to understand how seriously Kasey took her responsibilities…as a Christian mother and daughter. During Thanksgiving dinner, he'd overheard Pat whisper to her nephew, "I don't know where Kasey will come up with the cash to pay for Aleesha's new leg braces." Aleesha had added, "If Mom doesn't get the contract at the new outlet mall, I probably won't get braces on my *teeth*, either."

Add those concerns to the hundreds of everyday things Kasey had to worry about, like groceries and utility bills and maintaining a fifty-year-old house, and it wasn't any wonder that she'd been entertaining the idea of marriage to Buddy Mauvais.

Adam lurched to his feet and, punching a fist into an open palm, paced in front of his easy chair. There had to be something he could do to convince her the whole wedding notion was a mistake.

But what, Lord, he prayed. *What?*

Instantly, he realized that since meeting Kasey, he hadn't remembered to make a single delivery to the Delaney house. If he made a drop tonight, and left more than the usual amount in the envelope, maybe Kasey wouldn't feel she had to marry Buddy in order to take proper care of Aleesha and Pat....

Adam climbed the stairs two at a time, then dug around in his bureau for his black sweatsuit and knit cap. Stepping into his "uniform," he felt more certain than ever that he'd been doing the right thing all these years.

But wait...he couldn't make the delivery tonight, because the bank wouldn't allow him to withdraw more than three hundred dollars from the ATM. Tomorrow, as soon as the main branch opened, he'd fill out a withdrawal slip for double—no, *triple*—the usual amount.

He lay on his bed and, staring at the ceiling, tucked both hands under his head. There was a whole lot more to consider this time than just getting the cash into Kasey's hands. Unless he did something to prevent it, she'd marry Buddy, anyway, thinking the no-good, lousy bum had provided for her yet again. Adam didn't want credit. In fact, he hoped Kasey would never find out that all these years, *he'd* been her "generous benefactor," not Buddy.

Okay. So tomorrow night he'd make the delivery, and first thing the morning after, he'd pay Kasey a visit, tell her everything. It was a big risk, he knew—the biggest of his life—but one he felt compelled to take. Better to give up any chance he might have with her than stand idly by and watch her make the biggest mistake of her life by marrying Buddy!

Patting his jacket pocket, where he'd tucked the over-stuffed envelope, Adam grabbed his keys from the foyer table. He was feeling better about himself than he had in a long, long time, because tomorrow, everything would be out in the open; tomorrow, whether Mrs. Cameron was right about Kasey's reaction or not, he'd be able to breathe easy for the first time in fifteen years.

He took his time driving to her neighborhood, flicked off the headlights when he turned onto her street. As usual, he parked half a block from Kasey's house, taking care to stay in the shadows as he sneaked from his car toward her front yard.

A big pickup truck rounded the corner, its fog lights cutting a bright yellow swath across her road. Adam ducked behind a massive oak just in the nick of time, and waited there until the red glow of taillights faded before heading to Kasey's side of the street.

Her house was dark, he noted with a nod—a good sign. He'd still been in his teens when he figured out it wasn't wise to make deliveries on nights when her windows glowed with warm golden light....

Now, stepping onto her lawn, Adam took the fat packet

from his pocket and palmed it to ensure that no one inside would hear the crinkle of paper when he slid it into the mail slot.

The first porch step squeaked, and he froze. Holding his breath, Adam waited, counting slowly to ten. When nothing stirred inside, he eased his foot onto the next step, carefully trod across the white-painted floor. He got as far as a yard from the front door, when a loose plank groaned and popped under his weight.

What this place needed, he silently complained, was a man around the—

Beads of perspiration stood out on his upper lip as he admitted that if it hadn't been for his part in the contemptible prank, there might just *be* a man around the house.

Adam shoved the guilty thought aside. He could chide himself later; right now, he needed to concentrate on his goal.

Getting the old-fashioned wooden screen door open without making any noise had always been a test of his sneak-ability, but nothing challenged him more than keeping the brass mail flap from squealing as he opened it. Crouching, he balanced on the balls of his feet.

Finally, he reached the stage he'd dubbed Operation Let-Go. Holding his breath, he grit his teeth. The fingers of one hand opened the mail slot while the other hand prepared to slide the envelope into the—

"Ah-*ha!*" said a victorious, feminine voice, as a hand wrapped around his fingers. "After all these years, I've gotcha!"

Adam's pulse pounded in his ears as he tried to free himself. And he knew without a doubt that it had been Kasey who'd clamped onto him like a human vise, because he would have recognized that gorgeous, musical voice anywhere.

"Don't even think about moving from that spot, mister," she called through the door, "or you'll have four sprained fingers to show for your trouble."

So much for musical, he thought, grinning despite his predicament. Just as quickly, his smile vanished; even if he didn't already know how strong and stubborn she could be, Adam was scheduled to perform surgery first thing in the morning. Might prove difficult, he thought, with broken fingers.

If he could just catch her off guard, give one good yank, he could be out of sight before she disengaged the chain lock....

She squeezed harder. "I warned you...."

Pain ricocheted from his fingertips to his shoulder and back again. Then he heard the shuffling of slippered feet, heard the unmistakable release of the deadbolt. He couldn't help but wonder what would be worse...asking Wade to operate in his stead—or giving up and letting her open the door.

No sooner had he posed the question than she turned him loose. Too stunned to run, he shook his throbbing hand, stuck the fingertips into his mouth, then buried them under his arm. *Lord,* he prayed, *get me outta here!*

Somewhere in his miserable past, he must have done *one* good thing, because he heard Kasey mutter under her breath as she struggled with the chain lock.

"Thank you," he whispered, leaping from the porch. He ran fullout, and when he reached the car, took a quick look over his shoulder to make sure she hadn't followed. Thankfully, Adam found himself alone on the dark street.

He slid behind the steering wheel, jammed the key into the ignition and fired up the motor. Without turning on the lights, he shifted into reverse and did an abrupt U-turn, thinking as he sped away that if he'd worked that hard on the Centennial track team, he might've earned a full athletic scholarship.

Three blocks later, he flipped on the headlights. At the first traffic light, he reached over his head and turned on the dome light, and inspected his hand. Four angry welts glowed red on each digit. Whether the sharp interior of the mailbox or Kasey's fingernails had caused them, Adam couldn't say, but a few scratches were a small price to pay for keeping Kasey from finding out what he'd been doing all these years.

The light turned green and he pulled into the intersection. *You're gettin' too old for this espionage stuff, Thorne,* he thought, puffing air through his teeth. Still, he couldn't help but smile, because close call or not, he'd made yet another clean getaway. If he was lucky, this would be his last delivery; if he was lucky, Kasey would turn Buddy down flat…and say yes when Adam popped the question.

Suddenly, he thought of Mrs. Cameron's Bible. All right, so maybe it hadn't been luck that saved him tonight. When he got home, maybe he'd pray. Right now, Adam was too distracted by the picture of Kasey, dressed all in white as she and Buddy exchanged their first kiss as man and wife— especially on the heels of the way she'd responded to him.

I guess prayer couldn't hurt, he thought, pulling into the garage. As the overhead door slid down behind the car, he snapped the cap from his head. *"Okay, Lord,"* he said, scratching his matted hair back into place, *"here goes. Do Your stuff, 'cause You know better than I do that she'd be miserable with that—"* He cleared his throat, apologized silently for what he'd almost called Buddy. *"She'd be miserable, married to a guy like that."*

He slammed the kitchen door behind him and counted to five, waiting for the automatic light on the garage ceiling to turn itself off. When he heard the telltale *click,* he locked the door and headed upstairs.

Face washed, teeth brushed and alarm set, he kicked his shoes into the closet and tossed his sweats onto the chair beside his bed. Climbing under the covers, he turned off the nightstand lamp. *"Do Your stuff,"* he repeated, punching up his pillow. As an afterthought, he tacked on a heart-felt *"Please."*

Rolling onto his side, he closed his eyes and tried to picture Kasey as she must have looked, standing on the other side of her front door, squeezing his hand for all she was worth. The image made him grin, because if she'd looked even *half* as determined as she'd sounded, chances were pretty good that she'd ground down her molars a millimeter or two.

"Y'gotta love her," he said to himself, chuckling, "gotta—"

Suddenly, his lopsided smile faded; the impulsive admission had effectively struck him silent.

Because he did love her.

Loved her like crazy.

Earlier that evening, unable to sleep, Kasey got up, thinking maybe a cup of herbal tea would relax her. Every time she closed her eyes, it seemed, she got a picture of Adam's long-lashed eyes boring into hers seconds before their lips met.

Why the contact had had such an effect on her, she couldn't say. But Kasey knew this: she'd never been kissed like that before, would never be kissed that way again…unless Adam decided to repeat the performance.

If there's a husband in Your plans for me, Lord, she prayed, *couldn't it please be Adam?*

The very thought produced an audible gasp, and she be-

gan to pace back and forth in the darkened kitchen. No
need to turn on any lights as she poured boiling water over
the tea bag; she'd lived in this house since she was three
days old and knew it like the back of her hand.

She carried the steaming mug—and her pacing—into the
living room, stopping now and then to peer through the
sheer curtains hanging at the bay window. She saw the
newspaper man's boxy van coast by; when *The Baltimore
Sun* bounced onto Kasey's driveway, it startled Mrs. Moss-
man's cat. McClean yeowled, starting the Burokers' dog
yapping. Frisky's barking prompted Mr. Cavil two doors
down to bellow, "If somebody doesn't muzzle that mutt,
he's gonna be wearin' my boot for a hat!" A door
slammed, telling Kasey that Mr. Buroker had brought his
dog inside. "About time!" Mr. Cavil shouted, banging his
own door shut.

Grinning at the neighborly chain reaction, Kasey realized
it was going to take more than a cup of herb tea to make
her sleepy tonight.

Correction...this morning. As she'd stirred honey into
her mug, she'd noticed that the kitchen clock said four-
fifteen. Yawning, Kasey put her cup on the windowsill and
tied her robe tighter around her waist to fend off the chill
that wrapped around her.

Parting the curtains, she glanced skyward, saying a silent
prayer of thanks that the forecasted snow hadn't begun to
fall yet. The weatherman's prediction included an overnight
low of zero...far below normal for December in Baltimore.
And while it appeared he'd missed the "snow" target, he'd
hit the bull's-eye with the temperature outlook.

Hunching her shoulders against the nip in the air, she
gave serious consideration to turning up the heat. Money
was tight, but saving a few dollars on the fuel bill, only to

spend it on cough syrup and cold medications, didn't seem to make much sense.

She'd started for the thermostat, when a slight movement caught her eye. Instinct made her rub her eyes, curiosity forced her to stare through the opaque window covering. Kasey expected to see a neighbor's pet, a stray animal, even. But a second hard glimpse assured her she hadn't been seeing things.

Much to her dismay, it was a *man* out there on her front lawn, dressed all in black and skulking around, stoop-shouldered, like some crazed primate. Not once in all the years she'd lived here had she heard of a burglary in the area. But there was a first time for everything. Besides, could anyone outfitted like that be up to anything *but* no good?

Without taking her eyes off him, she patted the tabletop, searching for the portable phone, hoping as her fingers brushed the cradle that Aleesha had remembered to put the receiver back where it belonged. Kasey wouldn't know for sure unless she checked.

In the time it took to determine that the battery did indeed need charging, he'd disappeared. Craning her neck, Kasey gawked up the street and down again. Unfortunately, he seemed to have vanished, like ebony smoke.

She heard a quiet rustling on the front porch. One footstep, another. The hairs on the back of her neck bristled, and her heart hammered in her ears as a quiet *sproing* told her he'd opened the screen door, stretching the spring to its limit.

Kasey tiptoed to the foyer, intent on hurrying into the kitchen for the portable that hung on the wall above the canisters, when four beefy fingertips poked through the mail slot, followed immediately by the white corner of a fat envelope.

She licked her lips as instinct told her she had nothing to fear. This wasn't a burglar, but the man who'd been delivering packages of cash, once a month, every month, for fifteen years! She scurried closer...and with all her strength, took hold of those warm, manly fingers. "Ah-ha!" came her coarse whisper. "After all these years, I've gotcha!"

For a full minute after that, they played tug-of-war, pulling like their lives depended on it. If she could just hold onto him a moment longer, she'd know for sure if the gift-giver was Buddy...or not.

Not, she hoped, groaning under her breath and biting her lower lip, straining to maintain her hold on his fingers.

She heard him emit a low grunt. Odd, she thought, that she almost recognized it. Leaning against the door for stability, she grappled with the chain lock, the doorknob lock...and lost her grasp.

It seemed more important than ever to find out who he was. Flipping the deadbolt's latch, she flung open the door.

A cold blast of wind swirled onto the porch, and she squinted at the remnants of dried leaves that spiraled into her face. He was gone before she opened her eyes.

"Rats," she muttered, punching the air in frustration. Inside, after locking up again, she shook her head. "This close," she fumed, forefinger and thumb in the air. "I was *this* close!"

An hour later, when Aleesha's alarm sounded, Kasey was still pacing the semidarkened house. Yawning, she climbed the stairs to roust the girl from bed.

There was no earthly reason for Adam to pop into her mind at that moment, yet Kasey found herself wishing she hadn't gotten up earlier, because waking from dreams of his warm hugs and sweet kisses would be far easier to bear than memories of tussling with the man in black.

* * *

Adam stood on her porch and checked his watch. The operation hadn't taken as long as he'd expected, putting him at Kasey's at ten-thirty instead of noon. The unpredictable nature of surgery was precisely the reason he hadn't called first, to let her know he'd be dropping by.

As he rang the doorbell, he found himself wishing he'd phoned, after all, because what if she wasn't home?

"Adam," she said, opening the door wide.

He thought she looked adorable in her jeans and baggy sweatshirt, looked like a teenager with her hair pulled up in a ponytail that way. "I was in the neighborhood…" he began, unable to believe he'd actually uttered the timeworn cliché. Holding up a box of doughnuts and two foam cups of coffee, he could only hope his smile didn't look as stiff as it felt, because hers warmed him like a summer day.

The soles of her white sneakers squeaked on the slate foyer floor when she stepped aside to let him in. "What a nice surprise." Closing the door, she used her chin to point down the hall. "I'm baking Christmas cookies, so it's nice and warm in the kitchen."

He thought the house smelled delicious, and as he dogged her heels Adam told her so. "You do this every year?" he asked, scanning the cookie-strewn counters.

"'Fraid so," she said, taking two dessert dishes from the cupboard. "And I always make too many, so remind me to fix you a plate when you leave."

"You'll get no argument from me," he said, grinning. Adam tried not to think about the fact that, once he delivered his intended message, he'd be lucky if she didn't boot him out of there.

"Take a load off," she suggested, pulling out a chair. "I'd join you, but with this noodle strainer of a brain of mine, I'm afraid of burning the batch of cookies in the oven."

Content to watch as she slid tray after tray of fresh-from-the-oven chocolate chips and peanut butter puffs onto tea towels, Adam barely noticed the passage of time. He knew he'd never tire of listening to her chatter happily about the church's Christmas bazaar and the Nativity play at Aleesha's school. In fact, it seemed like an incredible shame to destroy this cozy mood by telling her the ugly truth.

But he had no choice. If he didn't 'fess up, Buddy might just succeed in talking her into a walk down the aisle. Adam would rather have her hate him for the rest of her life than stand by and let *that* happen. No sense putting it off any longer....

"How long 'til you can take a break from that?" he asked.

Kasey peeked into a huge bag of flour. "Oh, another couple of batches, and I'll be out of ingredients." She met his eyes, tilted her head. "Why?"

He shrugged, cleared his throat. "Because..." Taking a deep breath, he started again. "Because there's something I have to tell you."

"My, my," she said, grinning. She pulled two cookie sheets out of the oven, then sat across from him and folded her hands on the table. "This sounds serious."

Aw, Kase, he thought, groaning inwardly, *don't look at me like that.* It would be hard enough to tell his tale, without having to tell it to that flour-smudged, wide-eyed innocent face.

"More coffee?" she asked, pointing to the coffeemaker. "Won't take but a minute to brew up a pot—"

"No, thanks." He was shaking more than enough without adding another cup of caffeine to his system. "Remember Halloween night, when Wade and Marcy and Carole were talking about your dad's, um, accident?'' he began.

Kasey's delicate brows drew together as she nodded.

''Well, I know more about it than I let on that night.'' He hoped she couldn't hear the quiver in his voice.

She turned her head slightly and stared at him. ''What do you mean?''

''I mean…'' He gulped. ''I mean, I was there.''

Kasey sat back, blinking silently. Then she narrowed her eyes and said, ''You were where?''

''At the cemetery. Near the railroad tracks. The dummy they found…we made it.''

He couldn't bear to look into those big, glittering green eyes for another second, because if he saw even a trace of disgust or hatred there, it'd break his heart.

''Who's 'we'?'' she asked.

Adam noticed that her usually lyrical voice had quieted. But still he pressed on. Totally honest. He owed her that much. Let the cards fall where they may. ''Travis Garrison, Luke Matthews, Wade, Buddy and me.''

She clucked her tongue. ''Buddy!''

He shook his head. ''Yeah.'' Adam couldn't make himself say it was all Buddy's idea, because nobody had held a gun to his head. He could have walked away…if only he'd had the courage. No, Adam intended to take this on the chin, like a man. He folded his hands on the table and nervously tapped his thumbs together.

''We—I— Nobody was…'' He heaved a sigh. ''We weren't thinking. That's the plain truth of the matter. A bunch of juvenile delinquents is what we were.'' And running a hand through his hair, he added, ''Not that that's any excuse for what we did….''

Her silence was deafening. If she didn't say something,

do something soon, Adam thought he might die of misery, right there in her cookie-filled kitchen.

"How long have you known?"

He looked up, stared into her face. "Known what?"

She cocked an eyebrow. "Known that I'm his daughter."

Pressing his fingertips into his eye sockets, he said, "Since you came to the cabin that night. You looked familiar, right off the bat, but when you said your name—"

"Looked familiar?" She shook her head. "I don't get it."

Adam slid the wallet from his pocket, showed her the laminated article he kept in a credit card slot. "I've been carrying this around since the day after...to remind me what I am, what I was." Absentmindedly, he rubbed the welts on the back of his hand.

Kasey took the article, turned it over and over. Then her hand shot out and she grabbed his wrist. "What's that?" she asked, nodding at the scratches.

He slid his hands into his lap. "Nothing. Just some—" He cleared his throat again, and wished he'd let her make that pot of coffee when she'd offered, because he sure could use something to wet his whistle about now.

She lifted her chin, shot a suspicious glance at him, then turned him loose and read the article. Running the pad of her thumb over the black-and-white photo of her father's smiling face, she clenched her jaw. "You've been carrying this around with you—" Kasey's green eyes bored hotly into his "—for *fifteen years?*"

All he could do was nod.

"*Why?*"

Licking his lips, Adam swallowed. "Like I said...to remind me of what I was. What I am." He reached across the table and, palm up, waited for her to return the article.

When she did, he stared at it for a minute, then poked it back into its leather slot and returned the wallet to his pocket.

He could see that his truth had hurt her, hurt her badly. He knew, because tears shimmered in her bright eyes, making them look greener—if that was possible—making them look bigger and even more innocent. If there had been any other way to protect her from Buddy, Adam gladly would have seized it, because he'd rather cut off his right arm, give up cardiology altogether, than cause her so much as a moment's pain.

He'd given a thought or two to a direct confrontation with Buddy, but he knew the man well enough to realize that would only goad him into moving the wedding date up. And he couldn't have that. Adam knew Kasey deserved better than the likes of him, and she *definitely* deserved better than Buddy Mauvais!

"So tell me, Adam. What were you, Adam?" She leaned forward. "What *are* you?"

Frowning, he bowed his head. "Just a sorry excuse for a man." He met her damp eyes. "A man who thinks the world of you, despite how this looks...."

Pressing her fingertips to her lips, Kasey stared at the floor. "I don't mean to be rude, but..."

"...but you'd like me to leave."

She only nodded.

Adam got to his feet. He'd more or less expected that. Actually, he'd expected much worse. At least she hadn't said she hated him, that she never wanted to see him again.

He decided not to push his luck. If he went now, gave her a couple of weeks to think things through, maybe she'd give him another chance...a chance to prove how much he'd like to make it all up to her...how he'd love her 'til he drew his last breath.

"Wait," she said, standing. "You forgot your cookies."

Cookies? He must be hearing things! Surely she didn't intend to send him home with treats after—

"Which do you prefer, chocolate chips or cherry filled?"

He shook his head as guilt pounded in his heart. "Doesn't matter. Anything. Whatever you... You don't have to..."

But she'd already gathered a couple of dozen cookies, overlapping them in tidy circles on the plate. She was tearing off a sheet of plastic wrap when she said, "Don't worry about the dish." She tucked the cover around its rim. "You can bring it back whenever—"

He didn't know what possessed him to do it— The lost little-girl tone in her voice? The way she fussed over him, even after his confession?—but Adam couldn't resist gathering her to him. "Aw, Kasey," he groaned into her curls. "God knows I'm sorry—sorrier than you'll ever know."

He felt her tense up, sensed that maybe she was about to agree with him, and he held up one hand. "No...don't say anything. At least, not now."

Part of him wanted to hold her at arm's length, beg her pardon. And part of him was terrified to do just that, because what if he saw revulsion in her beautiful eyes? "Just don't hate me, Kasey, okay, 'cause much as I know it's exactly what I deserve, I don't think I could stand that."

He didn't deserve to be holding her, either, so he thanked God that she hadn't pulled away. If Kasey would let him, Adam thought he might just stand there for the rest of his days, hoping for her forgiveness.

"I could never hate you," she said after a while.

Only then could he summon the courage to take a cautious step back, to take a look at the exquisite face that he'd been seeing in his dreams since that night in his cabin.

Until she reached up and wiped a tear from his cheek,

he hadn't even realized he'd been crying. *Oh, you're a fine specimen of a man, Thorne,* he thought bitterly, swiping at the remaining tears.

"I need a little time," she whispered as the pad of her thumb brushed his damp lashes. "I hate to be such a big baby, but I'd like to think things through, pray, and—"

What's wrong with this picture? he wondered, acknowledging that she had, in so many words, just apologized to *him!* "Kasey…"

Her brows lifted slightly as she looked up at him. "What?"

Adam felt his lip quiver as he drew her close again. "Just…" he rasped, "I love you, that's what. And if it takes the rest of my days, I'll—"

She lay a finger over his lips, effectively silencing him. "Adam."

He looked into her face, into her wonderful, lovely face. She tilted her head, sent him a soft, sweet smile. If he didn't know better, Adam would have said her expression was…was *loving.* "What?"

"Just…"

So far, she'd echoed everything he'd said. Dare he hope she'd say—

"…just get outta here, and don't forget your cookies, okay?"

He didn't know what he'd ever done to deserve this second chance, but Adam intended to find out. Intended to repeat that deed, over and over. Maybe then the Almighty would see fit to let her utter those three, life-altering words.

He didn't deserve that, didn't think he'd ever live long enough to earn it.

But Lord knows, I'm just selfish enough to want it, anyway.

Chapter Twelve

As the yuletide holiday approached, Kasey's business more than doubled. Aleesha had been chosen to play Mary in the Nativity play, and Pat lost her eyeglasses—meaning Kasey had to chauffeur them both to and from the church between her own assignments.

Somehow, Kasey managed to get the Christmas cards in the mail on time, trim the tree and put the rest of the decorations up. With just over a week to go before the big day, she'd finished her shopping and gift wrapping, and except for hemming Aleesha's costume, felt ready to celebrate Christ's birth.

She thanked God for the many distractions that had kept her too busy to focus on everything Adam had said a week ago in her kitchen. Thanked the Lord, too, for allowing just enough time at the end of every day to reflect quietly on His Word.

Tonight, alone in her room, she slid her Bible from the bookshelf beside her bed and settled into the comfy old rocker that had been her grandmother's. Since childhood, Kasey had been playing a game she called "Talk To Me,

Lord''…opening the Good Book to a random page, then closing her eyes as her forefinger found the passage God had chosen for her.

In a voice that was barely more than a whisper, she read I Corinthians 13:4–8 aloud:

"'Love is patient and kind; love is not jealous or boastful; it is not arrogant or rude. Love does not insist on its own way; it is not irritable or resentful; it does not rejoice at wrong, but rejoices in right. Love bears all things, believes all things, hopes all things, endures all things. Love never ends….'''

It didn't take long to figure out what lesson the Almighty was trying to teach her; other scripture came to mind to back up her assumption: "'Love others as you love yourself'" and "'Put on kindness, humbleness of mind, meekness and longsuffering; forebearing one another and forgiving one another, even as Christ forgave you…and above all these things, put on charity, which is the bond of perfectness.'''

Kasey closed the Bible and held it to her chest, as, from out of nowhere, the image of Adam, contrite and humble at her kitchen table, formed in her mind. She saw yet again his trembling lips, his worry-furrowed brow and sagging shoulders—

And the bright pink abrasions that had scraped the backs of his fingers.

Emitting a tiny gasp, she lay the Bible in her lap and stared wide-eyed at her own fingertips, remembering how they'd unintentionally scratched the hand of the man in black.

She got to her feet, put the Good Book into its slot on the shelf and, face in her hands, stood stock-still in the middle of the room. *Buddy isn't my generous benefactor,* she realized, *Adam is.* All these years, it had been *Adam* who'd showed up, like a knight on a white horse to rescue his damsel in distress.

And rescue her he did. Somewhere in the depths of her soul, she'd always known Buddy wasn't the type to give so freely, so secretively; he wanted credit for every good deed he'd done...and some he hadn't done.

His drive to be spotlighted and highlighted whenever possible brought a slice of good advice to mind: When you do something for someone, do it because it's the right thing to do, with no thought of paybacks or praise; *that* was the true spirit of The Golden Rule.

If there had been any doubt about Adam's heart before, this newfound awareness erased it, like two-plus-two-equals-four from an elementary school chalkboard.

It was some lesson in humility, realizing what he'd been doing all these years. Remembering how he'd struggled that night to keep his identity a secret awakened something in her.

She understood something else, too.

The plain, simple truth was that Adam's gifts had been motivated by guilt. Guilt that, when he was still a boy, had bored deep into the very marrow of his bones, and grew like a cancer. His noble efforts to put on a brave face, to keep those around him from seeing his distress...well, that touched her, too. Because she'd seen the pain and grief on his handsome face, had wondered what had etched it there.

And now that she knew, Kasey intended to eradicate it, one furrow at a time.

Difficult as it had been, Adam had been true to his word and hadn't called Kasey, not even to suggest a time when he might return her cookie plate. He looked at the dish now, empty save one cookie and a chocolate chip. He'd meted out the treats to make them last.

Picking up the last peanut butter swirl, he took a bite—not much of a breakfast, but better than skipping it altogether—remembering how cute Kasey had looked, measuring out and mixing up the ingredients for the cookie dough, the whole time wearing a streak of flour on her cheek as a sugar crystal sparkled on the tip of her upturned nose.

Grinning, he put the treat back on the plate, gently blanketing it with the plastic wrap as if tucking an infant in for a long nap. He intended to stretch this out as long as possible, because for all he knew, it might be all he'd have to remember her by. That, and memories of the way she'd looked into his eyes every time he held her, as if his arms had been responsible for warding off the chill of a lonely lifetime.

Adam sighed, padded on white-socked feet into his family room and flopped into his recliner. He turned on the TV, was flipping through the channels for the second time, when the doorbell rang.

Smoothing his sleep-tousled hair, he glanced at the clock. Eight-fifteen. Way too early to be Wade, and besides, didn't his partner have an operation scheduled for nine?

The drapes were drawn, the doors bolted tight; he could sit right here and pretend he hadn't heard it, if he wanted to. Adam turned off the television, craned his neck and strained his ears. Had his early-morning visitor decided to leave?

"Adam?"

Kasey.

"Adam, are you in there?" She punctuated her question with a long, drawn-out period of knocking on the door: *Rat-a-tat-tat-tat-tat-tat-tat-tat.*

Silence.

Heart thudding, he sat up straighter.

Rat-a-tat-tat-tat-tat-tat-tat-tat. "Adam, I know you're in there. I heard the TV."

More silence, and then she said, "Are you aware this window beside your front door isn't locked?"

Almost able to picture her mischievous grin, he got to his feet. She was guileless, as evidenced by her clumsy attempt at subtlety. The fact induced a quiet chuckle.

"I wonder what your neighbors would think if I stood on the railing and—"

Adam opened the door. One look into her pretty face was enough to warm him, head to toe, despite the frigid temperatures that had her bundled up like an Inuit. "You're out and about early," he said, waving her inside. "Making deliveries?" When she breezed past, he inhaled the light, feminine aroma of her shampoo.

"I guess you could say that." Grinning, she held out another plate of cookies, this one piled even higher than the last.

"There's still some coffee from earlier," he said, closing the door. "Join me in a cup?"

She wrinkled her nose. "Nah. Too early for a swim," she said, shaking her head.

Adam groaned and rolled his eyes. "That one's old as the hills...."

"And twice as dusty." She winked. "But it's still funny."

Oh, how he wanted to take her in his arms! "Guess y'had to be there," he teased, instead.

"Is the kitchen in there?" She pointed down the hall.

"Uh-huh." Adam was so glad to see her, so thankful to hear the friendly tone of her voice, that he didn't care if he looked or sounded like an obedient pup as he followed her.

"I suppose Aleesha has told you she's playing Mary in

the Nativity play,'' Kasey said, setting the cookie plate in the center of his kitchen table.

Nodding, he said, "Not only that, but she expects me to get to the auditorium early enough to get a front-row seat."

"Did she tell you that Mom is narrating it?"

Another nod. *She looks gorgeous,* he thought. "Yeah, I think she mentioned something about that."

She sat down and folded her hands in her lap. "On second thought, maybe I'll take that cup of coffee, after all."

He was more than happy to oblige, and said so as he pulled a clean mug from the dishwasher. It seemed she planned to stay a while, and judging by her cheerful chatter, she hadn't stopped by to read him the riot act—something else to be thankful for.

"So how goes it at the outlet mall?" he asked. His fingertips brushed hers when he handed her the cup. Like a Cupid-aimed arrow, the warmth of it shot straight to his heart.

As she filled him in on what she'd been doing for her new contract, Adam sat across from her nodding and only half listening. The other half of his concentration was too busy reacting to the music of her voice, the spark in her eyes, the radiance of her smile. He loved the way she used her hands when she talked, and under different circumstances, he might teasingly ask if she was part Italian. For now, Adam was satisfied to bask in the warmth of her presence.

"So do you want to meet us there, or would you rather pick us up?"

Adam blinked, uncertain how to answer, because truthfully, he'd blanked out everything but those last words. "I, uh…" He shrugged. "Doesn't matter to me." *All I want,* he thought, *is to be with you.* He'd leave the where-when-how to the newspaper reporters.

"Just as I suspected," Kasey said.

He didn't have a clue what she was talking about.

Grinning, she narrowed her eyes. "You haven't heard a word I've said in the past ten minutes, have you?"

"Well, I, uh…" He chuckled. "'Course I have." *Sorta,* he added mentally.

She crossed both arms over her chest and tilted her head. "Oh, really?" There was a teasing glint in her eyes. "Then, maybe you'd like to sum it up in a sentence or two—big challenge, I realize, when I've been going on and on like a—"

"Do you have *any* idea how much I love you?"

If he'd known his honest declaration would shut her up so quickly, so completely, he would've made it ten minutes ago. But then, he hadn't planned to say it. Fact was, the words were as much a surprise to him as they'd been to her, though he'd whispered them that day in her kitchen. Still, if only she knew how precious she looked, sitting there all wide-eyed and slack-jawed….

And, oh, she was precious to him!

He watched as the pointy pink tip of her tongue dampened her lips, as thick dark lashes dusted lightly freckled cheeks. She looked up at him then, the green of her eyes dazing and dazzling and dizzying him.

Extending a dainty forefinger, she pointed. "Your coffee is getting cold."

The stuff in his mug had been there since earlier that morning, but he took a swig of it, anyway, and swallowed it with a noisy gulp. "Look who's talkin'."

She took a prim little sip from her cup, never taking her eyes from his. The moment lingered, sizzling like a burger on a hot grill, fusing them one to the other like an invisible cord.

Then she got to her feet and, with a never-you-mind look

on her face, walked around to his side of the table. She gave him a gentle shove, telling him without words that she wanted him to push back his chair.

When he did, Kasey plopped unceremoniously onto his lap and raked her fingers through his hair. "Ever heard of a comb, big guy?" she asked, tilting her head.

Adam wrapped a tendril of coppery hair around his finger, wondering how to respond when she ran her palms along his beard-stubbled cheeks. "Going for that Don Johnson look, eh?"

He felt the heat of a blush creeping up his neck, turning his ears hot and making his scalp tingle. Until that moment, he hadn't given a thought to what a wreck he must look, after a week of fitful nights. A barely audible groan escaped from him.

"Sorry," he said again, "if I knew you were coming I'd have—"

"—baked a cake?"

Her off-key singsong interruption reminded him of the old hit parade tune, and Adam chuckled despite himself. Leave it to Kasey, he thought, to turn an awkward moment into something fun. Leave it to her, he added, to make him feel good…even when he didn't deserve it.

He wrapped his arms around her and rested his head on her shoulder. "What I said before," he began, nuzzling her neck, "I meant it."

"Yeah," she said matter-of-factly, "I kinda thought so." And on the heels of a girlish giggle, she added, "You never answered me, though."

Adam could only shake his head. Grinning, he said, "What was the question?"

"Are you meeting us at the auditorium, or do you want to pick us up? Keep in mind, before you answer, that if you drive us, you'll have to get there an hour earlier and be stuck an hour later than everyone else.''

Stuck? Hardly the word he would have chosen. "I'd be happy to take you," he admitted, realizing as he did that the invitation itself meant that Kasey had forgiven him, that she intended to continue including him in her life.

Forever?

A guy can hope, he thought for the hundredth time since meeting her.

Suddenly, he remembered Buddy. Hard as it was to choke the words out, Adam said, "So will Buddy be joining us?"

"I doubt it."

She'd answered awfully fast, he thought. "Why not?"

Kasey lifted his chin on a bent knuckle, touched the tip of her nose to his. "Don't razz me, Thorne. You know very well that I told him to buzz off."

He'd been a cardiologist for years, knew most everything about the human heart, yet there he sat, wondering if it was possible for gratitude to make one explode.

She leaned back. "Aren't you going to ask me how he took it?"

"How he took what?"

She rolled her eyes. "My rejection, of course," she said, before breaking into a round of merry laughter.

"I know how I'd take it." *You'd go to your grave a miserable lonely old bachelor, is how,* he thought.

She blanketed his hands with hers, then frowned as she forced his hands to eye level. "You never said how this happened," she said, stroking the fading red welts.

A look of pride and self-satisfaction brightened her face as she inspected his mostly healed wounds, telling him without words that she'd figured out exactly how he'd earned the scratches.

"You really should be more careful, Adam."

She was right. He should've been more cautious, especially that night.

As though he'd rewound the tape, she went back to touching his face, teasing him because his hair was curling over his ears, chiding him for not taking better care of himself. "…now, if you were a girl," she was saying, "it wouldn't be so bad, because you could cover those dark circles with makeup. But—"

"Kasey?"

Smiling tenderly, she looked into his face. "Hmm?"

Adam pointed to his lips.

Giggling, she nodded, and kissed him.

Then, quick as a snap, she got to her feet. "I'm baking a ham and all the trimmings for Christmas dinner. Invited Wade and Anna and her brood, too."

That surprised him, and though he didn't say so, it must have showed on his face, because Kasey shrugged. "Makes perfect sense, if you ask me, since you're going to be spending so much more time around my house now."

Before he had a chance to respond, Kasey grabbed his hand. "You really oughta put something on that," she said, "because I love you, too, and I'd hate to see an infection spoil your Christmas."

He started to say that the wounds were well past infection stage, when she kissed his knuckles.

"…'cause even though I'm fairly fanatical about housekeeping, I hafta admit, I've never even thought about cleaning the inside of my mailbox…."

The breath caught in his throat as awareness dawned; she knew about the money deliveries, too!

Standing on tiptoe, she pressed a kiss to his chin. "From here on out, mister," she said, "no secrets. Got it?"

He could almost hear his guilty heart turning toward her

loving forgiveness. She'd dispensed with the expected "we have plenty of time to work out the details" speech, preferring, instead, to *show* him what their future would be like. Life with Kasey would be a lot of things, he realized, but boring wouldn't be one of them!

Pulling her closer, he whispered, "Got it."

"You bet you do," she said meaningfully. "You bet you do!"

*   *   *   *   *

Will Wade Cameron find true love
and accept the Lord's tender mercy?
Find out in

OUT OF THE SHADOWS

*by Loree Lough,
coming in July 2002 from
Steeple Hill's Love Inspired*

Dear Reader,

Though Webster's defines "guilty" as "the state of one who has committed a crime," the word means different things to different people: blameworthy, sinful, wicked, offensive... The list can be long and unwieldy, indeed.

The most difficult guilt to bear isn't the kind we assign to others, but that which we drape around *ourselves*...to protect others from our supposed corruptness, to protect us from dealing with their judgment.

Like Adam and Kasey in *His Healing Touch*, we've all done things we're sorry for. But Adam and Kasey learned that together they had the strength to shed their guilt—forever—and that's what I wish for you and me.

Next time guilt looms large in your life, try to see yourself through the eyes of God, for "great are His tender mercies" (*Psalms*—119:156) and "He delighteth in mercy" (*Micah* 7:18). I have faith I'll be surprised and amazed at how swiftly my own guilty heart will turn!

If you enjoyed *His Healing Touch*, please drop me a note c/o Steeple Hill Books, 300 East 42nd Street, 6th Floor, New York, NY 10017. (I love hearing from my readers and try to answer every letter personally!)

All my best,

Loree Lough

P.S. Be sure to look for my next Love Inspired title (a sequel to this book), *Out of the Shadows*, in July 2002.

Take 2 inspirational love stories FREE!

PLUS get a FREE surprise gift!

Special Limited-Time Offer

Mail to Steeple Hill Reader Service™

In U.S.
3010 Walden Ave.
P.O. Box 1867
Buffalo, NY 14240-1867

In Canada
P.O. Box 609
Fort Erie, Ontario
L2A 5X3

YES! Please send me 2 free Love Inspired® novels and my free surprise gift. After receiving them, if I don't wish to receive anymore, I can return the shipping statement marked cancel. If I don't cancel, I will receive 3 brand-new novels every month, before they're available in stores! Bill me at the low price of $3.74 each in the U.S. and $3.96 each in Canada, plus 25¢ shipping and handling and applicable sales tax, if any*. That's the complete price and a saving of over 10% off the cover prices—quite a bargain! I understand that accepting the books and gift places me under no obligation ever to buy any books. I can always return a shipment and cancel at any time. Even if I never buy another book from Steeple Hill, the 2 free books and the surprise gift are mine to keep forever.

103 IEN DFNX
303 IEN DFNW

Name	(PLEASE PRINT)	
Address	Apt. No.	
City	State/Prov.	Zip/Postal Code

* Terms and prices are subject to change without notice. Sales tax applicable in
  New York. Canadian residents will be charged applicable provincial taxes and GST.
  All orders subject to approval. Offer limited to one per household and not valid to
  current Love Inspired® subscribers.

INTLI_01   ©1998 Steeple Hill